THE
LOCH
NESS
PAPERS

THE
LOCH
NESS
PAPERS

Paige Shelton

MINOTAUR BOOKS
New York

This is a work of fiction. All of the characters,
organizations, and events portrayed in this novel
are either products of the author's imagination or are
used fictitiously.

THE LOCH NESS PAPERS. Copyright © 2019 by Paige Shelton-
Ferrell. All rights reserved. Printed in the United States of
America. For information, address St. Martin's Press,
175 Fifth Avenue, New York, N.Y. 10010.

www.minotaurbooks.com

The Library of Congress Cataloging-in-Publication Data is
available on request.

ISBN 978-1-250-12781-5 (hardcover)
ISBN 978-1-250-21885-8 (ebook)

Our books may be purchased in bulk for promotional,
educational, or business use. Please contact your local
bookseller or the Macmillan Corporate and Premium Sales
Department at 1-800-221-7945, extension 5442, or by email
at MacmillanSpecialMarkets@macmillan.com.

First Edition: April 2019

10 9 8 7 6 5 4 3 2 1

For authors Jenn McKinlay and Kate Carlisle. You two are the absolute best.

ACKNOWLEDGMENTS

Many thanks to my agent, Jessica Faust; my editor, Hannah Braaten; and editorial assistant Nettie Finn. Without the three of them, the following pages wouldn't be anywhere close to a book.

As well, thank you to everyone at Minotaur who works so hard to bring all these ingredients together—I'm amazed every time.

As always, much gratitude to my guys, Charlie and Tyler. Tyler's grown up now, living far away. Just in case he doesn't know how much I enjoy his phone calls, maybe he'll read about it here and keep calling. I adore and am so proud of them both.

THE

LOCH
NESS
PAPERS

ONE

The rain fell in sheets and the clouds grumbled angrily. I sought cover under a narrow brick awning, but the few moments I'd spent in the downpour had soaked me enough that my hair was sure to poof when it dried. I wrapped my arms around myself and sent the clouds an impolite thought or two.

It wasn't that I wasn't used to the rain. I'd been in Scotland for just over a year and I'd seen lots of rain. However, this July storm had caught me off guard.

Also, I was struck with an affliction; I had a hard time remembering to bring along an umbrella—a brollie, as some of my native Scottish friends called it. I'd purchased many over the past year, leaving behind forgotten brollies in my cottage, at my fiancé's house, and at The Cracked Spine, the bookshop in Grassmarket where I worked and spent most of my time.

After my evil eye up to the clouds, I looked around for a place I could pop in and buy yet another one. There were no shops nearby, no take-away restaurants selling fish and chips or fried haggis; no one seemed to be selling anything. But as I truly took notice of what was around me, my irritation with my ill preparedness as well as my desire to find a shop selling umbrellas dissipated. I'd never before ventured to this area inside the city of Edinburgh. Dean Village wasn't far from Grassmarket, just a quick bus ride, but it was as if I'd discovered yet another world. I'd disembarked the bus one stop earlier than planned because at that moment there had been no foreboding clouds above, and the walkway next to the Leith River, which ran through the village, seemed like the perfect place to stroll. It had been, just not for very long.

The village's old stone buildings, stacked on the slopes up from the river, reminded me of something someone would use as a model for a holiday display; sprinkle on some snow and voila! The 12th century architecture was all similar, except for the colors of the stones used. Some were white, some black, others red, and some even yellow. The varied colors gave the village a sense of playfulness and lent a cozy comfort to the close-set structures.

Originally populated with millers and weavers all those centuries ago, it was now mostly a residential neighborhood with old cobblestone roads, and structures repurposed to be apartment buildings and B and Bs. I'd learned that many buildings in Edinburgh had been rebuilt a time or two. The original wood structures had fallen victim to fire from flames that had been used to warm and illuminate. I wasn't sure if the stone structures I looked at today were original or replacements, and I made a mental note to research the answer.

Just as the enjoyable scenery began to perk me up, my eyes landed on what I suspected was my destination. Between me and the beautiful spires of the church on the hill were not only the river and the walkway, but a bridge and a forest. In all fairness, it was a small forest, exaggerated in my mind by the falling rain. It wouldn't have been a daunting trip under clear skies, but at the moment it seemed an expansive journey.

Fortunately, just as I was about to utter some unkind grumbles, the rain let up, and it transitioned from a downpour to a mist—the kind that still soaked you but did so slightly more politely than the torrential version.

"Go now!" I quietly exclaimed to myself, knowing my window of opportunity might close quickly.

I scurried up to the Dean Bridge and ran along Queensferry Road as cars and busses passed me by. I thought about trying to hail one, but truly, the church wasn't that far away. I could see its tall windows and the full view of its spires the second I stepped onto the bridge.

I had been told to use the red door on the side of the building located on Belgrave instead of the front doors. With my head down and my backpack lifted to cover at least a little of my hair, I took the corner onto Belgrave. Out of my lowered peripheral vision I spied the door, but not the person who must have just exited it.

"Oh!" I said as I skimmed a shoulder.

"Gracious," he said, his voice almost as wobbly as his legs.

I grabbed his arm gently to keep him from falling.

"I'm so sorry," I said, glad he stayed upright. "Are you all right?"

"Aye." He blinked up at me with clear blue eyes behind water-streaked glasses. A few strands of gray hair were slicked across the top of his head.

I continued to hold his bony elbow in my hand—I didn't want to let go until I knew he was steady.

"Aye, I'm fine," he continued. "Though I'd like verra much tae continue on. It's a wee bit blashie oot here."

I knew that "blashie" meant "rainy." I'd heard my landlords Elias and Aggie use the Scots word more than a few times now.

"Right." I looked around. "Can I help you get somewhere?"

"I think I'm fine. I live just across the way." He smiled with false teeth that shifted ever so slightly with the gesture.

He was old. I was caught between insisting on going with him and not offending him. Finally, since we were both so wet we couldn't get any wetter, I nodded.

"All right. Again, I'm sorry," I said.

"Not tae worry, lassie. It's not every day I get tae run into a young lovely." He winked.

I smiled and let go of his elbow. With sure steps that were a little hitched to the right—though maybe that was because of the big satchel he had over his shoulder—he walked around me. I thought for a moment that he was unsure of which direction to go, but after a brief hesitation, he seemed figure it out. I watched as he made his way across the street to a row of tall, narrow, brick apartments that reminded me of town houses, though I hadn't heard them described that way in Scotland. I thought about following just to make sure he was okay, but if Elias had taught me anything, it was that Scottish men, particularly those over sixty (and under too, probably), were proud enough that my offers of help might be more offensive than considerate.

I turned again and hurried toward the red door. Just as I put my hand on the knob I spotted something on the ground.

Inside a sealed plastic sandwich bag was a deck of cards. Protected from the rain by the plastic, the deck was facedown and secured with a rubber band. I crouched and carefully gathered the bag. I'd seen the illustration on the back of the top card before, and I knew it immediately. Nessie, the Loch Ness

Monster, in all her cartoonish glory, rose from the water and sent a vicious sneer to anyone who might be looking. I couldn't determine when the artwork had been created, but I'd re-searched enough about the old girl to know the deck of cards might come from as far back as the beginning of the last century.

I thought the cards might have fallen from the old man's satchel, but that was just a hunch. I took off in a slippery run across the street, but he was nowhere in sight. No one was in sight, probably because it was raining and no one in their right mind would remain outside. At least not without a brollie.

I needed to get in from the rain. I didn't hurry since I was now drenched to the bone, but with quick steps I made my way back to the church's door. I was glad it was unlocked as I did what I'd been instructed to do and made my way inside. Once there, I didn't know what to do but drip for a minute. As soon as I felt semi-presentable, I would seek out who I'd come to find, the woman who would hopefully help.

Despite the rain, the sweet man I'd almost knocked over, and the interesting deck of cards, I had a purpose in mind. I had a wedding to save.

Mine.

TWO

"Did you fall in the river?" the woman asked with one of the lightest accents I'd heard since moving to Scotland. Maybe no accent at all. "Or is it really raining that hard?"

I'd seen her a few seconds after I'd entered the building. She'd passed by, doubling back when she realized someone was dripping in the coatroom. She wore faded jeans and a black sweater. Her hair was cut boyishly short and her black-framed glasses made her look both intelligent and, surprising to me, feminine.

"Raining that hard," I said. "I thought a stroll would be fun, but I . . . well, you can see how that turned out."

"Here." She reached into a jam-packed shelf against a side wall, and somewhere in the mess of shoes, jackets, and other winter wear, found and grabbed a couple of towels. "Dry off. Though I feel like I should offer you a change of clothes."

"I'm okay." I dried my hands and extended one. "Are you Reverend Bellows, by chance?"

"That's me, but I prefer Reverend Nisa or just Nisa."

We shook; I cringed a little at my cold fingers. "Sorry about that. It's nice to meet you. I'm Delaney Nichols."

"Did we have an appointment, Delaney?"

"No." I put a towel to the ends of my ponytail, hoping I was calming and not feeding the frizz that was unquestionably in my near future. "I got your name from my fiancé's father, Artair Shannon. He told me to come in through the side door to find you quickly and easily. I need your help."

She smiled. "A lovely man. Well, any friend of his, and so on. Come through to my office."

I followed her down a hallway and into a small, pristine office. The bookshelves behind the desk were packed so evenly that they looked more like two-dimensional paintings than shelves with books. The desktop was vacant, even of dust, it seemed. Two colorful prints adorned two walls, both of them portraying golden and rosy sunsets. There were no windows, but the paintings were probably the reason the space didn't immediately feel closed off and claustrophobic.

"Have a seat," Nisa said.

I looked at the fabric on the chair. "Do you have any more towels?"

"It's fine. Please, make yourself comfortable."

I sat with a strained smile. I was going to soak the chair. I was going to soak everything in my near vicinity until I dried.

"How can I help you, Delaney Nichols?" she asked.

There was something about people who lived their lives for God. Not every religious person I'd met over the years had a welcoming and confident demeanor, as if they truly believed everything was always going to be okay, but Reverend Nisa had it. Artair had said I would like her immediately. It seemed he was correct.

"Since I showed up unannounced and don't want to take up too much of your time, I'll cut to the chase. Is there any chance you could officiate my marriage ceremony? Next Saturday." I smiled. I hadn't called first on purpose. I'd wanted to meet her, see her in person to know if I truly wanted to ask her to take on the task. Even if my bookish voices, those tricks of my intuition, remained silent, my gut instincts would surely kick in on their own and tell me if there was any reason at all why I shouldn't want her to be involved. My instincts *had* kicked in immediately, and I sensed that she would be a wonderful addition to one of the most important days of my life.

Her eyebrows came together. "In eight days?"

"Well, nine, if you include today. I know it's short notice, and though it's technically correct that you were my second choice, I didn't know about you at all until my . . . original officiating choice . . . well, he died."

"I'm so sorry."

"Me too. He was a sweet man. The reverend of a small country church."

"Dale O'Brien?"

"Yes, that's him."

"I knew him. He was a friend and his death came too soon." She fell into thought a moment. "Well, you *do* know Artair. And Dale was lovely . . . Aye, I think I can help, if the church is available. Normally, I like to spend some time with the couple, but if you were working with Dale, I'm sure he already did that part."

"He did. Tom and I both adored him, and he seemed to be happy that we were getting married, happy that Tom was finally settling down." I cleared my throat, wishing I hadn't added that last part, even if it was true. Tom had dated many women over the years, and his love-'em-and-leave-'em reputation had been front and center with everyone, including Dale O'Brien, a lovely man who'd had a pint or two in Tom's pub over the years, and had been a friend of my boss, Edwin MacAlister.

"Tom? Artair's son?" Nisa asked as if she was trying to place him.

I nodded.

"I don't think I've met him. Is he older than you by a bit?"

I smiled. She thought my comment about him finally settling down meant he was older. In fact, it was another reason altogether. "No, he's handsomer."

She blinked but picked up on what I was saying quickly. She smiled too. "And you're sure he's ready?"

"I am. Dale was sure too."

Nisa nodded. "I'd love to help, however, I would like to meet with the two of you. Just briefly. I wouldn't feel right just jumping in blind. Can you understand?"

"Sure. Tom would be happy to meet. When?"

"This Saturday morning?" she said. "Here? Oh, I don't even know if the church is available next Saturday. You'd think I'd know these things, but I have a secretary. Let me check . . ."

"Well, that's also something . . . We would like to exchange vows in the bookshop where I work. Then have a reception at Tom's pub. It's not fancy, and it's not a church. How do you feel about that?"

"Neither of you attend a church?"

"No, but I grew up going to church. So did Tom, back before Artair started attending your church. Neither Tom nor I have gone in quite some time."

"I see. Well, I have no problem with your plan, but I would like to know why you and Tom don't just have a secular celebrant officiate."

"I'll let Tom answer for himself, but my reason is—though I don't attend church and though my beliefs aren't traditional, I still have some beliefs that make me want a splash of religion in the mix." I held my breath. I was being as honest as I could be, but I didn't want to offend her. However, that was another part of the reason I was there, dripping in Reverend Nisa's office, to see if she would be offended by my beliefs and thoughts.

"A splash? I like that. Those of us who work in this world understand that sometimes even a splash is a good start."

I smiled and nodded expectantly.

Nisa's eyebrows came together as she tapped a finger on the edge of her spotless desk. She didn't think for long. "Yes, I would be happy to help." She stood. "Let me check my calendar. My secretary isn't here, but she keeps my schedule in her office. Give me a minute."

At least that answered where she kept her calendar. After she left, I wondered about all the other items that belonged on a desk. Once I was alone I looked around with more vigilant eyes. Where were all the things? Though my desk wasn't too messy, it usually had at least a few items on it. Pens, papers, tissues, and in my case, maybe one or two of the rare and valuable collectibles that my boss, Edwin, had accumulated over the years. Of course, not everyone was lucky enough to get to have their office like mine, but I couldn't remember ever seeing a desk this . . . vacant, nor an office this pristine. Reverend Nisa took the whole cleanliness next to godliness thing all the way up to the heavens.

My eyes finally landed on something I thought looked out of place. On a lower shelf, hidden mostly by the desk, were two books, askew on their sides as if they'd been put there hurriedly. I tilted my head and tried to read the spines. One book was written by a local author, Brodie Watson. In fact, Edwin and Brodie were "drinking mates," as Rosie, my grandmotherly coworker and Edwin's long-time friend, called them as she'd widen her eyes. I remembered being surprised by her exaggeration because, though I'd seen Edwin drink, I'd never seen him drink very much. At Rosie's description, Edwin had only lifted his eyebrows and muttered something about Brodie being a bad influence. I hoped to meet the esteemed author someday.

From my angle, the other book looked like a children's book, with a thin, colorful spine. I didn't want to get out of the chair and look, mostly because I would make telltale wet footprints on the tidy floor. I focused on the squiggly letters one at a time and said, "Oh!" aloud when I realized I was spelling "Loch Ness." The cards! Maybe they didn't belong to the old man; maybe they were Nisa's. I grabbed them out of my bag just as she came back into the office.

"I'm available both this Saturday morning to talk to you and Tom, and next Saturday for the ceremony," she said as she remained standing.

"That's great news. Thank you!" I stood too.

"Well, you are marrying into Artair's family, and he's one of the kindest people I've ever known. I look forward to meeting Tom, and maybe asking why he doesn't ever join his father for church on Sundays."

I nodded. "That seems fair."

"This Saturday morning, then?"

"Definitely." I cleared my throat. "I found something right

outside the door as I came in. I wonder if they belong to you?"
I extended the baggie-encased cards.

"Oh dear, I imagine he dropped them," she said as she
reached for the baggie. She looked up at me again. "We have a
church member who was here just before you." She hesitated
and I noticed something move over her face. Irritation? But it
passed quickly. "He's . . . well, he's quite into the Loch Ness
Monster. I suspect he dropped them. I'll get them back to him."

I didn't hand them over right away. "May I ask what you
mean by 'quite into'?"

She smiled, almost grimly. "Obsessed."

"Obsessed?"

"Aye," she said as she cocked her head. "Why?"

"My background includes working at a museum and with
many different types of collectibles. In a nutshell, I find collectible items, as well as obsessions with collectible items, intrigu-
ing. I would be happy to return these to him myself."

"I see." She studied me again, a longer moment this time.
When she finally spoke, I wondered if she had her own version
of bookish voices, or if her gut was just telling her I could be
trusted. "Norval Fraser is somewhat famous, locally. He's long
been obsessed with Nessie. There's a story there, and I suspect
he might tell that story if you stopped by his flat—it's right
across the street, along Buckingham Terrace—and let him
know you found his cards. His flat is overflowing with his obsession, and, frankly, he likes to show it off, to the right people,
I guess."

"Even better," I said.

But that look pinched at her eyes again. Something told me
her earlier meeting with Norval Fraser might not have been
pleasant.

"Everything okay?" I asked.

"Yes, of course." She smiled. "Norval was a wee bit upset this morning. He came over . . . and I'm worried about him is all."

"Oh."

She shook her head. "Sorry. I've got a lot on my plate this morning and my mind is going a million different directions. All is well. Yes, if you'd like to stop by Norval's, I know he'd like to have his cards back. Be prepared, his flat full of stuff is more claustrophobic than interesting."

In other words, I thought to myself, his flat was the opposite of her pristine office.

"I would love to introduce myself to him. I promise not to bug him, I'll simply return the cards if he doesn't want to talk to me," I said.

"Aye, certainly. He's just across the way, in the third-in, lower floor flat. Twenty-three. You'll see the number on the door. Tell him I sent you over."

"Thank you."

She walked me to the door and I told her I'd bring the towels back when Tom and I returned on Saturday. She said I could keep them.

I stepped out of the building and found clear, sunny skies. Maybe I would dry more quickly now. At least I wasn't too cold. I wondered if Nisa would break out into a cleaning fit over the water I'd dripped everywhere. I would have offered to clean up after myself if I knew I wouldn't just keep dripping or leaving wet footprints in my own wake.

I glanced at my watch. I'd darted out of the bookshop two hours earlier. Reverend O'Brien had passed away a week ago, and, bizarrely, finding a replacement hadn't even occurred to either Tom or me, until Rosie asked me this morning what we were going to do. I'd panicked a little, but then buckled down and got to work figuring out my options. Well, option; I'd only come up with this one. Unless Nisa ended up not liking me or Tom, it looked like I'd accomplished my mission.

And, cherry on top, now I was going to introduce myself to someone obsessed with the Loch Ness Monster.

Extra cherry on top: The rain had stopped, at least for now.

THREE

Each attached narrow section of Buckingham Terrace held three floors of separate apartments, and the doors leading to the upper floors looked just like the front doors of the bottom flats, not entries to stairways. Despite some momentary door confusion on my part, it wasn't difficult to find number twenty-three. However, once I knew I was at the right apartment I hesitated when I noticed foil covering the front window. I reasoned with myself that the cards needed to be returned somehow, and when I noticed the cartoon Nessie welcome mat, I sensed there was probably no real reason to be concerned for either Norval Fraser's stability or my safety.

I knocked and immediately heard a shuffling on the other side.

"Aye? Hold on a moment. I'm on th' way," Norval, I assumed, said from inside.

The door's creaky hinges protested even though he opened it only a crack. "Aye?"

"Hi, I'm . . . well, my name is Delaney and I'm the one who ran into you up by the church, but that doesn't . . . I found these." I held up the bag with the deck of cards. "Reverend Nisa said they probably belong to you. She thought it would be okay if I brought them over."

The door's hinges protested more loudly as he opened it fully. I tried not to let my eyes scan the space behind him, but I couldn't seem to ignore the stacks inside. Rudely, my eyes lingered behind the man and not on him.

"They *are* mine," he said with a smile. "Thank ye, lass."

"Happy to help," I said as I gave him the bag. When my eyes went back to him, I noticed that he'd extended his hand. "Oh, sorry."

He took the cards and looked behind himself, then back at me. "Aye, this mess? It's all part of my job, my work, I'm afraid. My work requires many pieces of paper, many things."

I gave him my full attention and smiled. "I admit, Nisa told me about your interest in the Loch Ness Monster, and I was curious."

"Ye're intrigued by Nessie?"

"Well, yes, but I tend to be intrigued by people who are intrigued by things. I've spent my career working in a museum and now in a rare and used bookshop in Grassmarket. I'm familiar with obsessions, even have a few myself."

Sometimes there's an invisible but real and immediate connection between people. I've never quite understood it, but my intuition has never once been wrong about it. I'd felt some of it with Nisa, but as Norval smiled up at me, the few hairs on his head still pasted to it, his glasses now dry, and his teeth still moving, a wave of real affection rolled between us. As if to underscore the moment, a bookish voice piped up.

What is a friend? A single soul dwelling in two bodies.

If it hadn't been so completely odd to do it, I might have an-

swered Aristotle out loud, telling him that maybe the connection to Norval wasn't quite *that* intense, but it was real
nonetheless, thank you very much. As it was, I simply digested
the old philosopher's words and returned the inquisitive smile
Norval sent in my direction.

"Which bookshop?" he asked a moment later.

"The Cracked Spine."

"Oh! Edwin MacAlister's place?" he said.

I hesitated. "Yes."

"He's been here before, right here at my hoose."

I nodded him on, and hoped their meeting hadn't gone
badly.

"Aye. He wanted my papers, all of them, he said. He said I
have the grandest collection of all, and if anything could prove
that Nessie is real, it's the work I've done."

"Sounds exactly like something he would do and say."

"Aye." His eyebrows came together, and he fell into thought.

"You weren't interested in selling?" I said.

"No! Of course I willnae sell my papers. I willnae sell anything."

"I understand," I said, working hard not to sound patron-
izing or confused.

His eyes snapped back to mine. "No, I willnae sell, but I
would like tae *give* them away, tae someone who will continue
my work. Ye might be surprised how difficult it is tae find someone tae carry on."

"I see."

"Mr. MacAlister said he wouldnae continue, but he would
care for my papers, maybe see that they made it tae a museum
or something, but he wouldnae continue." He paused, but only
briefly. "Would you?"

"Oh." Something stopped me from giving him an outright and emphatic no. Declining the offer *was* my first reaction, but something held me back, kept my dissent tamped down. "What does that mean, to continue your work?"

He blinked at me again. He must have felt that wave of affection too. Or maybe he just wanted company, because he said, "Would ye like tae come in and I'll show ye?"

"I would. Thank you."

I hadn't hesitated, but it did occur to me that at least Nisa knew where I was going. Someone knew I might be inside Norval's flat. Rosie and Tom knew I was stopping by the church to talk to Reverend Nisa. If I disappeared, the pieces could be put together. But, I admitted to myself, I couldn't have resisted going inside the apartment full of all things Loch Ness Monster, even if the wave I'd felt had been terror, not affection.

I wiped my feet vigorously on the mat and followed him inside, noticing that he placed the cards on the coffee table after he shut the door.

The light inside wasn't all artificial. Though foil covered the front window, there were three uncovered windows across the back, which was also where a small kitchenette and dining area were located. The dining table was covered with stacks of papers and other things; so were the chairs around the table. I could see either a garden or a bunch of overgrown green bushes outside one back window. The couch, chair, and coffee table in the living room were also mostly covered with papers, though there was an open seat at one end of the couch. The old, small television was turned off, its screen dusty and its top propping up another stack.

There was a lot to take in, but mostly I saw papers, notebooks, and photographs. I saw a toy or two, stuffed and plastic. My eyes skimmed over some items on the floor and tucked partway behind the chair: an old eight-millimeter camera, small canisters of film, and a projector that reminded me of elementary school from my parents' days.

"Take a seat." Norval nodded at the end of the couch. "Cuppa or some coffee? I think I have some hot chocolate. Would ye like something tae take off the chill?"

"I'm okay, but thanks. I'm still wet from the earlier rain. Maybe I should stand." I was now more damp than wet, but chances were pretty good that I would leave wet spots wherever I sat.

"Nonsense, have a seat."

The towels were useless, so I just kept them on my lap as I took the one seat on the couch. I wondered if and where Norval was going to sit.

"Give me a minute." He disappeared around the half wall to the kitchenette and dish noises ensued.

On the coffee table in front of me was a precariously stacked small pile of books. Kids' books about the Loch Ness Monster. I didn't recognize any of them, but it had been a long time since I'd paid much attention to children's books. A cute, worm-like creature illustrated the cover of *Nessie, the Loch Ness Monster.* *The Loch Ness Monster*'s cover highlighted a horrifying dragon-like creature, though still aimed at younger readers. I didn't want to tumble the pile, so I didn't try to see the other titles. I wondered if the book I'd seen in Nisa's office had come from this stack. Just as my eyes wandered down the coffee table and landed on an old manila folder with frayed edges and "2013" scribbled on its tab, Norval returned.

"Have a cup." He extended one in my direction, holding another in his other hand and a folding chair under his arm.

I inspected the cup, expecting to see a monster illustration, but it was just a plain ceramic mug.

"Thank you," I said.

He set his cup unevenly on some papers on the corner of the coffee table. He unfolded the chair, took a seat, and rescued his mug.

"What do ye think, lass? Will ye take care of my collections?" he asked.

I smiled after I took a sip of the creamy hot chocolate. He must have already had a kettle on. "I don't know what that really means. It looks like a pretty big job."

"Aye, 'tis." He looked around. "But ye have tae understand its importance. The truth is important."

When he didn't continue, I cleared my throat and asked, "And what is the truth? Is there a Loch Ness Monster?"

He looked at me with eyes that verged on fierce. "Oh, lass, of course there is. There might be more than one, mind. And, it's important tae never forget, never let anyone forget. More proof must always be searched for."

I opened my mouth, then closed it again, as I silently debated the best route to take. Finally, I said, "Norval, would you mind starting from the beginning? Of course, I've heard of Nessie, but I'd like to know what sparked," I looked around, "all of this. If you have proof that Nessie exists, I'd really like to know the story, your story, from the beginning, if you don't mind."

He took a sip from his mug and looked at me over its brim. He swallowed and then nodded.

"Aye, I think I'll tell ye. It's not what ye expect."

"Even better."

He paused again, purposely prolonging the drama, I

thought. Then, surprising me, his eyes clouded and filled with tears. He composed himself before he looked at me again.

"She killed my da, lass, took him from me, took him from us all," he said, his words shaky but certain.

I held my breath and hoped he would continue.

FOUR

He did continue, and his voice was strong, his tone so heartfelt I could feel the anguish in his words from the very first one.

"My da and mother and sisters, we lived in a village by Loch Ness. Wikenton. 'Twas during World War II, and Da couldna fight, ye see, because he had holes in his eardrums."

"How much war activity did you see in a village by Loch Ness?" I asked, though I felt like that was something I should already know.

"We covered our windows in blackout curtains, lived with rations, the sirens, the planes," he pointed a finger toward a long-ago sky, "went by overhead. Sometimes drills, sometimes the real thing."

"Was it frightening?"

"Aye, sometimes with the sirens, but most of the time it was just the way we lived. My parents were lovely people. They took good care of us. Weel, until . . . I'm getting off track."

"My fault. I'm sorry for interrupting. I'll try to be quiet."

"Oh, no, lass, dinnae be quiet. I like tae remember. My mind just goes back and forth so much these days."

"Take your time." I sipped the hot chocolate.

"Aye." He took a deep breath and let it out. "It was so, so dark that night. We had tae keep the lights oot, aye? Weel, there was no rain. No moon either, but clouds enough tae cover the stars. I couldnae sleep, and I'd been inside most the day. Cooped up because of the weather and the war. It was unnatural tae be inside so much but that's the way it was. Anyway, I was a wee lad of seven and I was too independent for my own good, according tae my mother. That night I needed tae get oot of the hoose. I climbed down from the loft I shared with my sisters and left, stepping out into a darkness so thick I had tae stand by the front door a few minutes before my eyes could catch even layers of shadows.

"I knew where I wanted tae go. I knew the path, I knew every path all around. It was home, even oot there in the darkness, next tae the water, it was home. I was sure-footed, and too sure of myself. Nevertheless, I didnae so much as spark a lunt," he caught my raised eyebrows, "a match, tae light the way." I nodded and he continued again. "I tripped once or twice, but only stumbles, as I made my way through the trees tae the loch." He paused again. "Lass, have ye ever seen water in the pitch dark of a night?"

"I don't think so. I've seen water at night, twinkles from the moon and stars and lights around it, but not in a pitch-black night." I thought about the view from Tom's house by the North Sea. The water at night always left me unsettled.

"As used tae it as I was, for it had always been there right outside my front door, it was and still is something that leaves me feeling hollow inside. Aye?"

"Yes, I understand."

"Like if ye fell in, ye'd just keep falling forever. Anyway, I stepped oot from the trees, and that's what I expected tae see, the same sort of scene I'd come on before, a black, smooth, never-ending dark. And at first, that's what was there. Just dark." He looked at me.

I nodded.

"But then, there was a noise. A rustle, and a voice, I was sure. I was startled, but I'd been well trained tae keep quiet because of the war, mind, and my hand sprung up to cover my surprise. I stepped back and moved behind a tree. I couldnae run even though I ken I should hurry back home, back tae the loft with my sisters, but I just couldnae. I was too curious.

"Soon, I recognized the voice, or I thought I knew it, even if it was part whisper. It was my da. He was somewhere near the shore, talking to someone. I was relieved and then even more curious. Why was he outside too?

"He carried a weapon on him and was careful, so I didnae want tae startle him too much. I worked up my nerve, because I was scairt tae let him know I was there, oot where I should-nae be, accidentally spying on him.

"'Da,' I said in a voice just above a whisper. 'Da, it's me, Norval.'

"It was what I heard in the next few seconds that I remember the most. A surprised noise from Da, hasty words spoken by him, and . . . and a moan, a groan, that didnae sound human. It didnae, lass."

"I believe you," I said, because it felt like the right thing to say.

"And then there was a splash. That's what brought me oot from around the tree. In a hurry, I came 'round, wondering if

Da fell into the water, but his dark figure was there tae meet me before the shore. He grabbed me and pulled me close.

"'Lad,' he said, 'are ye awright? Yer mother and sisters?' 'Fine, Da,' I told him. 'I . . . needed tae get oot of the hoose.' He pulled me close and said he understood."

Norval stopped again, and this time his shoulders slumped.

"Oh, Norval, are you okay?" I asked.

He sniffed and nodded and then sat forward on the chair. "Aye, it's that hug, he meant it, that still keeps me convinced about what happened. He wasn't acting as if he was scairt for me tae know what he was doing, like he felt guilty. He wasnae running away, lass. That's not what happened. It was . . . let me tell ye.

"'What are ye doing, Da? Who were ye talking tae?' I asked him.

"He hesitated then, but not for long. Soon he crouched and said, 'Norval, my boy, I came upon something and it's changed everything. I've been wanting tae share it with ye, yer mother and sisters too, but mostly you. I just wasnae sure how it would be.'

"'Tell me,' I pleaded.

"'Hold my hand, lad, and come with me tae the shore.'

"I took his hand and we made our way. We stood there a moment. I heard the water lapping at the rocky sand at my feet, but it was a calm night. The moon was covered by the clouds, remember. Da asked me, 'Lad, ye've heard about the monster, aye?' Of course, I had. Everyone had heard about the myth of the Loch Ness Monster. Pictures had been taken, most of them disproved, aye. I nodded up at him, but didnae speak. I sensed what was about tae happen. Even in the dark, he knew the nod was there and he crouched again." Norval paused the story and locked his gaze onto mine. "Lass, he said he'd met her, befriended her.

"Tears sprung tae my young eyes then. I was full of all things a seven-year-old boy should be full of—adventure, curiosity, energy, but there in the dark with the man who protected me from everything, I was scairt. Da sensed it and pulled me close again. He told me that she wouldnae come tae the shore that night, that first she'd need tae get used tae me. He told me tae look out about twenty meters into the water. It was dark, but I put my eyes there and looked hard as I blinked away my fear. I heard something before I saw it. I heard a splash and then another one and I looked harder.

"'There, there,' Da said. I looked and saw it." Norval paused again and turned back to me, his gaze even steelier. "The eyes of the beast, lass. I saw them, their glimmer, sure as I'm sitting here tonight."

I blinked. "The eyes only?"

He nodded. "The blue glimmer of the eyes. Sure as I'm here this day."

"There was no moon, no light or stars," I said. "What did they glimmer off of?"

"That's what I'm trying tae tell ye. They glimmered on their own. That's how I ken they were there. The sight lasted only a moment and then I heard another splash before the eyes, along with the rest of the monster, I'm certain, disappeared."

It would be impossible not to have doubts, but I didn't want to argue with the sweet, old man who missed his father. "And you've been searching for the monster ever since?"

"No! I've been searching for the monster *and* my da, lass. That's the rest of the story. And I cannae search forever. I need someone tae carry on. Da's long gone, certainly, but his bones, whatever's left, are somewhere, in the beast's lair, I'm certain. I've seen her, Nessie, but I need tae know her better. I need her tae take me tae my da. It needs tae be known that he didnae leave us on his own. He never would have. We must always search for the truth. We must never run away from it."

He was so sure. I saw it. I felt it. I was torn between my own doubt and sympathy. I'd known people who believed something so unbelievable before, but most of the time, they'd been un-well, unstable, mentally ill to some degree. Was Norval unwell? Or, and I wanted to believe this second option so much, had he just believed something for so long that it would be impos-sible not to believe it now? He'd wired his own beliefs, and after so long, they couldn't be untangled.

"What happened? I mean . . ." I said.

"I know what you mean. The next night . . ."

A knock pounded on Norval's front door. A surge of irrita-tion pulsed through me. However, at that moment I wouldn't have been surprised to see Nessie herself on the other side. Norval stood and put his hot chocolate down.

"Excuse me, lass," Norval said. "I should get that."

I felt abandoned. I made some sort of noise of protest, and then took another sip from my own mug.

FIVE

"Uncle Norval, did you forget our lunch, our meeting with the reverend?" The man stepped into the flat, appraised Norval's appearance, and then noticed my existence.

His pressed, gray suit and skinny red tie, along with his scolding tone, made me think about my hair and wonder how bad it looked. Pretty bad, if the man's surprised eyes when they landed in that general vicinity were any indication.

"And you are?" he asked me.

I stood and extended a hand. "Delaney Nichols."

I could tell he didn't want to shake, but he did. "I'm Gavin MacLeod, Norval's great-nephew."

"Nice to meet you."

Gavin looked at me and then at Norval. "Right. Well, Uncle, are we ready to go?"

"Not quite yet," Norval said. "I have a guest. And I met with Nisa by myself this morning."

"Ah, I see, and did the good reverend offer some of her advice again?"

Though he didn't make quotes in the air with his fingers,

his tone spoke the sarcasm. He wasn't a fan of Reverend Nisa's advice.

"She told me I didn't have to listen to you," Norval said.

A surge of the need to escape spread through me, no matter how much I wanted to hear the rest of Norval's story. Certainly, this should be a private conversation.

I wasn't sure if the younger man was ignoring the older one or keeping things civil because I was there, but he simply looked at the watch on his wrist. "I'm on a tight schedule, and I'd like to have some lunch at least. I need to get back to work in one hour."

Norval pursed his lips at his nephew and then at me.

"Norval, perhaps we can meet again. Soon?" I said.

"I would like that very much, Delaney," he said with an apologetic frown.

I wanted to take my mug to the kitchen, but it seemed wiser just to leave and let them get to their lunch. "I look forward to it."

"Aye," Norval said. "We were talking about Nessie, Gavin. Delaney might take over my papers!"

"I see," Gavin said stiffly.

I smiled. "I happened upon some Nessie cards he dropped and brought them by. That's how we met."

"I see," Gavin repeated, still stiffly.

"Thank ye for bringing them. I would have later wondered where they'd disappeared tae," Norval said as the three of us made awkward moves so that Norval and I could both get to the door.

"My pleasure." I smiled. "And such a pleasure to meet you, Norval. Thank you for your time."

With one more glance at Gavin—who forced a small

smile—I left the flat and headed back toward the church, ultimately back to the bookshop. I was grateful the rain hadn't begun again. I felt that void of disappointment that follows unrewarded anticipation, but I would talk to Norval again soon. He had mentioned knowing Edwin. Perhaps I could learn the rest of the story from my boss. I walked toward the bus stop I should have originally disembarked at.

But there was something keeping my steps slow. I was bothered by what I'd witnessed between Gavin and Norval. Should I have intervened more? Come to Norval's defense? Just because I liked him? Their relationship was none of my business, but I hoped I hadn't witnessed something that hinted at some sort of abuse. I wasn't quite sure what to do.

"Ms. Nichols," a voice called from behind only a few seconds later.

I turned and waited for Gavin to catch up. He moved gracefully in a quick jog, and I steeled myself for a lecture.

He smiled as he stopped in front of me. He was holding the bag with the deck of cards.

"I'm sorry to chase you," he said, his tone much friendlier than inside the flat, and not the least bit breathless from the jog.

"It's okay."

He seemed to suddenly notice that he held the cards. He put them in a pocket and rubbed his finger under his nose. "My uncle showed me the cards to prove why you were there. I understand, and I thank you for returning them."

"My pleasure."

"Right. My uncle . . . well, he's a wee bit eccentric."

"He's very sweet."

"Aye, but he's eccentric. That can't be denied."

"I suppose."

"People have tried to take advantage of him. His papers are . . . appealing to many, and I don't want him to be hurt or . . . well, I want to keep him protected."

"I understand."

"I'm sure he told you about his father."

I nodded. "Well . . ."

"Aye, his father was my great-grandfather. I'm Jean's grand-son, though she's passed on. Jean is Norval's eldest sister."

"He mentioned his two sisters."

"My great-aunt Millie is still with us. She had no children, never married, and sadly I've lost my parents too. I'm the last of the line, at least at the moment." He shrugged and continued to smile. I couldn't tell if he was just being friendly, or working hard to make up for *not* being friendly in Norval's flat. "Anyway, Norval's been . . . eccentric since his father disappeared."

"I see."

"But Norval's father wasn't taken by the Loch Ness Monster, Ms. Nichols. Surely you know that."

"I don't necessarily believe there's a monster, but that doesn't mean there isn't one, I suppose."

Gavin's mouth moved from a smile into a straight line. "Leopold Fraser, Norval's father, was having an affair, Ms. Nichols. He would meet a woman down by the loch. When he was found out, or when Norval happened upon him meeting with the woman, Leopold left with her. That's all that happened, though Norval doesn't want to believe it. There's been no way to stop him looking for his father and that mythological creature, all these years."

"There's proof of where his father went?"

Gavin shrugged again. "It's what my grandmother said happened. She had no desire to ever seek out her father, and he was long gone by the time I came along. It's a family story, that's all. We do what we can to take care of Norval, but he hasn't been . . . completely right since he was a wee lad. He can't keep a job. He can't be away from his papers for very long. When he was younger he'd have to travel up to Loch Ness when the urge hit him. He'd begin a job and then one day, go off for lunch and never return. We knew he was either with his papers or up at the loch. We've taken care of him, but it's been a challenge."

"I'm sorry. Has he . . . seen the monster? I mean, after . . . that night?"

"He says he has, but as many times as we have all asked him to show us the proof, it's just never there completely, available for him to prove. He claims we aren't worthy, or some such nonsense. It's buried under something or he misplaced it, or it's unclear." Gavin looked at me a long minute. "He told me you work at a used book and manuscript shop. The reason I chased you down, I just want to make sure you aren't scammed into giving him some sort of financial compensation for a bunch of junk."

"He said his things weren't for sale, but he would give them to whomever would continue his work."

"Well, I'm glad to hear that, but I wouldn't be surprised if he counters with some sort of dollar figure. Please just be aware."

"Thank you, Gavin. I will be," I said, not wanting to explain that I'd been in my business long enough that it would have been difficult for his great-uncle to fool me into believing he had enough proof of the existence of the Loch Ness Monster that I would pay for the evidence.

However, though I wasn't a believer, I wouldn't have minded being proven wrong.

"Good. Here." He reached into his back pocket, grabbed his wallet, and pulled out a business card. "Here's my information. Call me if you feel you need to. I'm pretty sure that now that Norval has met you, he'll become a part of your life. The fact that you work at The Cracked Spine only makes me surer."

"I would love to see him again," I said, and I meant it. I glanced at the card, but didn't digest the details other than noticing the word "finance" before looking back at him.

He frowned doubtfully. "Thank you, Ms. Nichols. A pleasure to meet you." He extended his hand and we shook again before we said goodbye.

Gavin took off with hurried steps but not back toward Norval's apartment. Before I set out for the bus stop again, I glanced back at Norval's door and foil-covered window. There was no sign of him peering out of either. I hoped he was okay.

I looked at the card:

GAVIN MACLEOD, EXECUTIVE DIRECTOR, MACLEOD FINANCE.

His office was located not far off the Royal Mile, and his card listed both his office phone number and his personal mobile. I didn't think I'd ever need the card, but I kept it nonetheless, tucking it into my pocket just as I noticed dark clouds coming my way again.

I'd only meant to find someone to officiate at my wedding, but I'd ended up with that and more. The entire world was fascinated by the Loch Ness Monster. I didn't believe the answer as to whether or not she truly existed was inside Norval's apartment. But a tiny part of me hoped that maybe it was. And maybe she did. And maybe I'd get to go inside there again and look for her.

I eyed the approaching clouds, and double-timed it to the bus stop.

a ponytail and everything, had retrieved a simple knit hat embroidered with the Edinburgh Managers' logo. I'd become better acquainted with soccer—I mean football—over the last year, but I wasn't sure I should be given the honor of wearing the logo. Football teams and their loyalties were taken very seriously.

"Is it really that bad?" I said.

"Aye," Hamlet said. "In fact, I've never quite seen it so." He waved his hands around his head.

I put on the cap.

"Looks lovely," Rosie said. It sounded like she meant: "much better."

I smiled, and Hector agreed. Once the hat was on he seemed to recognize me and think it okay to trot over for a proper welcome. I picked him up and we exchanged kisses and hugs. A little larger than the teacup that was sometimes mentioned in a miniature Yorkie's description, what the tiny, adorable Hector lacked in size, he made up for in loyalty and love. Everyone was in love with Rosie's dog, and he was in love with all of us.

The shop's phone rang. It was an old phone, plugged into the wall with a cord that snaked over the floor to Rosie's desk, and its ring reminded me of black-and-white movies I used to watch at my grandmother's house. A harsh, vibrating jangle.

The rest of the bookshop fit well with the old-fashioned ring, though it wasn't a harsh space at all. It was cozy, bordered on three sides by aged wooden shelves filled with books, most of them old and at least a little rare, but some contemporary too. We would be remiss not to have the occasional Harry Potter collection come through and graze the shelves until a customer in search of them came in, we'd all decided. A small shop, founded in the 1950s by Edwin, it had once been a bank.

Its back wall held a stained-glass window of scales weighted down with coins. I'd fallen in love with the space the moment I'd walked in. The rolling ladder along one side had cemented the love forever.

Stairs on the opposite side from the ladder led up and then over to the dark side, dark only because of the poor lighting from the exposed bulb in the ceiling of the collective space. However, the offices, loo, and kitchenette had some added lighting. My office, also known by us at The Cracked Spine as the warehouse, had its own lighting as well as some high-set windows. The windows let in natural light and kept me aware of the weather and general time of day, as I sometimes got lost in my job for hours on end. The warehouse stored Edwin's collections—items, some books but not all, that spanned the ages; some valuable, some not. It was my job to catalog everything in the warehouse. Well, that had been part of the original job description. I was now much more deeply involved with everything and found that learning histories sometimes only led to more mysteries, and mysteries could be quite distracting.

"The Cracked Spine. How may we help you today?" Rosie said as she answered. She smiled big. "Aye, she's right here. One moment." Rosie held the hand-piece toward me but then reversed it back to her ear. "We're so looking forward tae meeting ye verra soon. Aye. Here she is." She smiled as she handed it my way again. "It's yer brother."

"Hey, Wyatt," I said. I held Hector on one arm as I took the phone with my other hand. "I was just thinking about you."

"Sis, you are not going to be happy," he said.

"Uh-oh. What's up?"

My brother, three years my elder, was sometimes dramatic, and sometimes seemed bigger than life. He was the epitome of a stereotypical farm boy, even at thirty-three. A big guy, who often wore overalls and could lift a tractor's back-end with one hand as he opened a beer with the other, Wyatt Nichols was a bit of a legend in our part of Kansas. Also good-looking, he'd clung tightly to his bachelor status. He wasn't like Tom had been before he met me—love 'em and leave 'em. Wyatt had always been honest, using a specific line many times: "I'm going out this evening. I'll buy the beers if you want to join me, but there's no room for second dates in this deal."

And, as strange as it was to all of us, women joined him for the beers and the company. Wyatt had never been lonely. In fact, he'd never been alone; the flow of women in and out of his life was constant and constantly surprising. None of us even knew there were that many single females in Kansas, let alone in our town—with vast lands and a low population.

The strangest part of it all was that Wyatt remained friends with most of the women. In fact, he'd "dated" many intelligent, independent women who wanted the same thing he did. Nothing permanent. *Whatever floats your paper hat,* Dad had said more than once.

"Our flight got bumped a day. The airport up and moved us. We won't be there until Sunday now," Wyatt said.

"What? Why?"

I could hear his shrug. "They didn't tell us. They just said we would be a day later than planned. They didn't apologize or anything."

"Sunday, not Saturday?"

"That's right."

"Well. I suppose it could be worse. It could have been cancelled altogether, but I want you guys here as soon as possible, and I don't want any chance you'll miss the wedding. I was hoping for some good padding in the timetable."

"We want to be there. Still plenty of time."

I heard both the restrained concern in his voice and grumbles in the background.

"Is that Mom and Dad?" I asked.

"Yep. Here's Mom."

"Delaney, we're sorry!" Mom said, her voice full of distress.

Tears began to burn behind my eyes. It was only one day, but I missed them all so much.

"It's okay, Mom," I said after I swallowed hard. "You'll be here soon. Plenty of time for just us. We can work with this. I can't wait to see you all."

"Us either, sweetie." Mom paused, but only briefly. "And, we will not miss the wedding, I promise. We will swim if we have to."

I smiled. "Thanks, Mom."

"Are you sure we can't bring anything?"

Of course, my family had been surprised by the news, but they'd come to accept that I was old enough to make these sorts of decisions for myself. But all along the way, Mom had continually asked if she needed to send anything or bring something with her.

She'd been asking me the same question since we'd scheduled the flight. I sensed there was something behind it, but I had no idea what it could be. I wondered if it was just the sense of discombobulation I'd thrown at them. They knew I'd been dating a Scottish pub owner, but they were surprised by the engagement. I'd been surprised by the engagement. The distance made them completely uninvolved in my relationship with the man I was going to marry. I was sure it made them feel disconnected, and I wondered if Mom was just trying to find a way to bring a bit of Kansas to Scotland so I wouldn't forget where I'd come from.

After a pause that went on too long, one I could blame on the transatlantic nature of the call if she asked, I said, "Just yourselves. Safe and sound. I can't wait to see you."

"Okay!" Mom said with forced cheer. "See you soon. Can't wait."

In the background I heard my dad and Wyatt chime in with "Can't wait either"s.

I placed the handpiece gently back onto the cradle and my fingers lingered.

"What is it, lass?" Rosie asked.

I looked at her and smiled. "They'll be here. A day later is no big deal, right?"

"Of course not!" Rosie said.

But it was Hector's nuzzle into my neck that made me truly feel better.

"No, of course not," I said. I took a deep breath and let it out. It would be fine. They would be here. It had been over a year since I'd seen them, and I was looking forward to every minute of their visit. I felt robbed of twenty-four hours, one thousand, four hundred and forty minutes. I would have to suck it up.

"It will be all right, lass," Rosie said with a smile.

"Of course, it will," I said. "I know."

"Did you talk tae the reverend?" Hamlet asked.

"I did, and she agreed to officiate, but she wants to have a brief meeting with Tom and me first."

"Why?" Rosie asked.

"I think she wants to ask Tom why he doesn't attend church with his father. I guess she's curious." And she wanted to see for herself that he's ready for this, but I kept that part to myself. It had been the subject of many a discussion over the last year. No need to trudge it up again now.

"I see. Weel, Tom will answer her direct and it will be fine," Rosie said, somewhat doubtfully.

"He'll be fine," Hamlet said. He was wiping his hands on an old white rag and I smelled something that reminded me of elementary school.

"I smell paste," I said.

"That's probably because I'm pasting things," he said.

"Into the scrapbook," Rosie said. "Hamlet wasnae busy and we needed tae add some things I've been collecting."

"Scrapbook?" I asked.

"Aye, Rosie's book," Hamlet said. He noticed my questioning eyes. "We haven't told you about the scrapbook? Oh, that is a disgrace. It's one of our most important things. Rosie has basically written the history of the bookshop, perhaps a history even bigger than the shop but that's up for argument I suppose, with the scrapbook. Pictures, articles, notes, cards. It's quite the thing."

"I can't wait to see it. How have I missed it?"

"I keep it in my office," Rosie said. "I don't trust any other place, what with so many things coming and going all the time."

"I'd love to see it." I took a step toward the back table currently hidden by a partial wall but before I could go far, deep, dark shadows filled the bookshop and thunder rumbled from outside. Rain suddenly fell in sheets, rattling the glass in the front window.

"'Tis wicket oot there again," Rosie said.

Diverting our conversation further, the bell above the door jingled in tandem with another thunder rumble. We all, Hector included, turned to greet the customer.

Clad in a black rain jacket, a black cowboy hat, and with a black satchel over his shoulder, the tall man lowered his red brollie gracefully and pushed the button with a click and a splattering *whoosh*.

"Damn. I'm getting your floor wet," he said, his Southern drawl thick. Southern United States.

"It's all right. It sees rain quite aft," Rosie said.

The man blinked and I looked at Hamlet. I thought I knew what "aft" meant, but he'd confirm.

"Frequently, often," Hamlet translated.

The customer nodded at Hamlet and smiled at Rosie. "Is it all right if I just leave the umbrella by the door?"

His accent was so thick I wondered if Rosie and Hamlet felt the way I did about the thicker Scottish accents I'd come across, like Rosie's. I had to listen a little harder when she or my landlords spoke. Or, I used to have to listen harder. I realized with a bit of pride that I hadn't done that in some time.

"Aye, come in from the storm a wee bit. We've got coffee," Rosie said after she seemed to process the man's words.

"Well, thank you kindly, but I'm here for more than just an escape from the rain. Is Edwin MacAlister in?"

"Not at the moment. Can we help you? I'm Delaney," I said. I put Hector down and walked toward the dripping man, who seemed to want to stay where he was until he stopped dripping. I knew how he felt.

"Pleasure. Angus Murdoch," he said as we shook. "I . . . uh, well, I have something I need to tell him. I need to show

Mr. MacAlister something." He patted his satchel. "I can come back when he's in."

"It's up tae you," Rosie said. "Come in from the storm for a few minutes anyway. Look around or have a seat in the back if ye'd prefer."

Angus's eyebrows came together and he surveyed the rest of us. He'd been friendly, but his expression turned serious. "I'd love to, but I might not be all that welcome."

We looked at him expectantly. He patted the satchel again and continued.

"I'm soaked through and . . ."

"Och, come on in with ye," Rosie said when he didn't continue right away. "We've been dripped on afor. We'll not hang ye in the market or anything. It's raining hard oot there. Come in."

The man looked at me but resumed smiling. "I guess I didn't know a hanging in the market might be an option."

"Well, I suppose it used to be," I said with a shrug. "But Rosie's word is good. We won't hurt you right off. Come on in."

He took off his jacket and hung it and the umbrella on the coatrack by the door. He wiped his hands on the stomach of his long-sleeved black T-shirt, and Johnny Cash lyrics came to my mind, even more so when I noticed his black boots and the big silver belt buckle.

I hadn't meant to stare, but he caught me nonetheless.

"I'm here from Dallas, Texas. You're American?" he said as he moved away from the front door.

"Wichita, Kansas," I said. "Other parts of Kansas too, but most recently Wichita."

"Great basketball at that university," he said.

"My dad's a fan."

"How did you end up here?" Angus asked. "I'm assuming you work here?"

"I do. For about a year now. I was laid off from a museum in Wichita and I needed an adventure. I answered an online ad."

"I'll be. That sounds . . . wonderful."

"It is. Come on in."

When we were all comfortable at the back table, with coffees supplied by Rosie, Angus said, "I heard about this bookshop one time before, a few years back. A friend visited Edinburgh and stopped by. He said it was the most amazing place." Angus looked around a moment. "He was right. There's something about it that's welcoming yet mysterious. Anyway, this place came back into my life recently. I'll explain."

We waited, but when he didn't continue right away, Hamlet said, "The mysteriousness could be the dark clouds, but we do try tae be welcoming."

Angus looked around again. "I bet." He bit his bottom lip. He was struggling to find either the right words for his story or the right way to tell it. He moved his attention back to the satchel he'd placed on the floor, propped up against the leg of the chair. "Anyway, I brought this." He pulled out a book and handed it directly to me. "It was in my grandfather's things. A trunk I've had for over twenty years, since right after Gramps died, but I only recently opened it. I was close to him, and it took me that long . . . It was hard to lose him. He left me many things that are of no value to anyone but me, but this . . . I'm afraid this is worth something, and I'd already scheduled my trip to Edinburgh. It all seemed fortuitous, actually. I thought about just putting it on my shelf and pulling it down when I wanted to remember some of the reading adventures I had with Gramps, but I think that might be irresponsible if it is as valuable as I think it is. In fact, it might belong in a museum or something."

As I looked at the book, my curiosity transformed quickly—into shock, and then slight panic. I shared a look with Hamlet, whose reactions were equal to mine if a step slower.

"You don't think?" I said to Hamlet.

"It can't be," Hamlet said a moment later. "Later editions were printed. That must be what this is, a later edition."

I didn't want to touch the book. I put it back on the table, dropping it more than setting it. I didn't want human hands to ever touch it again. It was that big a deal.

"Should I get some gloves?" Hamlet asked as he stood and moved toward a shelf with a box of gloves.

"Yes, please."

"Empty." He held up the box.

"Here." I pulled my keys from my pocket and handed them to Hamlet. "I have some. If you wouldn't mind running over."

Angus didn't miss the hand-off and his eyes grew big when they noticed the old blue skeleton key.

"What's going on?" he asked.

"Hamlet's going to run over to my office and get some gloves. It's on the other side of the building."

"I got that part, Ms. Nichols. This book is . . . valuable, then?"

"I think so." I nodded. "You know the stories?"

"Of King Arthur and his knights? Of course. My grandfather and I enjoyed them all. I can't remember if he read to me directly from that book, but he read the stories to me frequently, written by a fella named Pyle. So, was this book really printed in 1634, like it says in there, or was that just when the stories were first written? I did a little research and found the author's name, Thomas Malory, but I don't quite understand how everything works together. Pyle, Malory?"

I shook my head. I still hadn't lifted the cover.

Wherein is declared his Life and Death; with all his glorious Battailes against the Saxons, Saracens, and Pagens, which, for the Honour of his Country, he most worthily achieved.

The bookish voice was Arthur himself, who spoke in my head, words from that title page. I'd only seen that page a couple of times, but my strange memory quirk piped up with an old, English accent. Tears filled my eyes, as they sometimes did when the voices spoke, and I blinked them away.

"I guess the simplest explanation is that there have been a few King Arthur storytellers over the centuries, but it is thought that Sir Thomas Malory was the first. This edition of his work—I believe it's the Stansby edition—wasn't the very first. Malory first wrote the stories in the late 1400s. This is a reprint. However, it's an old, valuable reprint, called the Stansby edition because the printer was named William Stansby. Over the centuries, lots of changes to the stories were made, so it's not so much author as rewriter who gets the credit, in my opinion. Edwin will know more, but I'm pretty sure Malory was the first recorded writer to put ink to paper about King Arthur. The printer got all the credit with this one and he made some changes to the original story. I'll need to check the inside to make sure, but you said you saw the date 1634?"

"Yes, ma'am."

"It's probably what I think it is, then. As I mentioned, other editions have been printed since then, including the collection authored by Pyle in the early 1900s, but if you saw the date . . . Wow, do you have any idea where your grandfather got this?"

Angus's mouth made a straight line as he took a deep breath

and let it out. "There's a parcel more to this story. The truth is the truth and it usually gets out there, and that's what I came here to do; get the truth set straight. My grandfather left me a note with this book." Angus cleared his throat. "He said that he stole this book from this bookshop many years ago. He wanted me to return it to Mr. Edwin MacAlister."

Rosie, who had been sitting quietly and observing the conversation with Hector on her lap, gasped lightly. Other than that small noise, a swallow of silence filled the bookshop. This was not simple theft, but something more. The book might be considered priceless. I sat back in the chair, feeling like the air had been let out of me.

"I see," I finally said a long moment later. I was looking at the book over my steepled fingertips as Hamlet came around the wall with the box of gloves I kept in the warehouse.

He stopped short when he saw my face. "What?"

"I think we'd better call Edwin," I said.

"Aye?" Hamlet looked at the book on the table, at Angus, and then back at me. "Aye. I'll ring him right away."

SEVEN

"Twenty years anon?" Rosie said.

"Yes," Angus said.

"It's no wonder ye cannae remember." Rosie looked at Edwin.

Edwin had arrived at the shop fifteen minutes after Hamlet called him. Though he wore his typical outfit of slacks, a nice shirt, and a tie, he seemed to be dressed up a notch or two. I noticed it when he walked into the shop and slipped out of his raincoat. I wondered now if there was some reason for his sharp style.

"I don't remember the book," Edwin said as he looked at Angus. His eyebrows came together and he looked at me. "I'm afraid I was even more disorganized twenty years ago than I was right before you joined us, lass. Who knows what was on my shelves back then."

There was no hiding my doubt. "But you know books, Edwin. If this book came into the shop, even twenty years ago, you would have immediately understood its value."

He shrugged. "Not if it came in a box and one of my em-ployees at the time didn't know. Maybe just put it on the shelf."

Rosie had worked with Edwin forever, but Hamlet was barely twenty himself.

"You might have hired people who wouldn't know this was an important book?" I looked back and forth at Edwin and Rosie.

They both shrugged, so casually that a simmer of anger blossomed under my skin. I could tell they weren't being com-pletely transparent, but why? I would think they would want to remember that book.

But as I looked at them more closely, I wondered if my anger was misplaced. They actually might not remember. I wanted them to know specifically what had happened so much that I didn't want to accept their memory loss, the passing of twenty years and many more books through their hands. I was too wound up.

Angus had been concerned but not embarrassed by what his grandfather had done. I sensed he'd probably come to Edin-burgh for the singular purpose of returning the book, that anything else he did while in Scotland was just extra fun. I had to give him credit; he could have made a lot of money with the book. He could have put it on his shelf. He could have just thrown it in the mail with a note to Edwin. That option made me sick to my stomach.

Angus's grandfather had apparently loved the stories of King Arthur. The ideal world of Camelot and the magical stories of the king, the knights, Guinevere, Merlin, and Lance-lot, were universally appealing—at least they should be, the bibliophile in me concluded.

Angus again claimed that until he opened the long-closed trunk, he didn't think he'd ever seen the book, that his grandfather had read him the stories from contemporary copies, not anything remotely monetarily valuable.

Though this copy was an old reprint, it was still a first edition, and it was pristine. Perhaps it was in the shape it was because it had been well preserved in a trunk for twenty years. That *might* have explained it.

However, I was having a hard time with all of it, even though it seemed everyone was doing the right thing. I couldn't pinpoint what was bothering me so much. Maybe a bookish voice could tell me, but I didn't want my attention to veer away from the current discussion.

"I'm a bit of an annoyance when it comes to the King Arthur stories," Edwin said. "Aye, Malory created the original, but very few of us have taken a look at those centuries-old versions. They're available to read online nowadays, but so long ago, writing was different. Misspelled words, no punctuation—a real mess when compared with contemporary writing. I give a lot of credit tae the editors, printers, publishers who polished and reprinted the stories, as well as Pyle, who wrote the stories most of us know today. Other writers have contributed stories too."

"Are you and Delaney saying that an editor and other writers should get every ounce of credit for the stories, not Malory at all?" Angus asked.

"Well, they were originally conceived in Malory's imagination as far as we can tell, unless he was just recounting history as he knew it." Edwin's eyes twinkled.

"You believe there was a real Arthur?" Angus asked.

Edwin laughed. "I don't have a strong opinion either way,

but I do like tae think about it, imagine maybe. And it was *editors*. There was more than one. This is William Stansby's edition. William Caxton was in there along the way too. I believe there was a Chalmers, and, of course, the Winchester manuscript."

We all looked at him.

"Aye. In the earlier part of the twentieth century, a manuscript of the work was found in Winchester, England, a rumored site for Camelot itself. In fact, there's a round tabletop now mounted on the wall of the great hall at the Winchester castle, painted with the knights' names."

"Really?" I said.

"Aye. But it's only something Henry VIII commissioned tae be created. Although, if old Henry's son had lived, he would have been a King Arthur." Edwin smiled again. "Besides, the original table in the stories was made to seat one hundred and fifty men. The reproduction in Winchester is much smaller than the genuine one would have been. If there really had been a genuine one."

For a brief instant, I saw the boy Edwin had once been, but he was gone just as quickly. That had happened a few times over the last year.

"Do you like the stories?" I asked him.

"Oh, aye," he said. "No matter who wrote them."

"You do, in fact, believe there was a King Arthur, don't you?"

"I believe there is much we don't know."

Angus added, "The stories seem too big and put Arthur in too many places at once to think he was real. I think what most fascinated my grandfather, and in turn, me, was what could possibly have sparked the stories? Who influenced the world at the time, even if we didn't quite understand what time in history they were actually being written in, in such a big way that the stories even came to someone? Much mystery there."

I nodded as a notion came to me abruptly. "Oh. Are you here to search for the grail?"

Angus smiled again. "No, in fact I'm not. I am however considering a trip to Winchester now. Sounds mighty fine, the tabletop on a castle wall and everything."

"There are a number of possible locations for Camelot," Hamlet piped up and then looked at me. "You considered one for the wedding. Arthur's Seat."

"Really? I didn't know."

"Arthur's Seat?" Angus asked.

"It's a popular hike." Hamlet nodded toward the correct direction. "The hills up from Holyrood Park. Arthur's Seat is the main peak. There's a beautiful view of the city from up top."

"I'll have to check that out too." He turned to me. "You're getting married?"

I kept expecting to hear him say "little lady" at the end of his sentences. It wasn't just the accent; there was a tone to his voice reminiscent of the movie star John Wayne.

"Yes, but the hike seemed too much to ask of the guests," I said.

"She means me," Rosie said.

"Not just you." I smiled at her.

Aggie, my landlady, had been taken into consideration too, and Tom's father, Artair, though I was pretty sure he could have handled it. Of the older attendees, Edwin and my parents would have been fine. I didn't know how Edwin stayed in such good shape, but he could probably beat us all up to the top. My farmer parents were both in great shape, if somewhat weary from their farm lives, and would have made it up without a problem.

"Aye, weel, hiking up there used tae be a fun adventure for me, but that was some time ago," Rosie said.

"It's not one of the more popular possible Camelot locations," Hamlet continued. "But it's brought up every now and then."

"I'll definitely give it a climb." Angus looked at me. "Where did you decide to have the big event?"

I was uncomfortable talking about my wedding right then, but I wasn't sure why. Maybe it was because I'd kept it such a small, personal event and his questions made him seem like an interloper. I was glad when Rosie answered for me.

"Right where the wedding belongs," she said. "Here, of course."

"That's a great idea," he said. "This place is mighty magnificent!"

"I agree," Rosie said, but she changed the subject back around. "Edwin, what are we going tae do about this book?"

He hadn't mentioned calling the police. I didn't think the police needed to be called either, but I was surprised by my boss's casual attitude about it all.

"I don't know," Edwin said. He looked at Angus. "Something makes me think the book should be yours. I wish I remembered the circumstances around it; I wish I'd known your grandfather. There's something about him having it for so many years that makes me think you should have it now."

"Oh, no, Mr. MacAlister. I won't be leaving with that book. It's yours, and I don't want it in my possession any longer. It's too much responsibility," Angus said. "I'm only staying put in this chair right now in case you want to call anyone and file charges. Besides it was raining cats and cows out there. I'd've just dropped it off or mailed it if I didn't want to make sure you felt everything had been paid up. Somehow, there's got to be some payback with interest involved. Know what I mean?"

"I do, young man, but . . . well, will you be in Edinburgh for a while?" Edwin asked. "Not for any sort of fence mending, mind, but just in case I'd like tae talk tae you about it. I'd like tae try tae remember your grandfather and tell you that story. Sometimes if I let things sit a while, I do remember."

"I'd like that. I'd like that a lot."

I'd been trying to judge Angus's age since he first mentioned that he hadn't opened the trunk for twenty years. Suddenly, he looked older than I'd originally thought.

"How old were you when your grandfather died?" I asked.

"Twenty-six," he said. "A full-grown man, but we were tight, he and I. I will miss him always, I expect."

"I'm sorry," I said.

"Me too," Edwin said.

Rosie and Hamlet nodded in agreement.

"Thank you, but it *has* been twenty years. I've gotten on with my life, which is as he would have wanted. Finding this book rattled all my cages, you know, but I have been living life."

"Let me think about it," Edwin said again. "Maybe I'll remember something useful—tae me and tae you."

"I'd rightly appreciate that." Angus slapped his own thighs, the sound making us all jump. "Alrighty, then, I'll be on my way. It sounds like there's a break in the rain." He stood and reached into his back pocket and handed Edwin a piece of paper with some handwriting on it. "Here's my number. My cell is on there, and I bought a UK SIM card when I got here. Feel free to contact me at any time. I'll be in the country another week or so."

Hamlet and I stood too. Rosie, with Hector on her lap, remained seated.

With his typical grace and good manners, Edwin escorted the man whose grandfather had stolen one of his most valuable books to the door and bid him a polite and proper farewell. I tagged along because it felt like the right thing to do.

After Angus shook Edwin's hand and thanked him, he took my hand and held it with both of his.

"You are one of our American beauties," he said. "Congratulations to your fiancé. The rest of us will have to regret we didn't meet you first."

His words disarmed me. They felt over the top and I wondered if he was being too sincere or sarcastic. Then, I remembered where he was from. Texas charm is a real thing.

"It was a pleasure to meet you," I said, my best polite-self keeping my response short and simple.

Once Angus was gone, Edwin and I rejoined Rosie and Hamlet.

"Edwin," Rosie said first, "I don't remember a thing."

"Aye?"

"Do you?" Hamlet asked him.

"Do you remember either the grandfather or the book, or maybe both?" I asked.

"No, not clearly, at least. I'd like tae think about it, see if anything comes back tae me, and then figure out the best approach. I have . . . a recollection of a book, but as time will sometimes do, the book I'm remembering isn't exactly this book." He looked at the rare tome still on the table. "Something's off, but I'm not sure exactly what."

"It's all very unbelievable," I said.

Edwin looked at me with more focus now. "Get caught out in the rain earlier?"

I put my hand up to the hat. "I did."

"The hat is charming," he said.

Rosie laughed. "We've some decorations tae talk about, Delaney. What do ye want tae do with the book, Edwin?"

"I think I'll take this one home with me," Edwin said, though his mind seemed a million miles away. He looked at me again. "Tomorrow, we have an appointment. Will you be available in the afternoon?"

"Of course." I'd learned not to ask more specifics unless we were alone, but I guessed we probably had an auction to attend. Though Rosie and Hamlet knew about the auctions, they didn't know, didn't want to know, all the details. Fleshmarket Batch, the group named after one of Edinburgh's more well-known closes, or alleys, was made up of a secretive bunch of very rich people. Rosie had enough on her plate managing the bookshop and Edwin's finances, and Hamlet didn't want details about anyone's money.

Without needing instruction, Hamlet grabbed a bag from a back shelf and put the book into it. He folded it over the top and handed it back to our distracted boss.

"Right. Thank you, lad." Edwin took the bag with the book. "I'll be off for now, but tomorrow, Delaney, all right?"

"I'll be here," I said, but Edwin wasn't looking at me; his attention was focused on the bag. I looked at Rosie, who was also watching Edwin.

We all watched as our boss left and then the three of us shared inquisitive looks.

"It's probably the book, that's all," Rosie said.

"Probably," I said.

"I don't know," Hamlet said in rare dissention.

We might have asked him more about what he thought the cause of Edwin's distraction was, but just then Hector sent out a tiny bark in support of Hamlet. We laughed, and the tension dissipated.

I would ask Edwin for more details tomorrow. Though we didn't have many secrets at The Cracked Spine, he seemed to have many himself, but he was sharing them with me bit by bit. And, he tended to prefer one-on-one conversations to group discussions.

I stepped around the table and looked out the front window. Neither Angus nor Edwin was in sight, and the rain had stopped. The sun peeked hesitantly from behind some clouds, giving a glimmer to the rain-soaked Grassmarket.

I hadn't had a chance to mention Norval Fraser, but King Arthur had trumped the Loch Ness Monster, at least for now. One crazy myth at a time.

Unease rattled inside me, but I couldn't place why. No bookish voices were talking, but something was off. It could have been my family's delayed flight, or the strange meeting with Norval Fraser, or the other strange meeting with Angus Murdoch. It could have been all of it.

Maybe it was just an uneasy kind of day.

I would put my focus on the wedding. That would surely get things back in line.

EIGHT

"Are you sure Aggie wants to do that?" I asked Elias as he steered the cab toward The Cracked Spine.

"Aye, lass, she was upset that ye hadnae asked her. I had tae convince her ye were just trying tae be polite. Ye need tae quit being so polite. It will be the death of me."

"But baking a wedding cake is so much work," I said. I had planned to order cupcakes from the bakery next to the bookshop. It was such a small wedding, with only family and the closest of friends. We were having dinner catered at the pub and I thought pretty cupcakes would serve the purpose. But I really should have known better.

My almost accidental landlords, Elias and Aggie McKenna, had become family just as much as everyone at the bookshop had. Elias and his cab had been outside the airport when I'd first landed in Edinburgh. I'd been drawn to him and, again, my intuition had proved to be on target. He and his wife, Aggie, had conveniently not only had guesthouses that they rented out but an extra cottage they could spare for me to live in for a ridiculously low rent. I loved my cottage. I loved my landlords, even if they were sometimes a wee bit overprotective. I didn't consider my meeting them a complete accident only because of that intuitive pull I'd felt toward them. It had been meant to be, and, of course, Aggie would feel slighted that I hadn't involved her in the wedding, thought to ask her to bake a cake.

"Lass, baking a wedding cake is also an honor. Particularly for Aggie. How do ye not ken that?"

Frustration pulled his voice into a tight wire. I tried not to smile with affection at him as I put my hand on his arm.

"I would love for Aggie to make the wedding cake. And it would be *my* honor to have her do it. Should I call her right now?"

Relief relaxed his furrowed brow. "No. Ring her this afternoon. She's cleaning the guesthooses this morning. She'll be thrilled tae the gills."

"Not as thrilled as I am, Elias. Truly."

"Good. Oh, aye?" he said as he pulled onto the narrow street in front of the bookshop. It was early, too early for my coworkers to be at work. The bakery nearby started baking at four o'clock, so its lights were on, but the other businesses on the short street, The Cracked Spine included, were dark. I'd wanted to get some work done before Edwin and I left for the appointment he'd mentioned the day before. As I'd walked out of my cottage and toward the bus stop, Elias had burst from his cottage with coffee mug in hand and told me he would drive me in this morning. He was fully dressed and shaved, so eventually I deduced he'd been waiting for me so we could talk about the cake.

The sun rose about five a.m. in July in Edinburgh, and set around nine thirty at night. I'd become used to going to bed when there was some lingering light outside. Often, I went to bed early when Tom worked late. I liked getting up extra early and getting to work, so Tom and I could fit in some time together in the afternoons. It was only five thirty by the time Elias turned into Grassmarket, but the sun was on its way up, and the clouds were few and far between, for now.

I followed Elias's line of vision to the bookshop's front doors. I blinked twice and wondered if I was seeing what, or who, I thought I was seeing in the dawn's leftover gloom.

I decided I was. Norval Fraser was there. He paced in a small circle and worried his hands together.

"Oh dear," I said. "I'd better talk to him."

"I'll come with you," Elias said.

I wouldn't have been able to talk Elias out of joining me even if I'd wanted to, and I didn't want to. Norval was mostly a stranger, and his great-nephew had been correct about him being eccentric, even if he'd seemed sweet and harmless too.

Elias parked the cab quickly. We both hopped out and approached the pacing man.

"Hello, Norval," I said as I tried to catch his attention. He was talking to himself, and his eyes were glazed as they darted everywhere but at me.

I looked at Elias as he sidled up next to me. I nodded and then put my hand on Norval's arm. He yanked it away.

"Easy there," Elias said. He wedged himself a bit more in between Norval and me. "How can we help ye today?"

"Norval?" I said.

Norval's eyes popped into focus and he looked at me. "Oh, lass, there ye are. I've been waiting for an hour at least."

"It's five-thirty in the morning, Norval. The shop still doesn't open for a while. What can I do for you?"

A frown pulled hard at his mouth as his eyes filled and then spilled over with tears. "Something's wrong with Gavin, my nephew."

"What's wrong?" I said.

"I dinnae ken. He's not answering his phone."

I put my hand on his arm. "Should we go inside and try to call him from here?"

"No, no. I want tae . . . I need tae get tae his flat."

"Where does he live?"

He sent a westerly nod. "Two blocks that way. I thought of you first thing when I couldnae reach him, lass. If . . . I mean . . . I want someone tae take my papers."

Elias and I looked at each other.

"How about a cuppa or some coffee?" Elias said.

"No, sir. I need tae get tae his flat."

Elias and I looked at each other again. Norval was clearly afraid of something, but I wondered if his fear was unreasonable, maybe some sort of night terror. It was no longer nighttime, I thought, as I squinted toward the edge of the brightening sky.

"Would you mind just driving us over?" I asked Elias. "We can talk on the way."

He nodded. "Aye."

Norval sat in the back seat as I sat in the front passenger seat.

"Okay, Norval, we're going over to Gavin's, but can we take a second and calm down a little, take a couple of breaths?" I said.

Norval looked at me as he did what I suggested. He took a deep breath, and then another. With clearer words and eyes, Norval gave Elias directions to Gavin's flat.

"I have my cell phone. Do you want me to try to call Gavin as we go?" I said, wishing I'd kept Gavin's card with me or taken the time to run inside the shop first. *I left the card on my desk,* I thought.

"I've tried all morning! We talk in the early mornings. It's how we start the day. He's up at three-thirty every single day. He works with money and money is worldwide, he always says. I ken something's wrong."

"Did you call the police?" Elias asked Norval as he sent me furrowed eyebrows.

"No, they . . . they dinnae like me keeping so many papers. They dinnae think fondly of me. I just need tae see for myself."

Chances were pretty good that nothing was wrong with Gavin MacLeod, but Norval's panic was contagious. The unease I'd felt in the bookshop the day before had disappeared, but it was sneaking back under my skin. *Something* was off.

I looked at my cell phone, thinking about texting Inspector Winters, a police inspector I'd come to know, but I didn't. Surely, this was about Norval's eccentricities more than something truly being wrong with Gavin. I needed to keep him calm and keep myself calm. Maybe I could distract him.

I turned and looked backward. "Norval, what happened the next night with your father, the night you were supposed to meet Nessie?"

He only blinked once before he remembered the conversation and its abrupt interruption.

"Och, lass, the next night my da wasnae there. He was gone. He wasnae anywhere after that. He disappeared. Into the loch with the beast."

"Oh, Norval, I'm so sorry," I said.

"No, I dinnae want yer pity, lass, I just want ye, someone,

tae do my work. Keep up the search for the monster and whatever might remain of my da. There, that building," he pointed,
"that's where Gavin lives."

With the speedy skill of someone who'd driven a cab for decades, Elias maneuvered his into a narrow space on the street
not far from the building.

We were out in a flash, Elias moving fast enough that he led
the way inside. He sent me a look that said, *This man with us
isn't in his right mind, and I'm going to make sure no one gets
hurt.* I adored Elias, but that thing that had been niggling at
my intuition made me want him on alert as he forged the way.
I sent him back some eyes that said, *You be careful.* He got it.

Even in our rush up the stairs of the old two-story building, I noticed it was in worse shape than I might have predicted.
Though I'd only met Gavin the day before, the impression he'd
made was one of affluence. Expensive clothes and a business
card that mentioned a finance company. Dingy floors and stairs
with a chipped paint railing hadn't come to mind.

"Which flat?" Elias asked backward over his shoulder.

"It's 2B, just the door up and on the left," Norval said.

Elias pounded on the door. "Gavin, man, we've got your
uncle here."

There was no answer.

"Do you have a key?" I asked.

"Oh! Aye." Norval reached into his back pocket and pulled
out a ring with only two keys. There was no fob, just the ring.
"I hate to intrude though."

If the man holding the keys hadn't been so old, feeble, and
a little confused or whatever was going on, I thought Elias
might have spoken his impatience loudly. Instead, Elias just sent
Norval a withering look, took the keys, and inserted one into

the lock. He'd chosen the correct one and when the door swung in, he leaned with it and said, "Gavin, your uncle's here tae see you."

Silence. The kind that makes it clear all is not well.

"Should we go in?" Elias looked at me.

I looked at Norval.

"Aye, here, let me." He pushed around Elias.

The door opened all the way, and Elias and I followed Norval. The front room of the flat was small, but extraordinarily tidy, with perfectly placed and smoothed brown leather couch cushions and a few stacks of books that climbed in straight biggest-to-smallest upward towers in front of a packed but equally organized bookshelf.

To the left of the front room was a small kitchen nook with a stark, skinny-legged white table and two chairs tucked tight underneath. There was nothing on the table, even, as far as I could tell, a crumb.

But beyond this front space and at right angles from it were two facing doors. One was shut tight, but one was open. It's what was on the wooden floor by the open doorway that changed everything. It looked like a pool of blood. We gasped in unison.

Elias held Norval and me back as we both tried to move toward it.

"Let me look first!" he commanded, using his arms as barriers.

It must have taken him only a few seconds to convince us to stay still, but as I looked at the blood, it felt like time slowed to a muddy beat, and an eternity passed.

I grabbed Norval's arm and we waited while Elias looked inside the room.

Peering in, he deflated. "Call the police, right away."

"Elias? What is it?" I asked.

"Call the police, lass," Elias said.

Norval was silent as he blinked and looked back and forth between Elias and me.

"Should we try to help?" I asked. "I mean . . ."

"No, there's no help for the lad. Call the police," Elias said. "I am sure."

Norval swooned and Elias and I both reached to grab him. It was an awkward save, but we managed it.

And then, before I investigated the room where I assumed Gavin's dead body lay, I did exactly as Elias said, I called the police.

NINE

Norval came to only moments later, and as he and I sat on the brown couch and the sound of approaching sirens became louder, he startled and his eyes opened wide.

I put my hand on his arm. "Hey, Norval, it's okay. We called the police. They'll be here shortly."

"Aye, I understand. He's dead then?" Norval asked as he worked the zipper on the jacket he wore.

"I believe so. I'm so sorry."

Norval looked toward the door where Elias stood as the siren sounds continued to become louder.

He didn't seem overly bothered by Gavin's death, but he did seem frantic. I watched him closely for signs of something I might be able to understand and offer some sort of comfort for, but mostly he was busy trying to wrangle the zipper. Finally, when he got it to move, he freed a file folder he'd had underneath and extended it toward me.

"Take this, Delaney. When Gavin didnae answer this morning, I ken something happened tae him, I just ken. The police are going tae blame me, but I would never have hurt that boy.

I'll need someone, Delaney, someone tae continue my work. You'll do it won't ye?"

"Norval," I said in shock, as I reflexively took the folder.

"Hide it now! Hide it under your sweater. There are things in there you'll need tae see, if you're tae take over my work, if you're tae help me."

I shook my head, but the sirens suddenly stopped wailing and even from the second floor apartment, I could hear car doors opening and closing and approaching footsteps.

"Hide it in your sweater, lass," Elias said. "Sort it out later."

I stuck the folder underneath my sweater just before Inspector Winters led a group of officers inside.

———

The police didn't arrest Norval. They didn't arrest any of us, though they did seem plenty suspicious.

They separated us at first and questioned us, or more precisely, just asked for a sequence of events. I assumed two things—that all three of our stories were consistent and that all three of us left out the part where Norval gave me a folder he'd hidden under his jacket and was now under my sweater. Once that was completed, we all moved outside and Inspector Winters told Elias and me that Gavin's death was officially being ruled a homicide, that he'd been stabbed.

"He was killed?" I asked stupidly.

"Aye," Inspector Winters said.

"A knife? Stabbed?" I asked.

Again, that's what Inspector Winters had just told us, but he must have been used to people needing to repeat the horrible truths they'd just heard because he remained patient with me.

"Aye," Inspector Winters said again.

In the last year, I'd become so acquainted with the police inspector that he even knew my friends, and I had wondered if perhaps I should introduce him to my parents and Wyatt when they got into town. Maybe I should have invited him to the wedding.

Tom had recently joked that the inspector was probably bothered that Tom and I were getting married, only because now I wouldn't be under any sort of time crunch to have to leave Scotland. We'd laughed at the thought that Inspector Winters might be tiring of my input on local crimes, but sobered quickly. Maybe Tom had been correct.

"This is horrible," I said. My stomach had been swirling since we'd come upon Norval in front of the bookshop. I'd known something wasn't right. I wished my intuition had been incorrect, but in a way it had been. I'd thought something was "off." Murder was much worse than that. We'd come upon a murder victim, a man I'd met just the day before and who seemed to be in a rough relationship with his great-uncle, a man who'd sought me out and then whose priority, after learning his nephew was dead, was to sneak me a folder. I looked over at Norval, who was still with another officer sitting inside one of the police vehicles. "Any ideas? Any clues?"

"Not really. Not yet." Inspector Winters looked where I was looking. "Mr. Fraser is . . . isn't sharing his story as clearly as we would like. We're concerned and suspicious. At this point."

"Inspector Winters, I think . . . well, I don't know if Norval is well. I don't know much about mental health, but there's a chance . . . anyway, please keep that in mind. Maybe be gentle with him."

Inspector Winters looked at me and nodded, but didn't say

anything. I was under the impression that he heard well what I'd said. I hoped so.

Elias cleared his throat and Inspector Winters and I looked at him.

"Excuse me," Elias said. "Are we free tae go?"

Inspector Winters turned his attention toward two other officers standing about half a block away. One held a phone to his ear and the other one stood with his arms crossed in front of himself.

"Not quite yet," Inspector Winters said as he looked at me again. "Tell me again about the circumstances of meeting Misters Fraser and MacLeod yesterday."

He was obviously stalling, but I was willing to go over the story again. And this time I learned a little more too.

"We know all about Norval Fraser's obsession," Inspector Winters said when I finished retelling the part with Gavin outside Norval's apartment. "His apartment is a fire hazard, but he's not breaking any codes yet. We can't force him to clean things up, but I think we'd like to, for his safety as well as others'."

"Is he a troublemaker?" Elias asked.

"I wouldn't say troublemaker. He's disappeared a time or two. I've never been a part of those searches but some of the other officers mentioned that he can get himself . . . lost easily, which might be an indication that your concerns about his mental health are valid, Delaney."

"Gavin mentioned that whenever Norval went missing, they could usually find him in his apartment with his papers or up at Loch Ness."

Inspector Winters looked at me.

"Sorry," I said. "I just remembered that part."

"Aye. I don't know where they've found Norval, but he has gone missing a time or two. Anything else you might've forgotten from yesterday?"

I thought as I looked toward the police car again. "I think one of Norval's sisters is still alive. Millie. Gavin's mother is gone."

"Millie." Inspector Winters jotted down a note. "Norval couldn't seem to remember her name, but we would have found it eventually."

"Do you think he really couldn't remember or pretended not to?" I asked.

Inspector Winters shrugged. "I don't know, but he's certainly upset."

"To be expected," Elias said.

"Aye."

A whistle sounded from one of the officers down the block and Inspector Winters looked over there again. I watched as the officer who had been on the phone gave a thumbs-up.

"Well, I've got good news and I've got bad news," Inspector Winters said to us. We looked at him expectantly. "They got prints from the knife. I'll need your prints. It won't take long and we can do it here. If you'd rather come down to the station, you may."

Elias and I gave our prints to Inspector Winters on an iPad, using an app. I'd never seen anything like it. I assumed that Norval gave his prints on another iPad inside the vehicle he sat in.

"We'll analyze everything, but you're good tae go for now," Inspector Winters said when we were done. "Don't leave the country or anything."

"We won't," I said. "Can we take Norval home?"

"No, we'll take care of him," Inspector Winters said before he turned and made his way back to the patrol car.

Elias and I watched as he got in and seemed to give instructions to the officer in the driver's seat. The patrol car turned and drove away. As it did, Norval looked out the back window at me, his eyes filled with a mixture of hope and fear. My heart went out to him.

I hoped he wasn't in some way responsible for Gavin's murder. I hoped the police would take good care of him.

"Ye say anything about the file?" Elias asked me when we were inside his cab.

"Not a word. You?"

"Of course not."

"Good." And then after a long pause, "I hope he's not a killer."

"Aye. Someone is, though."

I nodded. "Let's get somewhere where we can look through this file."

"Right away."

TEN

I picked up the handwritten note on the top of the papers in the file and read aloud:

"Delaney, if something bad happened to my nephew, somewhere in my things is something that will prove I'm innocent. I would never hurt Gavin, but the police probably think I'm capable of such behavior. The police don't like me. They don't like my papers. Please, if they take me away, see if you can find the truth, and please take my papers. Do what you will with them. Yours in friendship, Norval."

"What could he be talking about? What's in his flat that would clear him?" Elias asked. "How did he think to write such a dire message only after wee Gavin didnae answer the phone?"

"I don't know, Elias. It seems very . . . scripted, but maybe not. There's so much in his apartment, it would be difficult to know where to begin. The police *did* take him away, but they are making sure he's okay. They didn't arrest him."

"Yet, I suppose."

"Okay, yet."

"His trust for you came easily," Elias said.

We'd hurried inside the still empty bookshop and stopped at Rosie's front desk, both of us too anxious to open the folder to go any farther.

I thought about that. "I think I was just top of his mind, the person he'd most recently met. He knows Edwin and that might also have helped him trust me. Perhaps people are wary of him. I wasn't wary in the least. He can recognize someone who loves a good story and a good mystery when he sees one."

"Maybe," Elias said doubtfully as he peered at the file.

"What I don't understand is why he immediately thought that something might be wrong with Gavin. That's a quick rush to judgment. He didn't talk to him this one morning, and he's certain something must have happened to his nephew. He prepares a folder for me, stops by the bookshop. He was very upset."

Elias rubbed his chin. "Makes ye wonder if he *was* the killer. Or . . ."

"What?"

"What if he'd already been by Gavin's flat earlier this morning? He might have seen his nephew dead. Maybe he didn't kill Gavin, but he was paranoid that the police would think he killed him, so he created this elaborate setup. These are purposeful actions, Delaney."

"I might agree, except . . . one thing contradicts another. He's purposeful but he's disappeared before and the police and his family have had to look for him. He can't keep a job. Is he . . . 'with it' or not?"

"I dinnae ken, lass. Ye said he had foil over his window. He's a paranoid one, for sure. Paranoid folks can also be obsessed. Maybe Nessie and his papers are his singular focus, and you got in the middle of his focus at the wrong time and whether you like it or not. If he cannae reach his nephew, maybe his mind automatically goes to protecting his papers. I would say he's daft, but I cannae know anything for sure."

"It's all possible, I guess," I said.

"Things don't add up, that's certain."

"You think he's trying to set me up for something?" I asked.

Elias bit his bottom lip. "No, not really. Using you maybe, but not setting you up as a killer, though I could be wrong. Ye dinnae know the wee man. Proceed with caution."

"Of course."

The file didn't contain much, but the five pieces of paper inside it were interesting. It took us a few minutes to get a grip on the particulars of the contents, but ultimately we figured out that there were two copies of handwritten accounts of Nessie sightings, and three copies of photographs.

One account was dated November 17, 1956, and was signed with the flourished signature of Melba Mayerson. The writing was big, making its wavy squiggles somewhat legible.

Melba wrote, "I was just there, minding my own business, on the middle of the western shore, and she surfaced. Her head first, and then her long neck, scaled and thick. She looked me straight in the eye, hers had a funny blue glow even during the middle of the clear day. She blinked twice. I remember that more than anything else. Two lazy blinks and then she went back under the water. She was like a lizard maybe, maybe an old dinosaur. I don't know, but it was all over so quickly that as sure as I am of what I saw, and though I never see things that aren't there, I still wonder. Did I see her? Did I see what I thought I saw, or am I making it up? I think she was real, but I have no way to prove it."

Elias and I looked at each other.

"Anyone could have written that," Elias said.

"At any time," I added.

"Aye."

I pulled out the next account. This one was signed by Charles Grayson, and was dated July 17, 2015.

I read, "She's a crafty one, and a grand dame, if you ask me. The loch is an unforgiving strip of water that is unappealing in every way; dark, murky, and never calm. I didn't expect it to be so gloomy, but, of course, the dark clouds in the sky didn't help. I didn't expect to see the monster. In fact, before that moment, I didn't believe in her. I was just a tourist, one that wanted to return to Edinburgh, a city with so much more to offer than these dark waters gave me. Or so I thought.

"I figured that since I was there anyway, I might as well take a good, long look. I walked along the shore for a time and then stood still, just me and the water, looking at it, getting it out of my system, so's I could say I'd done it when I got back home. Not another person nor boat in sight. It's like she knew I was alone, knew there would be no other witness.

"There was a stir about twenty feet out. Like water circling down a drain. I was baffled, and wondered about that too— was I really seeing a cyclone of water? Then there was no further hesitation. She flew up into the air, looked at me in the eye, and then dove back under. It was all so fleeting. The only remaining strange moment was when the water foamed at my boots. Unconsciously, I'd stepped deeper into the loch.

"She was a beast, to be sure, eel-like, but more like a dinosaur probably. I feel a fool saying such things, and I'll never tell this story. I'm only writing it down for Mr. Norval Fraser because of his call for eyewitness accounts, and his promises of secrecy. If he shares this with another person, I will sue him for everything he's got."

I looked at Elias again.

"Not so secret anymore," he said. "But we'll not let Mr. Grayson know."

"Right," I said. "But why did Norval want me to read these? They don't tell me anything about why someone might want to kill Gavin, or why Norval wouldn't."

"Tempt ye tae take his papers, I expect."

I shrugged. "It could work."

The three photographs were in black and white, and seemed to have been taken consecutively, one after the other, as quickly as an old camera that used film would allow. The numbers 1 through 3 were handwritten in black marker on the pictures' corners.

"It's hard to tell," I said as I held the first picture up. "Black-and-white, copies, and the water is so dark. Here, it does look like the long tail of some creature, but it's impossible to be sure."

"Aye," Elias said doubtfully as I spread out the three pictures on the desk.

Picture 1 was allegedly a tail over the top of the water. Picture 2 was the tip of the tail sticking up to a point. And picture 3 had been snapped when the tail had submerged halfway under the water. But the "tail" could have just been a trick of light and shadows. Or something that had been manufactured or faked. They were copies, after all; who knew what the originals looked like.

"Not a believer, huh?" I said.

"It's not that. I believe anything could be possible, but I'm a big believer in seeing things with my own eyes. All the public accounts seem sketchy, many later proven tae be lies. I'm hope-ful she's a real thing, Nessie is, but I need real proof first, and I dinnae want tae get my hopes up."

As I lifted and moved the last picture, we noticed that a key had been taped to the inside back flap of the file folder.

"That's how you're tae get into his flat, I suppose," Elias said.

"That seems to be the clear message." I touched the key. "But I'm not going into his flat. He might be home now. I'll go over tomorrow, knock, and return the folder. He'll need a friend, but I'm not sure if I'm the right person for that. I'm sym-pathetic, but I don't think I should be the person he runs to when he's worried about a family member. Maybe I'll try to get in touch with his sister. I don't know."

Elias rubbed his chin and studied me. "Aye. Good plan."

"What?"

"I ken ye, lass. I ken ye're a curious one."

"I promise I'll be smart."

"Aye."

I put the pictures and papers back into the file.

The bookshop's front door opened and Rosie, with Hector in the crook of her arm, came through. "I thought I saw the light on when I turned the corner. Good morning, Delaney. Elias. Is everything all right?"

Elias and I shared a look. Murder always did upset Rosie, but I couldn't think of a way not to tell her.

"I'll go get some coffee," Elias offered.

Rosie blinked. In her experience, Elias had never gone to get the coffee.

"Uh-oh. What's the bother, lass?" she said.

"Come in, Rosie, and I'll tell you all about it."

ELEVEN

Rosie took the news as well as could be expected.

After we shared some scant details, Edwin and Hamlet arrived and Elias left. Rosie rang Regg, her on-again-off-again boyfriend, and took a few minutes for a private conversation at the front of the shop, sitting in her chair and looking out the window at the market as Hector curled on her lap.

"I didn't think they were together at the moment," I said quietly to Edwin as we sat around the back table with Hamlet.

"They reunited," Edwin said. "Rosie missed him and he was more than happy tae take her calls again."

Rosie and Regg had broken up and made up more than any fickle high-schoolers I'd ever known. I'd told her I was available to talk about it if she wanted to. She never wanted to.

"I hope she invites him to the wedding," I said absently. I cleared my throat. "I told her he was welcome, but it was up to her."

Edwin shrugged. "We'll see, I suppose."

My limbs felt strangely detached, my head foggy. Clearly, the shock of the murder hadn't hit me all the way yet, because

I was beginning to feel it more and more, sneaky waves of panic that shook me momentarily. I thought I was regaining my composure, but a wave suddenly hit me and made my fingers tremble. I took another deep breath and let it out.

"Lass, I think you should go home. Take the day, take off until the wedding if you want. Your family will be here in a couple of days," Edwin said.

"No, no thank you. That's the last thing I want to do, sit around with nothing to do but think about . . . everything. I'll stay busy when my family gets here, but I'd like to work until then. Besides, you said we had an appointment."

"Aye, but . . . I don't mind going alone," Edwin said. But I heard disappointment in his voice. We always did enjoy the auctions together.

"I'm good." I wasn't, but I really did prefer to be busy.

Hamlet, who'd reacted to the murder by falling deeply silent, looked like he wanted to say something.

When he didn't, Edwin prompted, "What is it, lad?"

"I've heard of Norval Fraser," he said. "But I think lots of people have heard of Norval. He's always seemed so harmless. I didn't know his great-nephew at all."

"He had his own finance company?" I said.

"That might explain it." Hamlet smiled sadly. "But I wouldn't have any use for that. I hope Norval will be okay."

I looked at Edwin. "Do you remember visiting with Norval? Did he ask you for any money for his papers?"

"It was about fifteen years ago, but I remember the meeting, if not all the details. He was a very nice man. I wouldn't take over his work, and I was honest with him about that. He didn't ask me for money."

"Me either," I said. "Gavin told me to be on guard about

Norval asking. Maybe neither you nor I got that far with him. He must have asked someone for money. I can't think of any other reason Gavin would warn me it might happen."

"Oh, I can," Edwin said. He frowned. "It's impolite to speak of the dead this way, but I wouldn't have been surprised if Gavin wanted Norval's papers for himself someday. Who knows what's there—could be nothing, but could be something too, something valuable. But that's just a guess. He was warning you away, making you think that if you stuck it out and be-friended Norval by telling him you'd do the work, you would eventually be asked for money. Perhaps if you were warned, you wouldn't bother."

"That makes sense," I said. "It didn't work, not yet at least. I still wanted to visit with Norval, but I can't say I would have wanted more than the rest of his story. After that, I don't think I would have been rude, but Gavin's warning might have made a difference."

"Do you think Norval could have killed him?" Hamlet con-tinued. "Maybe Norval found out Gavin was trying to manipu-late his friendships."

"I have a hard time believing Norval could kill anyone. And he's probably not strong enough to have . . . I don't know, man-handled, if that was needed, his nephew," I said.

"He was stabbed?" Hamlet asked.

"Yes. Elias saw . . . more than either Norval or I did."

Edwin said, "Well, I agree with you, Delaney, I don't think Norval could kill."

"I guess we don't know the whole story either. I mean the way-back whole story," I said. "What really happened to Norval's father all those years ago? What did Norval actually see? I'm sure that time in his life shaped who he is today. How could it not?"

A vision of Norval looking out the back window of the police car formed in my mind. The file. The key. His request for me to help. I shook my head. The police would handle this. Might they truly jump to the easy conclusion that the odd man obsessed with a fantastical creature had killed his meddling great-nephew?

I remembered that moment between Norval and me in the rain outside the church, that connection I'd felt. I liked him. I hoped he wasn't a killer and I didn't think he was. I did wonder, however, what he'd actually done this morning. Elias had thought that maybe Norval already knew what happened to Gavin by the time we found him in front of the bookshop. That made more and more sense.

"I might try to track down his sister," I said. "Talk to her."

"I will try tae help," Edwin said.

"Let me know if I can do anything," Hamlet added.

"All right. I'm sorry, but I must go. Delaney, I would like for you tae take some time off, but you're welcome tae come with me," Edwin said.

"I'm going with you."

Without further ado, I gathered my bag and joined Edwin in his Citroën. Once inside the car, I asked another question.

"What did you think of Norval when you *first* met him?"

"I didn't think he was mentally unstable, though I admit, I did think he wasn't quite right. It was as if he saw the world a slightly different way than the rest of us, but he was harmless, both tae himself and tae others. I was . . . well, for a moment

I was envious of him. It seemed the world's events didn't touch him the way they do the rest of us. The envy was fleeting, but for a moment I thought it might be wonderful tae be in Norval's world."

"Did you hesitate at all when you said you wouldn't take over his work?"

"No, not even for a moment," Edwin said as he turned onto a road I wasn't familiar with. The auctions were held at a few familiar locations, but there were surprises sometimes too. It looked like I was in for a surprise today.

The secret auctions had been taking place for years. The Fleshmarket Batch was made up of rich people who wanted to buy and sell expensive things—with each other. It had turned into a social club, a way for friends to come together and share, look at, talk about items that were more valuable than anything that my bank account would ever be able to afford. Originally, the members hadn't meant to be secretive, but when they realized their motivations might be interpreted as more arrogant and snobbish than a sharing of mutual interests, they decided to keep their activities to themselves.

I still wasn't privy to receiving early notice about the meetings and their locations. Maybe in another year.

"I would have loved to look through his papers, his pictures, and can you imagine what's on those films? I told him that if he ever just wanted someone to take care of his research, I was his man, but I didn't have time tae venture up to Loch Ness every weekend," Edwin said.

"That's how often he would go up?"

"Back then at least. I don't know if he was still going as often."

"I'm surprised he didn't just live there."

"Aye, I wondered too. He said his family moved to Edinburgh when he was young and he had tae stay close tae them."

I nodded. And now the one who seemed to take the most care of Norval was gone, even if he might have been a manipulator as well as a caregiver. Who would watch over Norval, help him now?

Edwin continued. "I wonder if he could have moved past his obsessions if he was left tae his own devices, had tae take care of himself. I certainly don't know enough about psychological or mental illness tae be able tae offer an educated opinion, but he's able tae engage. We were able tae converse. He could make eye contact. He's an intelligent man, who might have kept a job if he'd been forced tae have one tae pay his bills."

"Has his family enabled him more than helped him?"

"Impossible tae know."

We'd traveled about twenty minutes from The Cracked Spine. The metallic-tinged clouds were currently thin, with a promise that darker ones would roll in soon. I hadn't visited Loch Ness yet, but some imaginary sea air from there sent a chill down my arms. Or maybe that was still shock from the murder.

"We're here," Edwin said as he turned into a narrow driveway.

"A pub?" I said.

"A restaurant. We've got the whole place tae ourselves for a couple hours."

"It's more public than usual."

"Aye. The owner is a new member of Fleshmarket," Edwin said, his voice oddly high-pitched.

"What's going on?" I asked as we pulled into a large carpark behind the building. It was empty save for a few cars I recognized as being owned by members of Fleshmarket, along with one vehicle I didn't recognize. An old Volkswagen Beetle, refurbished with bright yellow paint.

Edwin parked his car. "Delaney, the newest member of Fleshmarket is a woman named Vanessa Morgan. She and I have been dating for some time."

I opened my mouth, but all the questions I wanted to ask got jammed up somewhere on the way out. It wouldn't have mattered if I'd asked them, coherently or not; Edwin had hopped out of the car and was moving around to open my door.

"I have questions," I managed to finally say as I swung my legs around and looked up at him.

"I have no doubt, but perhaps you could save them until after you've met Ms. Morgan. I think that would be best."

"I'm not sure I agree that it would be best, but I'll abide," I said as I unfolded myself from the car.

"Excellent," he said as he led the way inside, a nervous stiffness to his shoulders.

TWELVE

Bruno, a former Edinburgh police officer, was at the door to greet us. As he always did when on Batch duty, he wore his dress kilt and kept his muscled arms crossed in front of his barrel chest, even as he winked a private hello at me. Bruno and I were friendly outside of Fleshmarket. He enjoyed Tom's pub, and though the auction group was a secret, members could still socialize together, as long as no mention of the group was made in a public setting. You just never knew who was listening. Bruno and I had shared a few secret winks and conversations that purposefully didn't mention anything that had anything to do with an auction.

I'd come to learn that the word "secret" took on a slightly different meaning when it came to those of us at The Cracked Spine. Both Rosie and Hamlet knew about the auctions, though they didn't like to talk about them for fear they'd let loose the secret at the wrong time. The warehouse was my office and still the place where Edwin kept things he'd collected over the years. The police were now well aware of the warehouse and, in fact, Edwin had invited them in anytime they would like.

However, we still didn't discuss it with just anyone. In fact, we still denied its existence to many who inquired. It was a tricky tightrope sometimes, and it seemed the rules were changing all the time.

Secrets. They'd caused some big problems over the last year.

Once inside the restaurant I asked Edwin the first question that formed clearly in my mind. "Do Rosie and Hamlet know?"

"Not yet, lass. You're the first. I wanted tae make sure there was something there. I've courted her for three months, and I'm sure now. As sure as one can be. Rather than just drop her by the shop, I thought we'd begin here, with you." He paused and looked at me with tight eyebrows. "I've enjoyed the company of women every now and then over the years and it hasn't always . . . well, it hasn't always gone well. I think I would like for you tae meet her first and . . . maybe ease the introduction with Rosie and Hamlet."

I wasn't exactly sure what he meant by "enjoyed the company of" but whatever it was I was happy to hear he'd had companionship. I'd been under the impression that he hadn't dated much. Perhaps that was the impression he wanted me to have.

"I'd be happy to, but they'll like her if you like her," I said.

"I don't know, lass. I don't always see the forest for the trees."

I put my hand on his arm. He was genuinely nervous. "Are you at least ninety-five percent sure that you care for her?"

He fell into thought, but then looked at me seriously again. "About ninety, but heading toward more."

Suddenly, I saw a youthful Edwin again. And, again, it was fleeting.

Love is such an ageless affliction.

"Okay." I smiled back. "I can't wait to meet her."

"Good." He crooked his elbow and I put my arm through as we continued inside.

In a way, it had been a setup. It didn't take long to understand what was going on, and, frankly, I was touched. Even though Bruno was on duty, the gathering was small. Edwin; Birk Blackburn, one of Edwin's oldest, richest, and most flamboyant friends and someone I'd also become close to over the last year; and Towsen Mullins, a gentleman I'd met for the first time at the last auction, were the only members present. Birk had made all his money in international trade, which seemed to give the other auction members confidence enough to trust him with logistics and specifics that might come with buying and selling. Towsen had inherited his money from a rich uncle who'd owned oil wells throughout the world. Towsen enjoyed sharing stories of his time with his uncle, but every time someone mentioned the money, he seemed uncomfortable.

There was one more member, of course. The newest one. Vanessa Morgan.

It seemed this auction had been set up mostly so I could meet Vanessa. It would be Edwin's way. No simple dinner invitation for introductions, no grabbing a drink at a pub, but, here, where no one had to force any small talk, where we could all just see how it went. I suspected there was a meal planned, post-auction, and only if it seemed everyone was comfortable with everyone.

Birk had been called because he and Edwin were such good friends and it became clear quickly that he'd somehow been an integral part in the development of Edwin's new relationship, though I didn't get the specifics right away. Towsen was one of the sweetest men ever, so I suspected that he and Bruno were both asked to be there to keep this a "real" auction.

Towsen had probably figured it all out before I did, but he played his role perfectly.

"Ah, the lass from America. You are always such a delightful breath of fresh air among this stuffy crowd." He lifted a bottle of beer and saluted me. He was one of the few members who didn't drink whisky. He liked his bottled beer.

"Always good to see you, Towsen. Birk."

When I made it to Vanessa, I extended my hand. "I'm Delaney."

"Nice to meet you. I've heard only good things. I'm Vanessa," she said with an Irish accent.

Vanessa Morgan had a youthful sparkle to her eyes that easily won the battle over her wrinkles and gray-haired ponytail. She wore all her features well, but the sparkle in those eyes only reinforced that no one ages the same way.

We held onto each other's hands a bit too long as we looked at each other. Who had won my boss's heart? I imagined she was wondering: *Who is this woman the man I care for trusts so much?*

In those few long beats, I knew that Vanessa and I were going to get along. What route the friendship would take was still a mystery, but at least I could already see the destination.

The items for auction were hers; some Russian nesting dolls. They had all the indications that made me think they were extremely valuable. One determining factor of the value was the number of dolls in the set, and this set had eight. I'd once seen a set with twelve, but eight wasn't bad.

Edwin, still behaving as if this wasn't a meeting with ulterior motives, stated that the reason there were so few people there to bid was because most of the other members were either busy or not interested. I silently predicted that Edwin would be the buyer, but Towsen genuinely wanted the dolls and ended up making the highest offer. Once bidding and paperwork were completed, Towsen and Bruno left, feigning other tasks that needed their attention, but Birk, Edwin, Vanessa, and I, all of us getting along very well, sat down to a hearty lunch of tatties and neeps, shorthand for potatoes and turnips, that Vanessa prepared herself. She did not include the haggis that typically came with the Scottish meal, making me like her even more.

"I introduced the two of them," Birk said proudly before digging his fork into his turnips. "An Irish beauty preparing Scottish food in ways that very few Scots can accomplish. Then I had a conversation with her and knew. I knew she and Edwin would be a match." Birk chewed and swallowed. "Delicious. I was a wee bit jealous too. I would have wooed her myself if I hadn't thought the universe intended for her and Edwin tae be together."

Vanessa smiled graciously and I decided that she and Birk must not have known each other well enough for her to quip back with sarcasm. Or maybe she didn't do sarcasm.

She turned to me. "Delaney, I've been to Kansas. Kansas City, Kansas, and Kansas City, Missouri. I was traveling to California, and ended up with a two-day stop right in the middle of your country. My room was in a downtown skyscraper. I could see wide open land spread out from the crowded city."

"There's a lot of wide open country in Kansas, and the city you stayed in was probably on the Missouri side. The Kansas side isn't quite the same thing."

"That's what one of the flight attendants told me. I liked it, the modern mixed with all the space."

"It has its charms," I said, feeling a pinch of longing for my parents and brother.

"Aye," Vanessa said as she and Edwin shared a smile that made me feel like Birk and I were intruding. They didn't intend to make anyone uncomfortable; it was just clear that they cared for each other. A twinge of glee forced me to smile goofily at them.

Birk caught my eyes with his and sent me his own smile with some raised eyebrows. He was pleased with his matchmaking prowess. I was too.

"These tatties and neeps are some of the best I've had, but please don't tell my landlord Aggie I said so. She takes her neeps and tatties seriously." I smiled.

"I heard about your wedding next week. Congratulations," Vanessa said.

"Thank you."

"I'll be bringing Vanessa as my plus-one," Edwin said.

"That's wonderful!" I said.

"Well," Vanessa said, "I don't want to intrude. It will likely be my first time meeting Rosie and Hamlet, and I really want to make sure you're all right with that. Attention should be only on you and Tom."

"No! I mean, Tom and I would love to have you there. I think that's perfect, actually." I was impressed that she knew everyone's names.

"Thank you. I look forward to being there." She and Edwin shared another smile, but this one was conciliatory on her part, as if she was telling him he'd been correct in his guess to my reaction to her attending. She turned back to me. "Are you going tae remain in your house?"

I shook my head as my heart sunk a little. The decision had

been made recently. "No, my fiancé has a house by the sea. I'm excited to move there, but I'm going to miss my cottage something fierce. I'm going to miss my landlords even more than that."

"Elias, one of the couple and Aggie's husband, is a cab driver. He said he's going tae pick her up every morning and deliver her tae The Cracked Spine," Edwin said.

"I'm torn between telling him that's just too much work for him, and being thrilled he's offered. We'll see how it goes."

"It's lovely that you've become so close."

"It is. I've been very lucky. When did you move here from Ireland, and," I looked at Birk and back at Vanessa, "did Birk really introduce the two of you?"

"I moved here three years ago and bought this place. And Birk told the truth. He came in for dinner one evening, told me he had someone he wanted me to meet, and brought Edwin in the next night."

"The rest, as they say, is history," Edwin said.

I thought back over the last few months. Edwin had seemed . . . not happier, because he was naturally happy, but brighter, with a quicker smile. He'd always been a sharp dresser, but I had noticed a few new items of clothing, some of those also brighter than I was used to seeing him in. I suddenly remembered a peach-colored shirt that Rosie, Hamlet, and I had all commented on a few weeks back.

The signs had all been there. Maybe if I hadn't been so caught up on my own love life and planning my wedding, I would have noticed.

Edwin sat up in his chair. "Have either of you heard the news about Norval Fraser and his great-nephew?"

Vanessa shook her head. "Who?"

"The Loch Ness Papers man?" Birk asked.

"Aye."

"Not a word. What happened? Did he finally find the monster?" Birk laughed, but sobered when he saw the looks on Edwin's and my faces. "Oh dear, what happened?"

"Delaney, perhaps you should share the details," Edwin said.

All silverware was set down and three pairs of eyes watched me intently as I told the highlights of what had happened. I didn't mention that Norval had given me a folder stuffed with interesting pieces of paper and a key.

"How terrible," Vanessa said when I finished.

"That's a blow," Birk said. "I've met Norval a time or two, and, of course, I'd heard about him years before we crossed paths. He was well known about town. Odd, aye, but a sweet man. Losing his nephew will be rough."

The image of Norval looking out the back of the police car filled my mind again. "I barely met him but he told me he'd seen Nessie more than once."

"If anyone had, it would have been him," Birk said. He suddenly sat up straighter. "Hang on, Gavin MacLeod?"

"Yes, he was the man who was murdered. Norval's great-nephew."

"Do you know if it's the same Gavin MacLeod who runs a financial company?" Birk asked.

I had gathered Gavin's card from my desk earlier; now I fished it out of my bag and handed it to Birk.

"Oh boy, this lad . . . he's . . . I don't know because I never invested with him, but I've heard rumors for months. In fact, someone was just talking about him recently . . . Who was that? I can't remember right off but it will come tae me. Do you know what a Ponzi scheme is?"

Vanessa and Edwin nodded.

"I think so," I said. "The investment records are fabricated, and the money just keeps chasing money. New investors end up paying returns to those people who invested early, but nothing is really earning like it's portrayed. Something like that," I said.

"Aye," Birk said. "I think he was being investigated. I heard that many investors have lost significant sums of money. Oh dear, I wouldn't be surprised if an unhappy investor killed Gavin MacLeod. I'm sure the police are on the case, but do you think I should call them just in case they don't yet know his reputation? Goodness, I wish I could remember who was talking about him recently."

"Yes, you should call the police," I said. I looked at Edwin. "Is his name any more familiar to you now?"

"No, lass, I never invested with him and I don't talk money with many people. Only Rosie, actually. She knows more about my money than I do."

"Do you know the story of Norval's childhood?" I asked Birk.

"No," Birk answered. "I only know him as the Nessie hunter with all the papers."

Again, I snared my rapt audience as I told them about Norval's father and his disappearance.

"My goodness," Vanessa said as she wiped a tear from the corner of her eye.

"That is fascinating," Birk said. "I know some people who live up by Loch Ness. I've not heard of Wikenton."

"I don't know if it's there anymore."

"I'll ask my friends," Birk said. He looked at Edwin and back at me. "Would either of you consider selling Norval's papers at auction? I think we'd all be interested if Norval still wants you tae have them."

"No, if I take the papers, I won't ever sell them," I said.

"I wouldn't sell them either," Edwin said.

Birk shrugged. I wished I felt his detachment.

There was honor among the Fleshmarket members though. They would not intervene and try to get the papers before Edwin or I could. Well, I was sure that Birk wouldn't. I could only hope I was reading Vanessa correctly.

The conversation continued, turning away from murder and onto normal chitchat. I considered mentioning Angus and the book he'd brought into the shop, but decided now wasn't the time. There were still too many unknowns, and I thought Edwin was keeping some of that mystery to himself.

Still, it would have been fun to see Birk's expression when he heard about the book. He'd be over the moon.

I was so caught off guard when Vanessa and Edwin kissed before we left that I was stuck staring. It was just a quick, friendly kiss, but I blinked and apologized as I made my way out to Edwin's car to wait for him to join me.

I was happy it took him a few long minutes.

THIRTEEN

I read aloud: "Edinburgh resident and Loch Ness Monster Enthusiast, Norval Fraser, has been arrested for the murder of his great-nephew, Gavin MacLeod."

I dropped the paper back to my lap and looked at Tom. "I really can't believe it."

"Aye," Tom said as he pulled his car into a parking spot. "It's shocking. The whole thing."

It wasn't front page news, but the story made it to page three of *The Scotsman*. The police evidently hadn't told the reporter—a name I didn't recognize—about Elias and me, but other details had been included. The early call to the police, the discovery of the body, the murder weapon. And then, the worst part. "Prints found on the knife matched those of Fraser."

"Elias wondered if Norval was setting us up for something," I said. "He must have been right."

"I'm sorry, love," Tom said.

"But setting us up for what? He didn't frame us for the murder, at least as far as I can tell. And neither of us were further detained or called back in."

"Just having another witness tae finding the body might have been enough in his mind."

"But he forgot about possible fingerprints on the knife?"

Tom shrugged. "Impossible tae know, impossible tae understand, maybe."

"Maybe," I said.

It would have been impossible for Norval's paranoia not to play through my mind. *The police don't like me. They don't like my papers.*

Could they dislike him enough to accuse him of a murder he didn't commit? Frame him even? I hoped not.

But still, something wasn't right.

"He lives close to here?" Tom asked.

"Yes, right down there."

We were parked in the street, right next to the church and across from Norval's building. As we both looked down to where I pointed, we were surprised to see someone leaving Norval's flat.

"Oh," I said as I sat up straighter in the passenger seat.

"Know her?" Tom asked.

"I do. That's Reverend Nisa. That's who we're meeting."

"I see. And she was in Norval's flat?"

I looked closer to make sure she'd come out of the door next to the foil-covered window. "Yes, that's his."

"I think we should hop out of the car now so she knows we saw her leaving. Let's go."

I didn't quite understand why he thought that was important, but we both got out of the car just as Nisa made it to the street.

"Hello," I said.

She'd been deep in thought but looked up, startled. "Aye? Hello, yes, Delaney and . . . Tom. Welcome."

She approached each of us and shook our hands, but she was distracted.

"Everything okay?" I asked.

She sighed and hesitated before she finally spoke. "I'm afraid not. You'll see it in the paper today, but Norval was arrested for . . . oh, goodness, the murder of his great-nephew."

"I know," I said. "I saw the article. It's terrible."

"It is. I hadn't seen him since two mornings ago. After I saw the article this morning, I thought I should make sure he hadn't left anything on in the flat—the cooker, the clothes dryer. I worry about those things. He's forgetful."

"Did he leave anything on?"

"No, in fact . . . well, the flat seemed tidied up a bit."

Or she'd tidied it up, which was a terribly suspicious thing to think, even if I didn't quite understand why or how the idea had come to me. I tried to push it away.

"That was very thoughtful of you to check," Tom said.

"It's the least I can do. I hope he's okay . . ." She looked off toward Norval's building.

"I'm sorry," I said.

I didn't know what else to say and I wasn't going to tell her what else I knew, how I'd been at Gavin's flat too, or even how I'd also met him. But I thought I understood why Tom had wanted us to get out of his car and let her know we'd seen her. To see her reaction. Had she in any way been behaving guiltily?

It had just been odd, that was it. At first glance it was strange to see her leaving Norval's flat, but her explanation made complete sense. And there was no crime scene tape warning anyone away. She hadn't done anything wrong.

The most random of thoughts flitted into my head. "I forgot the towels!"

"Don't worry about them," she said as she sent us each a smile and her demeanor switched gears. Whatever duty she'd just done at Norval's, it was now time for Tom and me. "Welcome. Let's go in."

Under a clear blue sky, we followed her through the red door and to her pristine office. I looked at the spot where the two off-kilter books had been. They were no longer there. If they'd been shelved properly I couldn't see where.

She began the conversation. "It's a pleasure to meet you, Tom. I know your father quite well, and he's one of my favorite people. You look like your mother. I've seen pictures."

"Pleasure's all mine."

As we sat in the sparse room, suddenly an air of the principal's office surrounded us. I gave myself a silent pep talk. No matter what, I was marrying the man sitting next to me. I was 100 percent sure. On the other hand, no one knows everything about anyone, right? Would Nisa expose something about Tom that would change my mind? What about something about me that would change Tom's mind?

Deep breath, Delaney.

It wasn't quite an interrogation, but Reverend Nisa did have a fair amount of questions. First of all, she wanted to know if we both felt the same way about religion.

"Do the two of you believe in God?" she asked.

"I believe in something that I can't name. I don't know exactly what I believe, I just sense that something is there," I said.

Nisa nodded and looked at Tom.

"I believe in something akin tae karma, I suppose."

"Do unto others?" Nisa said.

"Aye," he said.

"Will you want your children to go to church? What if they want to go and you don't?" she asked.

"I grew up going to church," I said. "In an ideal world, I would love for my children to be exposed to different beliefs and hope that they choose what fits for them. I would support that even if I found their beliefs difficult to understand myself. However, I also understand that chances of that happening are slim. Children typically believe what they were raised around."

Nisa smiled and looked at Tom again.

"I would drive them wherever they'd like tae go, but once they were old enough I probably wouldn't attend any services with them. I would never be angry at their choices. Again, though, that's an ideal world. I think that's how I would behave. Until you're in the middle of something, it's hard tae really know, aye?"

Nisa's eyebrows came together as she remained focused on Tom. "You believe differently than your father. Your father is here every Sunday. Did something happen to change your beliefs? Was there an event?"

"No, I think it's just the changing times," he said.

Nisa looked at me.

"Same," I said, though I silently wondered about Tom's mother's death and if that was part of his changing views. Personally, I knew there was no one event in my life that had been a catalyst.

She smiled. "Well, that's all good news. I don't feel the need to give the 'differences in religion can be challenging' lecture.

Mixed religions in marriages can work, but some extra understanding and patience might be required. All right, this next part is mostly my curiosity and just to see if the questions spur any other questions from you. There are no 'right' answers and it's okay to say the answers are none of my business."

She had a number of questions that did, indeed, seem personal, and things she didn't necessarily need to know. She had many more questions than Reverend O'Brien had, but somehow I didn't find them intrusive. In fact, there were a few things Tom and I hadn't discussed. I knew about Tom's aunt, old and in failing health, but I had no idea he sent some of his pub profits to an Alzheimer's association to honor her. Nisa fired off her questions so smoothly that we were both surprised we answered everything quickly and without taking time to think about what we were going to say.

"I never thought tae run that by you, but you will know all of my finances," he said. "I won't hide anything."

"Tom, I love that you donate to the Alzheimer's association. I won't hide anything either, though there's not much to not hide. Edwin pays me well, but I don't have the same sort of accounting you're responsible for as a business owner."

"Will you also be a co-owner?" Nisa asked.

"Aye, she will," Tom said. "In whatever capacity she wants."

"I'll keep working at the bookshop, but I might actually hop behind the bar every now and then. I don't know yet."

Nisa smiled. "That's been discussed?"

Tom and I nodded.

"Have you talked about how many kids you each want?" Nisa asked.

"Aye, but we haven't come tae an agreement," Tom said as he smiled at me and rubbed his finger under his nose.

"I think two is a good number. But not right away," I said.

"Tom?" Nisa looked at him.

"I'd like many and I'd like tae start right away."

"That's interesting," Nisa said. "Particularly for someone with . . . well, pardon this term, with your reputation. I've heard you . . . dated a number of women before meeting Delaney."

And there it was, I thought, the crux of the matter. Nisa had been waiting for a moment to insert something about Tom's reputation. I was both impressed by her convenient timing as well as what I thought was a touch of discomfort. She wanted to get to know us, but she hadn't wanted to be quite that personal. She'd only gone there because of the slip I'd made when first meeting her, my comment about Tom's reputation. She thought she was asking something I needed to hear answered.

"That is true," Tom said as he reached over and put his hand on my knee. "You can't make yourself fall in love with someone, and you can't stop yourself from falling either. It's either real or not. I'm afraid I'm a quick study. I could determine quickly that I didn't love any other woman enough to commit tae any of them for the rest of my life. I knew the second I . . . the second Delaney and I looked at each other that she was the one. My whole world changed. My outlook changed. It's forever, I have no doubt." He looked at me with a serious cobalt gaze.

I'd become lost in his words, but I swam up and out of them as quickly as I could. "Me too. Me too." I smiled.

By her smile, I was pretty sure that Nisa was convinced too.

"Well, if you're both being honest, and I have no sense that you aren't, you're going to be just fine. It would be an honor to officiate at your ceremony."

Tom and I smiled at each other.

"I . . . uh," she interjected quickly. "I have another matter I'd like to discuss. It's delicate, and not as cheery as a wedding discussion."

Tom and I looked at her again and waited. She sat forward and seemed to switch gears again.

"Delaney, did you take the cards back to Norval?" she asked.

"I did," I said.

"Oh good. I . . . I actually looked for them when I was there this morning. I didn't see them."

"Were they something you needed returned tae you?" Tom asked.

"No, no, not that. I wondered if Delaney had stopped by, is all, and I wondered how Norval was. If he seemed okay."

"He was great," I said. "He did tell me the story of his meeting Nessie, and his father. He wanted me to take his papers and continue his work. I didn't decline outright but even after I thought about it awhile, I would have told him no." I still didn't want her to know I'd met Gavin or had been there to discover his body. It suddenly felt like too much to explain. "Why?"

"Gavin only recently started attending church with Norval. I thought it was a good thing at first, but then I sensed that maybe it wasn't, though I couldn't put my finger on why."

"I'm so sorry," I repeated, again not sure what else to say to fill her pause.

Nisa nodded. "From my point of view, Gavin took good care of his uncle. There was never a real problem that I could see . . . until very recently. The two of them were having some sort of row. They were to come talk to me later the day you met Norval. They never showed for the meeting. I tried to get

Norval to give me the details by himself that morning, but he didn't. He said something about not wanting to be told what to do by Gavin anymore, and he brought me a couple books. He was cryptic, but I told him he didn't have to do anything he didn't want to do. I was just trying to calm him down. I hoped to talk to them both later. I meant to get back to them to find out if we needed to reschedule, but I never did."

"The books, were they the one by Brodie Watson and the Loch Ness book?" I asked.

She blinked at me. "Well, yes."

"I saw them on your shelves. They were the only things out of place when I was here. I couldn't help but notice them."

"I understand. Yes, those were the books."

"I get the Loch Ness Monster book. Norval probably has lots of those. But is he a fan of Brodie Watson's? Are you?"

She brought her eyebrows together as she studied me. "You know who Brodie Watson is?"

"I do."

"Interesting. I hadn't heard of him until Norval brought me the book. He said the author, a local man, approached him recently, seeming only to want to chat and leave him a book. I thought perhaps the author had actually approached Norval for some Nessie research, but Norval was pretty sure that the author was simply visiting. I was going to bring it up again in the group meeting we were scheduled to have, see if Gavin knew about it—only because I sensed that Norval was somehow bothered by the whole thing. He wasn't interested in reading the book so he brought it to me."

"Did you think Brodie Watson was trying to somehow take advantage of Norval?" I asked.

"I have no idea. Norval was just . . . I don't know, overly consumed by their meeting, at least for a good few moments. But, and this is important to know, Norval can easily become obsessed. Obviously."

My mind was whirring, but going nowhere, really. I still hadn't quite accepted what I'd read in the article, let alone processed this new information. How could any of this be important to Gavin's murder?

"Do you think I should tell the police?" Nisa asked.

"Honestly, I have no idea, but I don't think it would hurt," I said.

Tom agreed.

"All right. I'm going to try to see Norval if the police will let me," she said. "I need to see if he's okay, see if I can understand what might have happened."

"Nisa, this isn't your fault," Tom said.

"I know," she said unconvincingly, "but it would be impossible for me not to wonder what I could have done differently. I am Norval's religious advisor, after all. Surely, there might have been something I could have picked up on. At this point, I'd like to try to understand and try to . . . help, I suppose."

"I doubt anyone could have changed anything," I said, feeling a little guilt myself. *Was there something I could have done differently?*

She forced a weary smile and it seemed the dark circles under her eyes became deeper.

"I look forward to next Saturday. Stay well and safe, and we'll have a beautiful wedding," Nisa said.

I realized that she was doing her job. That's what you had to do when you were involved with so many different people, be happy for some, sympathetic for others, and sometimes despondent for even others. Sometimes all at once, sometimes transforming in the blink of an eye. I didn't envy her job, and I was suddenly grateful to have found her.

"Thank you for doing this," I said.

"My pleasure," she said.

Nisa walked us to the red door. The hallway was busy. Some people smiled and greeted us, but others were too busy to even notice us. Nisa sent them all a friendly hello, as if nothing was weighing on her mind.

As we said goodbye, I realized that I hadn't had even a tiny doubt about marrying Tom; in fact, I was now even more convinced that it was the right thing to do. Nisa's interview had been much more about Tom and me than Nisa's curiosity.

She was very good at her job.

FOURTEEN

"Delaney?" Tom said.

I had stopped moving toward the car, my attention pulled back across the street. "Is that crime scene tape over Norval's door?" I nodded toward the row of homes. "Before we went into the church, I actually had a thought that there was no crime scene tape there. The police must have been there while we were inside." I glanced at my watch. It had been about an hour.

"It looks like it, and I wouldn't be surprised."

"There are no police cars nearby. They were quick."

"Do you want tae walk over there?"

It had been a good idea to leave the key behind. The temptation to use it was only growing. I would love to make my way into Norval's apartment and take my time looking through his papers. Even if I did it under the guise of trying to find something to help him.

"No, that's okay," I finally said.

Tom laughed. "You don't sound convinced. Are you sure?"

"I am. Well, I'm curious, but it seems . . . wrong, I guess."

"He gave you the key, so it's not wrong that way. He

shouldn't have asked you for your help; that was asking too much. It's natural tae be curious, particularly for someone who is already such a curious person anyway. But crossing police tape might not go well."

Absently, I nodded, and muttered quietly, "I really wonder if he had anyone else to trust."

Tom said something else, but my attention jumped to some movement I saw out of the corner of my eye. Someone was walking around the corner of the church building. Someone I recognized immediately, but it seemed like such a square-peg-in-a-round-hole kind of moment, that I had to move through bewilderment before I got to recognition.

"Well, I'll be. It's Delaney, right?" a thickly twanged voice said. Boot-clad bowlegs came in our direction.

"Angus?" I said.

"Yes, ma'am." He tipped his hat just like any good cowboy. He extended his hand to Tom. "You must be the lucky guy. Delaney mentioned the upcoming nuptials. Good to meet you. Angus Murdoch."

"Good tae meet you. Tom Shannon." Tom shook the cowboy's hand.

The two men made a striking pair, movie star–like in their own ways and oozing with so much male-ness, I wondered if they'd stop passing traffic.

"Angus brought a wonderful rare edition book into the bookshop," I said.

"Aye? Well, you picked the right place," Tom said.

"I have no doubt." Angus blinked as if he pondered whether to share the rest of the story with Tom, but he didn't.

"What are you doing over in this part of town?" I asked, making polite conversation.

"Sightseeing." He nodded backward. "Dane Village over there is quite the place. Like something out of a fairy tale."

Neither Tom nor I corrected him with "Dean" but his description was spot-on.

"It's a great place," I said.

"I saw this church from over there yonder, so I walked over the bridge to take a gander. I thought about going inside, but just because this is a tourist town doesn't make every church a tourist place." He looked up at the steeple and back at us. "Does it?"

"If the front door is unlocked, I'm sure you're welcome tae look inside," Tom said.

"Good point. I think I'll give it a try." His smile this time was half-sided as he hitched up his jeans.

At that moment, he struck me as so Texan, so American, that even though Kansas wasn't Texas, a memory of my parents' farm filled my mind. For an instant I could smell the tilled earth, the same earth that made up Scotland, but different in ways that had to do with space and sky and their congruity. I would never be able to explain how lovely the wide-open plains of Kansas were to me.

"Hey," Angus continued. "Y'all told me about Arthur's Seat."

"Yes. Hamlet mentioned it," I said.

"Can you point me in the right direction?" Angus asked.

"Sure, it's that way." Tom nodded his head and held back a full smile. "You won't want to walk from here. Take a bus maybe. Up from Holyrood Park, other side of the university. Any of the bus drivers can help you."

"Huh. I thought I was closer. Got off track, I guess." Angus laughed. "My mom always said I couldn't find the one cow in the barn, so . . . there it is."

Angus glanced across the street and toward the row of houses, and he noticed the same thing Tom and I had.

"Is that crime scene tape down there?"

I looked at Tom.

He answered before I could. "Not sure."

Angus looked back and forth between Tom and me. We must have both looked like we were keeping secrets. "Do you know what happened there?"

"Not really," I said, cringing inwardly. I wished I'd said that more convincingly.

Angus tipped back his cowboy hat and smiled again. "Not really?"

I looked toward the tape, fluttering in a breeze I couldn't feel. "I recently met the man who lives there, but I don't know what's going on."

"I see. Well, I'm sorry for whatever it is," Angus said.

"Good to see you," I said. "Come visit us in the bookshop again. Tom and I should probably be on our way."

"Right," he said, and he brought his attention back to me. "Oh! Did Edwin remember anything else about the book?"

"I don't think so. But I'll have him call you if he does."

"I just hope he remembers something. I think my grandfather would be glad that any mystery his thieving ways might have conjured was solved."

Tom raised one eyebrow in my direction.

"I don't think Edwin is concerned," I said.

Angus smiled again, sadly this time. "Pleasure to meet you, Tom, even if I wish I'd met her sooner."

His compliment, if that's what it was, was unsettling. It felt less like a compliment and more like I was being objectified. Fortunately, Tom, not surprised by much, remembered his manners.

"Pleasure tae meet you too, Angus, and feel free tae come by my pub before you leave. It's in the Grassmarket, not far from the bookshop. First one's on me," he said with a smile.

Angus tipped his hat again and Tom and I got into the car.

"That was interesting," I said without moving my lips too much, in case Angus was watching us.

"Och, he's a friendly fellow, a bit out of his element. Remember how you felt when you first moved here?" Tom said.

But I knew Tom well enough to know that Angus hadn't sat right with him.

"Did he bother you?" I asked.

"Not really. He's just so larger than life. There's no question that the man comes from Texas. He's so like the American television shows and movies that take place in Texas. He wears it well, and very proudly."

"You think he's working too hard to be genuine?"

Tom thought a moment. "No, I just think he is what he is and he wants tae make sure everyone knows it. Nothing wrong with that, but I'd like tae hear about the thieving ways of his grandfather."

"Okay, only if you drive me over to Cowgate, let me out of the car, and drive away quickly."

"You really don't want me tae see the dress. I promise I won't peek. I'll wait for you outside."

"Nope, not an option. A girl's got to have some superstitions, right?"

Tom laughed, and as he drove me to the errand he couldn't

take part in, I not only told him all the details about Angus and his priceless book, I added the part about Edwin's new girl-friend.

He was equally intrigued by both stories.

FIFTEEN

I waved as Tom reluctantly pulled away from the curb. It was a little more than being superstitious about the dress. He had plenty to do, and I didn't like people waiting for me.

Besides, Rosie bought into the superstition completely and had begged me not to let Tom see the dress before the wedding. I'd promised her.

Located in Cowgate and tucked in between a tobacco shop and a butcher shop, Petal Dress Designs was a pocket of a place that would have been claustrophobic if it hadn't been filled with so many beautiful dresses to distract one from feeling like the walls were closing in.

The dress I'd found was as simple as a dress could be, but I'd tried on a few others. In fact, since my mom couldn't be there with me, I'd tried on a few and texted her the pictures. The comments had been varied:

-Almost.
-Not quite.

-Beautiful, but is it you?

-Oh no.

And then . . .

-That's the one!

It had been the perfect one, except for the way it fit. It was a bit tight up top and a bit loose on the bottom. But then I'd met with Bonnie Warren, the shop's seamstress. In a flurry of measuring tape and taffeta that had been absently wrapped around her neck, she'd proclaimed that my "difficulties would be fixed." At least, I thought that's what she said. Her accent was as strong as Rosie's.

Once Tom was well out of sight, I pushed through the shop's door, the bell above it jingling.

"Welcome to Petal," a voice called from the back.

I made my way carefully down the short and narrow aisle, thinned because of the skirts poofing from the racks. The side walls each held two rows of dresses, as did the four circular racks on the floor. Most of the dresses were white or off-white, but some bright colors sprouted here and there.

The owner appeared from the back, a pencil in her mouth and two dresses folded over her arms.

"Oh, hello there. You here tae see Bonnie?" She took out the pencil.

"I am."

"She's just in the back. G'on."

The back of the shop was even more cramped than the front. Bonnie's workroom was at the very back. Small and cramped with dresses and a sewing machine, I wondered how she managed to get anything done in the space.

I stuck my head through the doorway.

"Bonnie, hi. It's Delaney Nichols."

She looked up and put a hand over one of her eyes. "Och, lass, I have yer dress right here."

I was perplexed that she'd covered one eye, but she uncovered it as she began the search for the dress. She found it quickly and held it out toward me.

"It's a lovely frock, aye?" she said as the eye she'd covered closed, seemingly involuntarily.

"Bonnie, are you okay?" I pointed toward my own eye.

"Och, aye, I've a bad eye, lass. Happens when ye get old. Things stop working, one at a time. My eye's aboot the fourteenth thing tae go."

"I'm sorry to hear that."

"Not tae worry. What do ye think of the dress?"

It was something I'd envisioned Audrey Hepburn would wear, a long-sleeved, white satin frock, with a scoop neck and fitted bodice, a loose skirt that fell just below my knees. There was no lace, nothing other than the silky material of the dress. I loved it.

But something seemed wrong as I looked at the dress.

"Bonnie, it looks great . . . except . . . well, did you loosen the top, tighten up the waist?"

Bonnie looked up at me with furrowed brows. "Lass, it was the opposite. I was tae tighten the bust, loosen the waist." She looked me up and down. She looked the dress up and down. "Oh, dear."

"Should I try it on?" I asked, trying to be helpful.

"I doubt you'd get it over your neck and down tae cover . . . well, tae cover yerself." She put one fist up to her mouth and I thought I heard a snicker. "Lass, it's that one bad eye, that must be it. I read my notes all wrong."

As another chuckle escaped her lips, any terror that might have been creeping up my spine because of the disaster that was now my wedding dress dissipated. I felt laughter bubble up my own throat.

I looked at Bonnie and she covered her bad eye, trying hard to also cover her laughter.

"Oh, Bonnie," I finally said with a real laugh of my own. "It's not only wrong of me to laugh about you having a bad eye, it's downright rude. I'm so sorry."

"Lass, it's the liveliest thing that has happened tae me in many months. I'm so sorry I didn't . . . well, I didn't read my notes correctly. I will fix your dress. Will two more days cause any problem?"

My mom would be there in two more days. "Not at all! Thank you!"

And then we both collapsed into laughter. Later I might realize that it really wasn't as funny as all that, but we both must have needed the release. I couldn't wait to introduce Bonnie to my mother. I suspected they'd get along very well.

I left the shop with a smile still on my face. The only thing that would have been better would have been for my mom to be there too, for that fitting. She would have also laughed. I'd tell her all about it.

I boarded the bus to head back to The Cracked Spine, and let my thoughts roll around in my mind. By the time the short trip was over, I had solved nothing, come up with no answers, and only felt worse for Norval Fraser. I could not imagine him killing anyone, no matter what.

I was so lost in my thoughts that it wasn't until I disembarked the bus that I noticed a police car outside the bookshop. It was parked normally on the street and its lights weren't flashing. Maybe whoever it belonged to wasn't even inside the shop, or maybe it was just Inspector Winters visiting. I quick-stepped my way to the front window. I craned my neck and spied Inspector Winters inside at the front desk, talking to Rosie.

Though he was a friend, he also was an officer of the law, and there had been a murder, and I'd been somehow in the vicinity of it—again. No matter friendships, a surge of anxiety went through me. I wished for a bookish voice to let me in on what might be going on inside before I joined them. But the bookish voices didn't work quite that way, and they were stubbornly silent.

The bell jingled above the door as I entered, and Inspector Winters and Rosie looked in my direction. Hector was stretched out on the floor, playing with a sock that had been knotted on the end. He stood, barked once, and trotted toward me as if he hadn't seen me in years. I scooped him up as I eyed a scrapbook lying open on the desk. It was *the* scrapbook, the one I'd heard about the day Angus came into the shop and diverted everyone's attention before I could take a good look at it.

There were no other customers in the shop and shadows were coming and going as clouds rolled over the sun. It was my favorite time of the day; I called it the lazy time, and if I happened to be in the shop instead of the warehouse, sometimes I would grab a book from the shelves, find a comfortable seat, and read an hour or so away. The perks of working at the shop were endless, but that was one of my favorites.

"Delaney, my dear, we've been waiting for ye. As luck would have it, Inspector Winters stopped by tae speak with ye. I've been showing him some things," Rosie said. "I had some memories, and the scrapbook was nearby anyway."

"Hello. Memories about what?" I carried Hector to the desk.

The scrapbook's binding had long ago been ripped and stretched. The spine was probably about six inches high, broken and thready, but the pages sloped up to about twice that size at their outer edges. I peered at the newspaper clippings on the exposed pages.

"Aye, look here." Rosie pointed at a picture of two men, one of whom I immediately recognized as a younger Norval, "this is the man ye met with, the one who's been arrested, God rest his poor great-nephew's soul. This is another man who lives for Nessie, maybe not in the same way, but is also obsessed."

"I came in tae talk tae you about Norval being arrested," Inspector Winters said. "I didn't know the paper would have a story this morning. I'm sorry if you were surprised."

I relaxed and looked closely to see if he was just saying something that would make me let my guard down, but I didn't see anything other than sincerity. He continued, "Rosie was telling me about the feud Norval was a part of about ten years ago."

"It's okay. Thanks. What feud?" I said.

"Aye. That's what I was remembering. It made the newspapers. I thought maybe I clipped the stories. And I did! This other man," she pointed, "his name is Albert Winsom, he said that Norval told him he could have all of his papers."

"That's what Norval told me," I said. "I believe that's what he told Edwin. We could have his papers if we promised to continue his work."

"Aye, but ye and Edwin said ye wouldnae carry on the research. Norval claimed that Mr. Winsom reneged on taking over the research so Norval refused tae give him the papers. Mr. Winsom claimed that taking over the work was never part of the deal. They both felt cheated and it somehow became more than just a personal argument; 'twas an interesting Edinburgh scandal for a day or two. Not long, but there was talk of fisticuffs."

I had a hard time imagining mild-mannered Norval lifting a fist, no matter the situation, but as I'd pondered already I also had a hard time seeing him as a killer. There was a chance I needed to admit to myself that I simply didn't know him very well. I glanced over the scrapbook but didn't see a picture where it looked like he'd taken a beating.

"How is Winsom obsessed with Nessie?" I asked.

"He's a chemist," Rosie said, "but his shop is filled with souvenirs and what he calls artifacts. He claims he's seen her a time or two but has no photographic evidence." She put a finger on the picture in the scrapbook. "He said he would display the important parts of Norval's collection, but he'd be the one tae determine which things were important. I believe that bothered Norval too, someone else deciding what was important and what wasnae."

A chemist was the same thing as a pharmacist. I looked at Inspector Winters. "Were drugs in any way used to kill Gavin?"

"No, the medical examiner has determined the manner of death conclusively. Death by stabbing with a knife."

"Are Rosie's memories important to the case?" I asked.

"Aye, believe it or not, maybe," he said as he scratched his head.

"Of course, this is important," Rosie said. "How could it not be? Did ye read the article this morning?"

"I did, but not well, perhaps," I said. In fact, I had skimmed much of it, the important fact that Norval had been arrested needing some digesting before I moved deeper into the article.

Rosie pursed her lips. "Gavin MacLeod's clients." She lifted the edge of the scrapbook and fished out the flattened newspaper from this morning. She held it up. "Mr. MacLeod's investment firm has recently become the subject of a Ministry of Finance investigation. It doesn't list the details as tae why, but that wee bit tells me that he had some unhappy clients. And then the paper goes about listing some of his clients. I ken a number of the names, but the one I zoned in on is Albert Winsom! That's how I remembered."

I looked at Inspector Winters. Birk had mentioned some possible issues with Gavin's company, but it seemed a much bigger deal now. I wished I'd read the article more thoroughly. "Who released this to the press?"

"I'm not sure. In fact, I wondered if by some chance it was you," Inspector Winters said. I shook my head. "Right. We've already begun looking at his clients, but until Rosie told me I had no idea that Mr. Winsom and Norval had such a public row. It was a time ago and who knows if the connections mean anything, but in a way, there could be motive there. We'll take a better, more informed approach with Winsom now."

I smiled at Rosie. "Good job."

"Thank ye, lass."

"Am I in trouble?" I asked, turning to Inspector Winters.

"Not at the moment," he said with a half smile. He looked at Rosie, seeming to debate if he should continue in front of her. She didn't look like she was going anywhere. Inspector Winters forged ahead. "Not only was I curious if you knew the list of clients, I also wanted tae let you know that I'm making sure Norval gets some help with his mental health. I believe you are correct that he's not well. Though he's our suspect, I'm aware that other issues might be at play."

"That's great," I said.

"Aye. He's . . . fond of you. Are you certain you just met?"

"Yes, but he . . . well, he was worried the police might try to set him up because they don't like him, think his apartment is a fire hazard."

Inspector Winters shook his head. "No, lass, of course you know that isn't true."

I didn't, but I hoped not.

Inspector Winters cleared his throat. "He was under the impression that you might be helping clear his name. If so, how?"

I nodded. Time to confess. "He left me a key to his flat. He's convinced there's something inside that would help prove his innocence, if need be."

"If need be?"

"Yes, he prepared a note for me and didn't give it to me until after we found Gavin's body."

"I see."

Inspector Winters knew all the implications of Norval's pre-preparation. "You didn't tell me that in your statement."

"No, I'm sorry. It wasn't . . . quite what it turned out to be."

"What do you think is in his flat that will help him?"

"I don't know. Did he give you any indication what it might

be? I mean, you guys have searched the place, right? I haven't gone in yet."

"We have." Inspector Winters bit his bottom lip. "We're done, though. There's a lot of junk in there, and nothing that could serve as any sort of alibi for Norval. Nothing yet that points our suspicion in any another direction."

I sensed that Inspector Winters wanted Norval to be innocent. Maybe he'd grown to like him too. "Tom and I were near there, at the church across the street this morning. Crime scene tape was over Norval's door. We didn't go in. I didn't take the key with me. I haven't used it. It seemed . . . wrong."

Inspector Winters nodded. "The tape is mostly tae keep out curious reporters and the like, but I thought it was put up yesterday. I'll have to check the timing."

"Do you know who Brodie Watson is?" I asked.

Rosie huffed a noise that made it clear that she knew exactly who he was.

"The writer?" Inspector Winters asked.

"Yes, he'd been by to visit Norval recently, at least according to Reverend Nisa. The reverend at the church by Dean Village. You should go talk to her too."

"Really? Brodie Watson?"

"Yes. I'm afraid I'll get something wrong if I go into more detail. What I learned was according to Nisa, and I don't want to misspeak. Norval didn't mention Brodie to me at all."

As Inspector Winters fell into thought, Rosie and I exchanged raised eyebrows.

Finally, Inspector Winters looked at me. "If you're inclined, go on into Norval's flat. There's . . . well, there's so much there. Our people looked thoroughly, but you are used tae those sorts of items. You might know more. Let me get one more final assurance that we're done, and if you want tae, please go on in and look around. I'll talk tae my chief-inspector and let you know later today." He paused, then looked at me. "Is that something you'd like tae do?"

Of course it was, but not for the reasons he might think. I'm always up for working to clear an innocent man's name, but if proof that Nessie existed was somewhere inside that apartment, I was sure to become quickly distracted by those items. A thread of shame choked off any phony altruism I might have felt.

"I would," I said.

"Good. I'll let you know. What do you make of Norval's obsession?"

"You mean, do I believe in Nessie?" I said. Hector barked.

"That's my boy," Rosie said as she reached over the desk and patted his head. "Of course, Nessie is real. It's foolish tae believe otherwise."

"Really?" I said.

"Aye, of course," she said as she placed her hand on the scrapbook again. "In fact, it's all here in this book, I suspect."

Inspector Winters and I looked down at it again. The idea of going through it was daunting—terrifying, actually—even for people who liked tedious tasks. It would be easier to find a needle in a haystack, proof of Norval's innocence inside his apartment, than finding any real evidence inside that overstuffed book.

"Take it if ye'd like," Rosie said to Inspector Winters. Even she thought it was too big a task. "It's all yours."

"Thank you, Rosie," he said, but he didn't reach for it immediately.

"Do you believe in Nessie?" I asked him.

"I do not," he said with a careful glance at Rosie. She lifted her eyebrows as if to say she didn't care whether or not he believed anything. "But I wonder what Norval might have in his flat that would prove me wrong, or make me rethink. I don't know." He looked at me. "And I know you wonder the same thing."

"Possibly."

"Good. Well, Rosie, I might come back for the book, but I think you've most likely shown me the pertinent items inside it. May I return if I need it?" he asked.

"Aye, I'll keep it ready for you," she said.

"Very good. Ta," he said.

Still carrying Hector, I walked Inspector Winters out to his car.

"I'll ring you, Delaney, but don't feel obligated," he said. "I think your eyes would give us all a fresh perspective, though."

I felt more and more obligated every minute that ticked by. "I won't."

He got into the car and drove away and I looked at Hector. "It appears I have some work to do."

Because he was the most perfect dog ever, he licked my cheek in complete support.

SIXTEEN

I didn't take Hector with me over to the dark side, the side that held the warehouse, my work space. It had been Edwin's space until he gave it to me. He had behaved as if removing himself to a boring old office after so many years of becoming one with the warehouse was no big deal. It had been, I was sure. He was as much a "thing" in the room as everything else was. He belonged there just as much as the old books, the antique mousetraps, and the ancient scalpels. I belonged there too, and was always happy whenever Edwin visited, but for the most part it was just me and the things, and the stories that went with them, occasional visits from my bookish voices, and my quiet hours of work.

Today, despite the collection of old Edinburgh castle prints that I had been planning to research, I turned my attention to Gavin MacLeod and Norval Fraser.

However, I decided to start at the beginning. Nessie. The Loch Ness Monster. I began a search.

Though I'd never dived deeply into Nessie stories, I'd heard or read about the monster over the years. I didn't think I'd be surprised by what I found today. I was wrong.

It seemed there was some debate regarding the first sightings of the old girl. "Dubious" accounts were made as far back as 564 A.D. An Irish monk, Saint Columba, might have fended off the beast simply by making the sign of the cross and proclaiming that the monster should go away. Apparently, Nessie listened.

Modern interest wasn't sparked until July 22, 1933, though, when George Spicer and his wife came upon something they described as a "most extraordinary form of animal" crossing the road in front of their car. With a thick neck, no visible limbs, and a large body, to them it certainly looked like a monster.

Hugh Gray's photograph, allegedly taken on November 12, 1933, while he was walking his dog, also churned more stories. The photograph was questionable, however, and some alleged it was just a depiction of Hugh's dog grabbing a stick from the water. The original negative was lost, but later Maurice Burton came upon some lantern slides of the negative. It was ultimately decided that the picture was simply an otter in the water.

On January 5, 1934, Arthur Grant was taking a midnight motorcycle ride along Loch Ness's northeastern shore and claimed to see a long-necked, small-headed creature cross the road and slip into the water. He drew a sketch of what he saw. It has been claimed that Arthur, a veterinary student, might have exaggerated his story, or perhaps he'd just come upon an otter or a seal, misshapen by the poor lighting.

The most "infamous" moment, and the one I'd most heard about in Nessie history, was tied to two photographs, and was set into motion in April of 1934. One photo that looked like a dinosaur's neck and head sticking up from the water, and another with a similar head in a diving position. It was the first photograph that many still clung to as evidence of the monster, despite both photographs being later exposed as part of an elaborate hoax involving a London gynecologist, a disgruntled employee, a willing relative, an insurance agent, a toy submarine, and some wood putty.

Other notable "sightings" or hunts had occurred over the years, but my interest turned only to the stories that mentioned Norval Fraser. He had frequently been spotlighted or mentioned as an "expert." Writers of most of the articles seemed to stop just short of making fun of him. They all seemed to portray him as a sweet old guy who might have lost his marbles. I understood their reaction, even if I felt the journalists could have done a better job of remaining impartial. I made a mental note not to treat Norval that way if I ever saw him again, and, of course, if he wasn't a killer.

Then it was on to his great-nephew. Gavin MacLeod had, indeed, built a successful business, or that was what it seemed at first. Happy clients making money were the highlights of the early reports. But more recent articles told a different story. Gavin might have been up to no good, doing what Birk had already mentioned, running something akin to a Ponzi scheme. I couldn't find the word "Ponzi" in anything I read, but clients as well as government officials had become concerned about strange returns on some investments. According to a few articles, investigations had been underway for some time. At least Inspector Winters now knew about the tie to Albert Winsom. Rosie had done a good job.

My research also uncovered more information about Mr. Winsom. For decades, the relationship between the two monster-hunters had been made up of differences in opinion, a competition of conspiracy theories, as far as I could tell. They both believed in Nessie, but Winsom would never acquiesce that she might have taken Norval's father. In fact, Winsom was adamant that Nessie was a friendly monster with a sweet disposition and would never hurt a human.

Norval, of course, thought Nessie was evil and wicked.

But even though their rivalry had given heed to one noted physical altercation, the real contention had only begun recently, because didn't arguments about money make everything more contentious? Albert Winsom had been quoted as saying that Gavin MacLeod had stolen his money, and he thought that Norval Fraser, fellow monster hunter and conspiracy theorist, had somehow influenced that theft. In my opinion, them's were the fighting words.

"Ugh, it's in writing and everything," I muttered to myself, thinking that Albert Winsom's motive, many of Gavin's clients' motives, in fact, were now one hundred times stronger than Norval Fraser's. Had Inspector Winters come to that conclusion already? Or did it not matter? Were the fingerprints conclusive? They were usually considered pretty good evidence, but I knew there could always be something else at play. I'd heard that fingerprints alone weren't reliable evidence.

A little more research later and I found Mr. Winsom's shop's address. Surprisingly, not on the Internet, because I didn't know the name of the apothecary, but there it was in an old card file Edwin kept in the warehouse. I'd theorized that the file might contain addresses for every single person in Edinburgh. The long wooden drawers surely began their lives as part of an old library Dewey decimal system; they even had tarnished metal card frames on the fronts of each of the eight drawers. There, in the thick group of Ws, was an Albert Winsom, chemist and collector, his shop's address written with blue ink in Edwin's handwriting. I took a picture of the card with my phone.

Once the file drawer was closed and put back on the shelf where it belonged I sat again in my chair and stared at my laptop screen. I hadn't learned anything new. Not really. I'd just confirmed things and refreshed my memory, and added another layer of mystery to the Nessie stories.

I was anxious. I realized now, with a surprisingly strong conviction, that I believed that Norval did not kill his great-nephew. Was my gut just trying to tell me something? If a bookish voice wanted to pipe up, I'd listen. I lifted my eyebrows, but no one spoke. Then it came to me like a light bulb. It was Inspector Winters who kept my doubts alive. The fingerprints evidently weren't enough to convince him of Norval's guilt or he wouldn't have asked me to look around Norval's flat for something. I didn't know if that something would help or hurt Norval, but I hoped it would help.

"Hang on," I said aloud. Where had Norval lived as a boy? Wikenton. I began another search.

Wikenton was still there, but not really. No longer an incorporated village of its own, the sites I found online highlighted its glory days, back during the war. It had been home to thirty-six families, most of whom had been fishermen and farmers. There had been a small post office, a grocery store, and a candle shop. Though a few still lived in cottages on the village cove's shores, it was no longer part of a postal route, and those who remained had to claim Inverness addresses.

A few more clicks and I came upon an article I hadn't seen during my earlier research.

LOCAL MAN GOES MISSING, SON SUSPECTS
THE LOCH MONSTER

Mr. Leopold Fraser, local shoe cobbler, who was cursed with bad eardrums and wasn't given the privilege of going off to war, went missing nigh on two days ago. His seven-year-old son, Norval, told this reporter and a rapt audience of fellow villagers the story of his father talking to Nessie the night before and promising the boy a real introduction the next day. But when the next day came, there was no Leopold, nor sign of any monster. Leopold hasn't been heard from or seen since.

I read on, but it was more of the same; twists on the Fraser tragedy that didn't seem as entertaining or funny as the writers were attempting to make them.

Norval probably blamed himself, in the way young children tended to blame themselves for their parents' behavior. Villagers had other ideas. Some thought it feasible that Leopold fell into the loch and drowned. Some thought he ran off to fight in the war despite his eardrums. And then there were a select few who thought Leopold might have been up to no good in one way or another, one of those ways being that he ran off with another woman. In fact, the woman was named, but with a first name only—Flora.

"Did you run off with Flora, Leopold? And who is Flora?"

Try as I might, I found nothing more on the mysterious woman named Flora and where she might have come from or gone to.

But I found something else, a couple of nuggets of information I could try to mine. In the story about Norval's take on what had happened to his father, it was mentioned that the boy stood outside his house with his mother, his sisters, Jean and Millie, and his best friend, Ava MacMasters, as he told his story. Gavin had mentioned to me that Millie was still alive, and though a long shot, maybe Ava MacMasters was too. Best friends from their childhood would be a long time ago, but it was the only lead I had.

I found plenty of Millie Frasers in and around Edinburgh, but none that I could pinpoint as someone who might be Norval's sister. Surprisingly, Edwin's card file held no cards with the name Millie Fraser. My theory about him knowing everyone was debunked. I'd ask Inspector Winters if he'd talked to her.

I moved on to Ava MacMasters, predicting I'd run into another road with too many forks, but this search proved easy. I found her. Again, nothing in the card file, but I found Ava Mac-Masters Keaton, a resident of Wikenton. And, there was a phone number.

It was at least worth a try. I grabbed my phone and dialed.

"Hello?" the voice, tinged with both age and impatience, said.

I cleared my throat. "Mrs. Keaton?"

"Aye. What do ye want?"

"My name is Delaney Nichols and I'm a friend of Norval Fraser's," I began.

"Who?"

"Nor-val Fra-ser. You were childhood friends."

"Och, wee Norval? I ken him."

"Oh good!" *That was easy.*

"Is he dead?"

"No, ma'am."

"Then why are ye calling me?"

"I wanted to ask some questions about when you were children."

After a beat of silence, Ava Keaton laughed a gravelly snort. "Well, lass, ye're a wee bit late. I dinnae remember back that far, and I hate these infernal telephones. Come talk tae me in person and we'll have some tea, but I'm not going tae talk tae ye anymore on the telephone."

Then, true to her word, she hung up. She didn't slam down the handset, but she didn't hang up gently either.

I looked at my watch. Loch Ness was only about forty-five minutes away, but today wasn't a good day to make the trip. I had other commitments, and I would want Elias to drive me there. It wouldn't be fair to ask him to do so on such short notice, even if he would be willing.

Besides, I had another idea, another time in mind, and as I thought about it, it seemed like a good plan. Or good enough.

SEVENTEEN

My throat was so tight that I had no choice but to let tears fall down my cheeks, or I might completely cut off my oxygen. I could honestly say that I had never, ever been happier to see Gregory, Sylvia, and Wyatt Nichols. Not at my high school graduation, college graduation, not even at the goodbye party they held in their Kansas farmhouse the night before I left for Scotland.

They were, suddenly, the most beautiful people I'd ever seen. And, perhaps, the most ruffled. And the most exhausted. But still, the best ever!

Before moving to Scotland I'd never been out of Kansas. My parents had been to Missouri and Florida a few times, but the flight across the ocean was sure to have been a challenge, even if exciting. My brother had been to Iowa and Missouri, but most of his time had been spent in Kansas too. We were an educated bunch, but I suspected my family's horizons were going to be tested and stretched over the next week or so.

At least after they'd had a chance to rest a little. Unfortunately, rest wasn't on my immediate agenda.

My parents held hands as they walked toward me, though keeping a good distance from each other. It was as if they didn't want to lose each other, but still didn't want to participate in even a small public display of affection. My brother tailed behind but since he was so much bigger—taller and filled out like a good farm boy should be—than the rest of us, he stood out the most, particularly when he sent me the widest, weariest smile I've ever seen. I smiled back and sniffed and blinked away the tears.

Since they'd met, my parents had been inseparable, in that "I adore you but I need my own space for a while" way. The flight, with the two of them crammed right next to each other in close seats, might have tested their love a tiny bit, but they'd get over it.

My dad, in jeans and a lumberjack shirt, his thick hair now gray but at one time red, puffy, and unruly, looked just like he always had, except for the off-kilter glasses on his nose. He'd worn the same gold frames for so many years that his nose and the sides of his head had permanent imprints.

Mom, in cuffed jeans and tennis shoes I was sure she'd thought long and hard about (must wear the proper shoes for the proper occasion) looked just as strong and beautiful as I remembered. Her jet-black hair might have gone a little grayer, but she still wore her long ponytail tied low and with the smooth grace of a movie star. She also wore glasses; today's had bright pink frames. She was stepping up the style and I knew she would get along great with Rosie. She wore a denim jacket too, and it was something I recognized quickly. She'd worn the same jacket, even in brutal Kansas winters, for as long as I could remember.

Wyatt was also recognizable in his jeans and rock and roll

T-shirt, this one emblazoned with artwork from the 1975 Led Zeppelin tour. I'd know that winged man and colorful background anywhere, including in the Edinburgh airport. He swiped his hand through his short curly hair; he was the only blond relative in the pack, even when we came together for large family reunions.

"Delaney!" Mom said as she let go of Dad's hand and hurried to me.

We hugged and cried and looked at each other a minute, before it was Dad's turn. He held his hugs a little tighter than Mom did, but usually, not as long. Not the case today.

"My girl," he said when he finally pulled away. "You are a beautiful sight."

"I was just thinking the same thing about you three," I said with a sniff. "Oh, we've got to stop crying—there's so much to do!"

"Hey, sis," Wyatt said as he gave me one of his characteristic bear hugs.

"Where's Tom?" Mom asked.

"I told him I wanted to come alone. Well, my landlord is waiting for us outside the airport, but I . . . well, I have an idea and Tom has to work."

"Your landlord? Elias?" Dad asked.

"Yes."

"Can't wait to meet him," Dad added.

"Good, good, yes. I want to meet Tom as soon as possible, though," Mom said with a somewhat forced smile.

"You will. Soon. And he can't wait to meet you."

Though my parents were thrilled by my happiness, it was all a little too good to be true for them. A little too fairy-tale.

It was still hard for them to believe I was marrying a pub owner in Scotland. How was this man with his perfect kilt knees and amazing eyes so interested in me? I wasn't offended, and it wasn't that they didn't think I deserved the very best. They were just concerned something other than simple romance was going on, something that included a handsome Scot with some sort of ulterior motive. But soon they would meet him and feel better about the whole thing. I hoped.

I hooked one arm through Dad's and one through Mom's and led everyone to the baggage claim.

We chatted about the long flight, the Kansas summer weather, my parents' neighbors—who weren't actually right next door because of all the farmland in between—and the runaway cow that had somehow found its way onto my parents' porch, waking them up with some panicked mooing.

My brother sprung the news that he was planning a move to Detroit, where his mechanical engineering skills had gotten him a position with one of the big car companies.

"It's a big job," my mom said to me with raised eyebrows. "We're very proud."

Wyatt laughed. "Yeah, I know none of you thought I had it in me, but, well, I got this."

"Son, we've always believed in you," Dad said. "Just maybe not as much as you did. We like the pleasant surprise, and we don't mind being proven wrong."

My family didn't believe in blowing smoke. They were very honest, maybe sometimes too honest.

Wyatt winked at me and then grabbed the bags from the turnstile. I led us and the three large bags out to Elias and his waiting cab.

You might have thought Elias and my dad were long lost brothers. They were certainly cut from the same cloth—hardworking, loyal folks who put family first. I should have recognized the similarities earlier. It was no wonder I'd become so fond of my landlords. I was lucky to have such good men in my life.

Elias took my mother's hand and kissed the top of it as he told her what an honor it was to meet her. There was nothing forced or unnatural about the moment and I was duly impressed.

"It's such a pleasure, Elias. Thank you to you and Aggie for taking care of our little girl," Mom said.

"She is delightsome," he said. "Aggie is looking forward tae our dinner this evening."

"Oh, I hope she's not going to too much trouble. And you letting us stay in a guesthouse. Delaney has told us how wonderful they are. We don't want to be an imposition," Mom said.

"We wouldnae have it any other way," Elias said.

"Wouldnae—oh, I'm going to love this accent," Mom said.

"I know what you mean. So," I clapped my hands together, "are you three up for a little sightseeing, a small trip?"

My family blinked at me.

"Well, we're a little tired," Dad said.

"I'm ready for anything," Wyatt said, but I noticed his tired eyes too.

"Yes. Perhaps we could nap a bit first," Mom said.

I remembered the jet lag I'd experienced. It was so enveloping that I thought I might fall down in the street once the adrenaline of meeting my new coworkers was tapped out. I'd slept for fifteen hours straight.

"Well, maybe you could nap in the back seat of the cab?" I offered. "I'd like to take a small trip and today's a good weather day. I think you'd enjoy seeing Loch Ness, and I don't know how much time we'll have later in the week."

Honestly, I was a horrible daughter. I should have let my family get to some beds, but when the thought of making this trip with them today had come to me yesterday, I couldn't let go of the idea.

"Loch Ness?" Dad said. "The monster? Nessie?"

"That's the one," I said.

Mom and Dad exchanged looks and I caught their you-only-live-once shrug.

"I don't believe in Nessie, but I'm certainly game," Wyatt said.

"All right," Mom said.

"Verra good," Elias said.

It wasn't a huge cab, but it was big enough to wedge my parents and me into the back seat as Wyatt took the front passenger seat. Elias put two pieces of luggage in the back of the cab and then stacked and secured the other one on top. It seemed a dubious setup and I wondered if we should run the bags to the guesthouse before making the trip to Loch Ness. Elias didn't seem concerned and I think he had ideal travel times in mind. Running back home first might put us in some thicker traffic.

Only about three miles into our journey, as I was telling them about Norval Fraser, I felt the first head plop onto my shoulder. My mom had fallen asleep. I looked at my dad; he was out too.

I couldn't tell for sure so I quietly asked, "Elias, is Wyatt awake?"

He looked at the passenger. "No, lass, he's oot like a light. Ye remember the jet lag?"

"I do, but I managed a trip to the bookshop first."

"Aye, I remember. It's quite a journey though and they were delayed. I imagine they're forgnawed."

"That must mean exhausted."

"Aye, lass." He looked at me in the rearview mirror as my sleeping parents bookended me.

I was transported back about a year, to when I'd first seen those eyes in that mirror. It had been a good year.

"Should we run them back to the guesthoose?" Elias said. "I can take ye up tae Loch Ness by yerself."

I thought a moment. "No, they'd love to see it. I'd hate for them to miss it and I really don't know when we'll get the chance to go up again. We'll let them rest on the way. We'll wake them when we get there."

"Aye. Whatever ye say, lass."

EIGHTEEN

I'd never been to Loch Ness either, and, as often happened in Scotland, the weather changed from nice to foreboding as we approached the loch. My family slept soundly through the pouring rain, and the tight two-lane-road journey. My parents had me well tucked in place. The seat belt kept my brother secure, but his head rolled back and forth with the curves.

Fortunately, Elias was an excellent driver and his windscreen wipers and lights were in perfect condition. My family slept through a torrential downpour that curtained the passing hills and villages. At least the unruly weather meant they weren't missing much of the scenery, always better appreciated with clearer skies.

When I first moved to Scotland, the image in my mind of the legendary loch was something round, a tub of beautiful blue water for the monster I didn't believe in. It didn't take long to learn that the loch was actually a long stretch of dark, peaty, unwelcoming, and deep fresh water, its depth plunging down not far from the shore. Along each shore were some hotels and homes and places like Wikenton, where some villages still existed. I shared the results of my research, so Elias knew how to get to what was left of Wikenton, but he wanted to make a stop first.

I'd seen pictures of the Urquhart Castle, but I didn't expect Elias to take us to a spot where we could see its stone remains. When he pulled off the road to a hidden graveled nook, I was glad the rain had lessened enough that I could see out the windscreen and across the loch to the castle. Topped off with dark clouds—even though many of the stones were lost to time—the sight spoke to me in the ways Scotland always did: fierce and loyal, just like Elias and my dad.

"Do ye want tae get oot and take a look?" Elias asked me.

"Well. I would like to, but I'm not sure I can get out. Though I should wake them up anyway. I mean, it is Loch Ness."

"See if ye can climb over them. If they wake up, then it's meant tae be. If they sleep, I'll bring them back later in the week."

I smiled. "They're so cute, huh?"

"Aye." Elias smiled too. "They are happy tae see ye, but they'll be even happier when they're rested."

"All right, here we go."

I crawled over my dad, and he didn't wake up even a little bit. Elias plucked me out of the cab, and we both peered back in at my family.

"Do you think they were drugged?" I asked.

Elias laughed. "No, lass, don't ye remember how ye felt when you first arrived? They'll feel better after a wee snooze."

"If you say so."

"Come along. They'll be fine. Let's take a quick walk tae the shore afore the rains come again. Aggie and I love this place. Years ago, I came up here a time or two with some mates. We stumbled upon this fishing hole and stayed, told each other our lies. I brought Aggie when we first met and it's a tradition that we have tae stop whenever we're in the area. Ye and yer sleeping family are now part of the tradition."

"This is a great view of the castle ruins," I said, pleased that it was barely raining anymore.

"Aye." Elias rubbed his chin. "Ye've heard of King Arthur?"

"Yes. In fact, more than usual as of late."

"Aye? Well, there are many rumors about where Camelot might have been located if it really was a place . . ."

"This is one?"

"No, but it's rumored that Guinevere spent a night here. She ran from Arthur and Lancelot tae talk tae her father, who was the king of Scotland. She stayed here for the night but went back home tae her husband. If she was here, she probably spent a stormy night in a drafty castle, reminding her that perhaps Scotland's weather wasnae as lovely as Camelot's."

"Really? I'll be."

"What is it?"

I shook my head. "Sometimes things come in groups. You know when you start focusing on a number or something and you start to see it everywhere? That's what's going on with King Arthur right now. He and Camelot have come up a lot lately."

"Aye. Weel, if he was real, this country was his home . . . Arthur's Seat is another rumor, for a visit from the king and his knights."

"I heard that recently too."

Oh, to know for sure. It wasn't a bookish voice, just a wish that spoke inside me.

"See, we would set up some chairs right there and throw oot lines into the water," Elias continued as the water lapped in and came almost to my toes.

I stepped back. "You said you weren't a believer?"

"No, lass," he said, but I heard the hesitation.

"What?"

He looked at me with a half smile. "Dinnae tell Aggie, but I just dinnae ken for sure. If she thinks I have any doubt at all, I might never hear the end of her ideas."

"I'll keep it to myself."

"Let's just say that I wouldnae be surprised. I've seen things and wondered. 'Tis a mysterious place tae be sure."

In fact, the water and the surrounding countryside weren't the stuff of storybooks, at least those with happy endings. It was a beautiful place, like every other place in Scotland I'd seen, but more menacing. Maybe it was the dark clouds or the dark water, stretching far and long. Maybe the decrepit castle remains deepened the drama. I tried to imagine Norval's life as a little boy.

I searched the water for a head, or a tail, or something that might look like a monstrous creature, cartoonish or not. A shape in the water caught my attention, but it only took a moment to realize it was a piece of driftwood.

I saw nothing suspicious.

"It's beautiful in a very powerful way. Not like the ocean, but still commanding," I said.

"Aye. Commanding. I like that."

We watched the water as a tourist boat passed by. Many of the rain-cape-clad passengers had their phones or cameras up to the windows around the middle of the boat. I wanted a ride like that someday.

A cold spray hit my cheeks and I shivered.

"Ready tae go?" Elias said.

"I think so," I said.

We turned to step away from the shore and Elias took my arm as we made our way through a slightly more exuberant wind and the slippery gravel. Halfway to the cab, we heard a splash. It was distinctly a splash, not the lapping water, not a strange wave that might have come ashore, but a definite splash.

In unison, we turned back to look.

"Did you hear that?" I asked Elias, though I knew he had.

"Aye," he said doubtfully as both of us scanned the water.

"It was like something . . . someone jumped into the water, right?" I said.

"Aye, but it could have just been . . . something else."

"What?"

"I dinnae ken. A fish?"

"That would be one big fish."

"Aye. A big fish. That's what it was."

"Okay." I scanned the water again. "Would there be a fish that big here? It was a big splash."

"Aye. There must be. Or, if we heard what we think we heard, the water would be disrupted where it happened. We might be mistaken." Elias was trying to explain the sound to himself just as much as to me.

"I don't know. That's some pretty active water. Evidence might be hard to see."

Elias lifted and replaced his cap and then rubbed his chin. "Let's get back tae yer family."

"Right." But I couldn't take my eyes off the water. "Elias, you don't think. I mean, is it possible that a monster exists and knows when it's being talking about? Maybe knows how to tease its hunters?"

Elias pursed his lips and then rubbed his chin again. "No, lass, that's not possible."

"Of course," I said a good long moment later. Finally, I turned my attention from the water and we made our way back to the cab.

Gregory, Sylvia, and Wyatt Nichols were still sound asleep. I crawled back to my spot without disrupting anyone. I checked their noses for air movement and was relieved they were still breathing.

"Do you think their necks will be okay?" I asked Elias when he got into the cab.

"I think so. Might be a bit sore when they wake up. I wouldnae rouse them, lass. They'll be fine."

"It seems I couldn't even if I wanted to."

Elias chuckled. "On to Wikenton?"

"Please," I said, just as both of my parents rested their heads on my shoulders again.

NINETEEN

We thought we were headed in the right direction, but we weren't finding the correct turn. Because of a poor Internet connection, I couldn't search on my phone as we drove. We pulled off the main road next to the loch three times before we discovered the right road. The rain had stopped again, or I think Elias would have turned us around and taken us back to civilization instead of inside the overgrown cove.

Elias steered the cab around too many alder trees to count. We knew we'd made it to Wikenton when we came upon the old painted sign, hanging with one side of a broken chain. But we could still see that, in maroon paint over a weathered white background, the sign said: WIKENTON.

"This is the place," I said.

"Not much of a place."

As we traveled along the inner curve, we came upon a small house that looked lived in, and well-loved with peeling, whitish paint. However, the red door looked like it had recently seen a fresh coat and it shone even under the clouds above.

"Do ye think that's where she lives?" Elias asked.

"I don't see any other houses," I said.

I glanced along the cove's curve. There were only trees, no other structures.

"Wait, I see something over there," Elias said as he looked across to the other side of the curve.

I had to squint, but I thought there might be a structure over there too, painted light blue.

"Let me knock on this door and see. Maybe we'll get lucky," I said.

I wedged myself out of the cab again and followed a cobblestone path to the front door. I looked over my shoulder once to check the water for monsters, but the water was mostly hidden by the trees. However, it felt like something whispered on the back of my neck. My imagination was in high gear.

Considering that Ava had told me she didn't like to talk on the phone, I assumed she might be hard of hearing. I knocked on the red door with a little extra force.

"Coming," a male voice said from inside.

As the door swished open, I was greeted by a bushy gray mustache and the pipe underneath it. When the smoke reached my nose, I sniffed once. I couldn't place the scent but I thought it pleasant.

"'Elp ye?" he said, though I couldn't see his lips at all.

"Hi, I'm . . . well, I'm looking for Ava," I said.

"She's 'cross the way. The blue hoose," he said as he began to close the door.

"Uh, okay . . ." I said. I didn't want to let him go yet. "May I ask you a question?"

He might have frowned. "Aye?"

"Well, have you . . . have you lived here a while?"

"All my life."

"I'm Delaney." I stuck out my hand, which he shook, though I didn't think he wanted to. He didn't offer his name. "I've recently become friends with Norval Fraser. He's in Edinburgh now. Do you know the Frasers?"

He shrugged and took out the pipe. "I havenae seen a Fraser in nigh on forty years, but aye, they lived over there." He nodded to his right. "But their house is long gone, taken by a wicked winter storm. 'Twas empty at the time, so no one was hurt."

"Oh, that's good. I'm sorry about the house, though."

He shrugged again.

"I, uh, Norval's very into the monster, Nessie," I said. If he hadn't heard already, I didn't want to be the one to tell him about Gavin or Norval's involvement in that tragedy.

"Last I heard, Norval Fraser was certain his father was taken by Nessie herself."

"Yeah, he told me that story. What do you think about that?"

Another shrug. "Anything's possible."

I smiled. "Have you seen Nessie lately?"

He cocked his head. "Lass, are ye sellin' something?"

"No, not at all." I sighed. "Norval asked if I would take over his work, his search for the monster. I'm trying to figure out if I should."

"Weel, I cannae tell ye what tae do, but Nessie willna show herself tae ye if she doesnae want tae. She picks and chooses."

"She's real?"

I know he smiled now because I could see it in his eyes. "I'll never tell, but, lass, I really dinnae think that Norval Fraser's father Leopold was taken by the monster. He ran off with another woman. If I remember correctly her name was Flora, not

Nessie. Ava can tell ye aboot Flora if ye ask nicely. She knew everyone."

"Great—thank you for your time. I'll head over and talk to her now."

He continued. "I dinnae ken if she's back. Her son picked her up this morning. She cannae hear all that well, so go on inside and just yell her name. It's what everyone does."

"Go into her house? Without knocking?"

"Aye. She never hears the knocks. If she's not there, no harm done."

"Okay." I nodded. "Thank you again."

"It's the other house, the blue one," I said as I peered in at Elias and my still sleeping family. "I'll walk over. Meet me there?"

My mom stirred. I held my breath, hoping she'd open her eyes. Instead, she mumbled something incomprehensible and then snuggled her head back into my dad's shoulder.

"I'll meet you at the hoose."

I set off on the short hike and was quickly rewarded. Amid more alders was the ruined remains of one structure that might once have held three different businesses. This must have been the small downtown. There was no glass left where windows used to be, and vines snaked in and out of the openings and over the outside of the entire roofless structure.

"Probably the post office and the shops I read about," I muttered to myself. Elias's cab was far enough away from the walking path that he wouldn't hear me. I could hear the cab's engine on one side and the water on the other.

I thought of the ghost towns throughout the United States and had an idea. I was going to ask Elias and Aggie to come with me on a visit to Kansas someday. Aggie would love ghost towns, and Elias would go along without much of a grumble. I stepped out of the trees and onto Ava's property.

Though matching in shape and small size to the other man's cottage, Ava's blue house was in better shape than the one with the red door. I had a notion that it could either be a welcoming place, sure to have comfortable chairs and delicious sweets inside, or the home of a wicked grandmother who liked to trick children inside her oven.

"I'll wait here again," Elias said as I walked past the cab.

"The gentleman on the other side told me to go in, that Ava can't hear well and everyone just goes in."

"Sounds reasonable," Elias said.

As my barometer for proper Scottish behavior, his "reasonable" assured me that I wouldn't be overstepping, and chances of being thrown in the oven were slim. And, he was close by. Though it seemed my family would be useless if saving the day was in order.

I knocked even more loudly on this door than the other one and then I turned the knob, leaning to look inside as I called out, "Ava!"

There was no answer, so I made my way in, leaving the door wide open. I had surely stepped back in time. Last Christmas I'd been in a place that seemed to take me back to another time. I didn't dwell on those moments much because they were still somewhat unexplainable. But a chill ran up my arms as this place felt eerily similar to that one.

At least I could look out the front door and still see the cab, which kept me solidly in my realm.

"Ava?"

Still no answer. The small front room was walled off from the back of the house, and it only took two steps to reach the area behind it. A tiny kitchen with a too-tiny-for-even-a-child-to-fit-inside cooker took up one corner of the back space, and I could peer into a doorway to see the bedroom and adjoining bathroom on the other side.

Ava wasn't anywhere to be seen, but I couldn't resist taking a moment to get to know her.

The white appliances had probably been made back in the 1950s. They seemed clean but aged with a few scratches and maybe a fingerprint or two. The old wood floor was worn but would have caused renovators back in the States to cheer with glee if they'd discovered it under some carpet.

Some sort of sweet bread had been wrapped and was sitting on the counter, and my mouth watered reflexively. There was just enough space for a small wood table with two chairs tucked underneath. A white crocheted doily had been placed in the middle of the table, and cat-shaped salt and pepper shakers sat in the center.

Warmth emanated from a potbellied stove on the other side of the table. It probably warmed a kettle or two and seemed to be what heated the entire cottage.

The bed inside the bedroom was covered in a quilt of reds and yellows, handmade, I guessed, but it seemed too intrusive to walk in the bedroom to inspect further. I searched for the phone Ava had spoken on and found it attached to the wall. An old dialer, just like I'd expected, black with a knotted cord.

I pulled a pen and piece of paper out from my pack and wrote a quick note, letting Ava know I'd stopped by and that I would try to call her again later. I left the note on the table and then turned to go.

I hadn't noticed the picture on the wall just inside the front door, but I saw it now.

It was an old black-and-white photograph of a young girl, maybe a teenager smiling at the camera, but it was what was in the background that was the most interesting.

A tail. Or, maybe a tail. It was something with a tip that might have belonged at the end of a reptile. Except that it was sticking out of the water, probably the water right outside this cottage.

"No way," I said as I looked even closer. There was no mistaking its shape, but it could have been a trick of the light, or a trick of something. I took out my phone and snapped a picture of the picture. It wouldn't be easy to study, but I couldn't help myself.

I closed the door behind me and hurried back to the cab. Everyone inside was now napping. I tried to climb in quietly, but Elias's eyes flew open.

He cleared his throat. "How'd it go?"

"She wasn't there, but her house is adorable, and I almost stole what I thought was a homemade loaf of banana bread from the kitchen."

He smiled and shrugged. "Ye ken, if she's the type of woman I'm guessing she is, she wouldnae have minded a bit. Might be offended that ye didnae."

"I'll apologize. Also, I took a picture of a picture." I handed him my phone. "What do you think?"

Elias looked at my phone. "I think it could be the tail of a lake monster, or some sort of shadow, or . . . it's difficult tae know, lass."

"I know. But I couldn't resist."

"I expect not." He handed me back the phone.

"I feel terrible that I did this to my family."

He smiled in the mirror. "They can say they've been tae Loch Ness now."

"I guess."

"Home?" Elias asked as he put the cab into drive.

"Yes, home."

"We'll be there bedeen." He caught my questioning eyes in the mirror. "Quickly."

It was my turn to nap.

TWENTY

"Come in," I said as I opened the door. "They're all in the kitchen waiting for you."

I'd never once before seen my pub owner nervous. He was always cool under pressure, cool while my cheeks reddened with embarrassment at what his eyes could do to me. But today he was, for him, a wreck.

He took a deep breath. "Aye, and I'm anxious tae meet them. Lass, did ye see the paper this morning?" He'd tucked a copy under his arm and handed it to me.

"No."

"There's an article about Gavin's murder. Let's get tae your family, but I think you'll want tae read it when you can. No hurry. It's right there on the front page."

"Will do."

I was deeply curious about the article, but there were currently more important things to consider. I put the paper on the coffee table and then placed my hands on Tom's arms. "It's all good. They're going to love you."

"I hope so."

"I have no doubt."

The first thing my family had done on the day they woke up refreshed from their fifteen-hour naps, which was the same amount of time I'd needed to recover, was demand to meet Tom. They'd knocked on my cottage door and hoped he'd be in there with me. He hadn't been.

So, I'd called to invite him for breakfast. I'd invited Elias and Aggie too, but they thought we should have a meal as just a family first.

"This is Tom," I said as we came into the kitchen.

They all stood and greeted him with handshakes and hugs, and Mom said, "Goodness, you are a looker, aren't you?"

"Oh, Mom," I said.

"Mom," Wyatt added.

"Almost as much a looker as my little girl," Dad said.

Wyatt laughed, one quick snort. "Sorry, but, well, I mean, yeah, she's okay but . . . boy, am I hungry."

Tom had educated himself on my family's farm, going so far as to learn about the harvesting cycles. He asked intelligent questions that gave my parents a chance to talk about what they did with their days. Wyatt sent me some lifted eyebrows and a wink or two of approval.

And when Tom answered Wyatt's questions about Scottish whisky, I knew the two of them were destined to be friends. Tom promised Wyatt a full tutorial with samples and Wyatt didn't hide his enthusiasm at the idea.

Curiosity got the best of me and as their discussions continued, I didn't feel a need to supervise. I snuck away to the front room to look at the paper.

As Tom had said, the article I would be most interested in was right on the front page:

"Local Loch Ness Monster Hunter, Norval Fraser, Released but Detained and Moved to Medical Care."

"That's interesting," I said aloud as I sat on the couch and read.

Not only had Norval been hospitalized in an undisclosed location, the evidence against him had come into question.

"Charges have been dropped against Mr. Fraser," the article said. Though a caveat was included—he wasn't free from suspicion yet. However, now there were others who the police were also looking at. The others weren't named.

"Were there fingerprints or not?" I spoke to the paper again as dread rolled through me with another memory of Norval's warning about the police not liking him. Had they tried to get away with something, but failed? Or just hadn't succeeded yet?

I read on, hoping for an answer. I didn't get one, but I did learn more. Gavin had been stabbed to death with a knife that had a Nessie handle, a knife that it seemed "might" belong to Norval Fraser. The article even had a picture of the weapon—though the knife in the photo wasn't bloody, so I couldn't be sure if it was the actual murder weapon or a reasonable facsimile.

Though the article didn't name the other suspects, I wondered if Albert Winsom, chemist and fellow Nessie enthusiast, led off the list. Who else? Gavin's clients, probably.

I reached for my phone. I was going to call Inspector Winters, but then I thought better of it. He wouldn't tell me who the other suspects were. I had no right to know. But he did want me to go to Norval's apartment and look around. He'd texted me late the night before, telling me he'd received clearance from his Chief Inspector. He didn't mince words this time. *I'd like for you to have a look around*, the text had said.

I wondered if I could talk to Norval again. I looked at the phone in my hand. No, I would look around the apartment first and then call Inspector Winters. I could slip in all my questions, and hope for some answers.

"Sis?"

I looked up. My brother was so big, he seemed to take up the entirety of the small hallway to the front room from the kitchen.

"Sorry, I got caught up in an article." I put the paper back on the coffee table as I stood. I lowered my voice. "How's it going in there?"

"Great," Wyatt whispered back. "You're marrying a great guy."

I smiled. "You really think so?"

"He's either a terrific actor or he fell head over heels. Hard to know."

I smiled again. "I appreciate your support."

"Anytime."

"Let's go back in," I said.

I tried not to be distracted through the last few minutes of breakfast, but I probably was. And then I had one more task that needed attention before I could think about Norval or anything else again. I simply couldn't put it off, even for a police-requested "look around." Once Tom left, with confident hugs all around, I told Dad and Wyatt that I needed Mom to myself for a little while. Elias would take us on the errand and Aggie would be over to show them some spots she recommended they visit while they were in town.

"Hopefully, she'll have suggestions that won't put us to sleep," Wyatt said as he looked at me.

"I'm sorry about Loch Ness. We'll try to go up again," I said.

"I do find it odd that we slept through the whole thing," Dad said.

"Jet lag is real," I offered, helpfully.

My family and Elias and Aggie looked at me as if I might have more to add, but I didn't. It was a little crazy that I'd made them sleep in the cab, but that was yesterday, and we couldn't do much about yesterday, at least that's what Mom always said.

"Sorry about that," I said again.

Once Mom, Elias, and I were inside the cab, I said, "We're going to go get my dress. It needed one final alteration and it should be ready this morning."

Mom's eyes brightened. "Oh, Delaney, thank you for saving this for me!"

"I wish you could have been here the whole time."

"It's okay. The texts and pictures have kept me in the loop."

She put on a brave face, but my wedding had always been something she'd looked forward to, even more than I had.

Elias steered the cab toward Cowgate and I tried to point out some of the sights. The statue of Greyfriars Bobby and the story that went along with the much-loved dog captivated her.

I got so into telling it that I didn't notice something I should have noticed quickly. But Elias noticed. He uttered some Scots' curses under his breath as he looked toward the dress shop window.

"What?" I said as I looked over too. "Oh, no, that can't be. They're just switching things out. We must . . . there must . . ." Dread rolled through me.

There was no display in the shop window. Where there had

been a quaint display of a couple of mannequins in dresses, there was now nothing.

I jetted out of the cab and hurried to the window.

"No, no," I said again as I peered in at nothing but one lone white hanger on the floor, broken in two, strangely resembling a hand-drawn broken heart. How fitting. "How is this possible? There must be a sign somewhere or something."

There was. It was taped on the door.

"We are sorry to announce that we've had a family emergency and have had to close the shop. Our sincerest apologies."

"Is there a phone number?" Mom said over my shoulder as she fished her mobile out of her bag.

"I'm not seeing one. Both of you look too." I grabbed the door handle. Of course, it was locked, and didn't budge a bit when I shook it, even when I shook it really hard. "There has to be one, though. I paid for the dress. The seamstress was just fixing it. She probably has it with her." I peered in again. "Unless it's in that back room still. Do you think I have a right to break the glass?"

"No!" Elias and my mom exclaimed together.

"We'll find it or her, Delaney," Mom said. "Let's keep our wits about us."

I nodded. "Right, but . . . how is there no phone number?" I rattled the door handle again.

"What was her name?" Elias said as he took out a pencil and piece of paper from his pocket.

"Bonnie. Bonnie Warren," I said. "Any chance you know her?"

"No, but Aggie can find her. Or Inspector Winters, maybe. Should we call him?" Elias asked.

"Yes! That's brilliant!" I said as I took out my own phone.

"You're calling the police?" Mom said.

"Oh, yes," I said.

Ultimately, I was glad that he didn't answer. The message I left made my "urgent" situation sound ridiculous. Could he find the owner of a seemingly abandoned dress shop, or the seamstress who worked there? I doubted the police got many calls for such a thing. Still, desperate times and such.

I suddenly had a memory of years before, when my grandmother said that all weddings should be elopements. It was right after she told me the story of my own parents' wedding, one that had been fraught with one minor disaster after another until the major one hit. The barn that was supposed to have been the location of their ceremony burned down the night before. Fortunately, no people or animals were hurt, but all the decorations and some flowers were lost.

I looked at my mom and remembered that they'd ultimately had to share their vows at the local diner because another couple had booked the church, and it had been raining cats and dogs, mixed in with some ash from the barn fire. I hadn't interpreted her stories to mean that we as a family might be wedding cursed, but it crossed my mind now.

"Aggie's going to be bealin' when she hears aboot this. It'll give her something tae do with all that energy," Elias said.

"Bealin'" must be angry, boiling angry probably. I knew the feeling.

Time to get a grip.

It was just a dress. I could get married in anything. The good news was that Tom had his own kilt and I already knew it was ready for the ceremony; cleaned, pressed, and pleated.

"Thank you," I said. "It will be fine. I'm . . ."

"Weddings are stressful," Mom jumped in. "But Elias is

right. It will be fine. And this is a good omen. You know, your dad and I have been married thirty-four happy years and we had one disaster after another. Come on, let's let Elias take us home. I'll tell you a story or two that will curl your hair. Or your toes, or something."

I hadn't been aware of the burn of unshed tears behind my eyes, but I became aware of it as the tears dissipated. I reminded myself that it was, indeed, time to get a grip. Maybe this was how it was supposed to go. However, I still heard my grandmother's words in the back of my mind. Maybe all weddings *should* be elopements.

TWENTY-ONE

"Hello, lass!" Edwin said as Mom, Elias, and I walked into The Cracked Spine. "Welcome tae your celebration!"

Mom leaned toward my ear. "We couldn't tell you. It was meant to be a surprise. I know you're upset about the dress, but act happily surprised. We wanted a party to celebrate the wedding mostly, but everything else too. Your job, all these wonderful people you've met, everything!"

Elias sent me a tight grin, probably hoping I'd do what my mother said. I would.

Everyone was there. Dad, Wyatt, Aggie, Edwin, Rosie, Hamlet, Tom's father, Artair, Tom, and even Regg. Hector too. He trotted over to me before anyone else could and demanded to be picked up and have full access to my slightly wet cheeks for some of his kisses.

The burn gave way this time and real tears fell, just a few of them, and they were happy tears.

"Edwin wanted it tae be a surprise," Tom said as came forward and hugged me. "Are you all right?"

"I am better than all right. This is perfect," I said.

My parents and brother were treated like they were royalty. I was touched by how important it was to my Scottish family that my biological family feel welcomed and comfortable. Even Artair joined in and offered himself up for the role of tour guide. He had the week off from his job at the University of Edinburgh library and was available to take people wherever they wanted to go.

No matter, though, that it was the best party I'd ever attended; my mind eventually went elsewhere. Though I cared about the dress, I had to push it to the least of my concerns. Suddenly, I couldn't stop thinking about the article and the Nessie knife, and the fact that I hadn't looked inside Norval's apartment as he and Inspector Winters had wanted. Inspector Winters had all but driven me over and dropped me off. In fact, he might do just that if I asked him to. Instead, I'd used a call to him to report a defunct dress business. I hadn't even added a quick post-script asking who the other suspects were.

Yes, weddings were stressful, but there really wasn't a good reason why mine should be. It was small and simple. I looked around. In fact, everyone was there right then. We could have the wedding now, maybe just get it over with. My eyes landed on Edwin—no, everyone was not there. Edwin's new girlfriend, Vanessa, was conspicuously absent. Maybe now would be a good time to call her to come over for introductions.

Edwin noticed me looking at him and approached. "Delaney, lass. You'll show your family the warehouse, won't you?"

"Of course, but maybe not until later. They're hoping for some sightseeing today. Did you hear what I did with Loch Ness?"

"No."

I told him about our visit to Wikenton and my sleeping family, and he laughed.

"I've heard worse stories, I suppose," he said.

"I owe them a trip up there, but I really wanted to talk to Ava. I . . . I'm feeling remiss in not visiting Norval's place now. I think I should have done that first thing this morning."

"You don't know the wee man well. You don't owe him." Edwin put his hand on my arm before I could say anything about Inspector Winters' enthusiastic request. "I understand." He looked around. "I got a message from Birk. He wanted tae talk tae me about something he remembered before he called the police tae tell them—he didn't want tae discuss it over the phone. I'm tae go see him in a couple of hours, and there's . . . Rosie showed me the pages in the scrapbook and told me about her visit with Winters. I saw the article from yesterday morning, and I wondered if Albert Winsom might be a suspect." He shrugged. "I'm curious more than anything."

"I read the article too and had the same thought. Do you know him?"

"I met him once, inquiring about some items. I deemed them trinkets and not collectible."

"Loch Ness monster things?"

"Aye. He was none too pleased that I wouldn't purchase them. He might not remember meeting me, but I thought I'd swing by and . . . I don't know, I was just curious. We could stop by Norval's flat too. Do you want tae go?"

"I do!" I looked around. "But . . ."

"I know, you have obligations. Get to Norval's when you can and I will report back."

I sighed. "No, I'd like to go. Give me a minute."

Nothing like leaving your own wedding celebration party, before the gifts were even cracked open. In fact, I was surprised to see gifts tucked under the back table, but there they were, lovely in their wrapping paper and ribbons.

However, Tom and Artair were enjoying my parents, and Hamlet and Wyatt were deep in discussion about American football.

"Sorry," I said to Tom as I pulled him aside. "This probably seems rude."

Tom smiled. "Not at all. We'll tell secrets and stories about you while you're away. It's the best way for families tae get tae know each other."

Frankly, there wasn't much to tell, but he did have a point. If someone wanted to air any of my only slightly soiled laundry, while I was gone might be the perfect time.

"Thanks, Tom."

"For what? Being the luckiest man in the world?"

I looked at him a long moment. "Kind of."

"Whoa, sis, get a room," Wyatt said good-naturedly as Tom and I kissed.

Ultimately, no one much cared that I was leaving with Edwin. Hector seemed the most disappointed. But as we reached the door, a hand landed on my arm.

"Mom and Dad want to see a museum," Wyatt said. "Not my thing, but your future father-in-law is excited about taking them. I can head out on my own, but I wondered if I could tag along with you two. I'd love to know more about what you do with your days."

"Of course, lad," Edwin said.

"Sure," I said, trying hard to keep the hesitation out of my voice. I didn't really think Edwin wanted Wyatt to join us, but he sounded sincere. I hoped he was. "Sure, come on."

Wyatt climbed into the back of Edwin's car and said, "So, what are we doing?"

I looked at Edwin and then at my brother in the back seat. "Investigating a murder."

Wyatt blinked and looked at me. "Well, that's damn cool, sis. Let's go."

Edwin nodded his approval and we were off.

TWENTY-TWO

I filled Wyatt in on what was going on, beginning with my first meeting with Norval. I told him everything, and in turn Edwin too. Wyatt understood why Edwin and I were curious about who might have killed the financial investor, but he thought the case was pretty cut-and-dried.

"Norval wouldn't have killed his great-nephew, even if he was mad at him. One of Gavin's clients must have had enough of being stolen from and lied to. Norval's pretty easy to frame, considering all the Loch Ness nonsense, so throw in a Nessie knife and, boom, you've misled the police. The real killer didn't have to be all that crafty," Wyatt said.

"That's probably exactly what the police think, lad, even with fingerprints that might or might not be Norval's," Edwin said as he pulled the car up to a curb parking spot. "And the gentleman you are about tae meet was not only a client of Gavin's but a rival of Norval's."

"Well, that's even better. Surely, the police have talked to him," Wyatt said.

"We might find out," Edwin said.

The pharmacy was part of a long block of attached businesses, but its storefront was different from the other modernish facings. The window had the words CHEMIST: ALBERT WINSOM painted on it, and the intricate woodwork on the facade made it feel like a place from an old-timey village, perhaps like Wikenton had once been.

"Albert is a chemist." Edwin stated the obvious as we all stood on the sidewalk and looked at the window.

"A pharmacist," I told Wyatt.

He nodded as he rubbed his chin, deep in thought.

"Aye, that's what you call them in the States," Edwin said.

I looked at the shop again. "Eye of newt stuff in there?"

Edwin laughed. "It does seem particularly wicked and old-world, doesn't it? Wait until you see the inside."

Immediately through the door we were greeted by an array of scents; a combination of things I was sure I'd never smelled before. I sniffed enthusiastically, noticing layers of lavender, yeast, coconut, and something woodsy. There were other scents there too, but I couldn't identify them all. I'd expected something unpleasant, like when you first opened a container of vitamins, but there was nothing unpleasant about the smells in this place.

The inside was even more old-world than the outside. Rows and rows of dark walnut shelves were built into the side walls, each shelf packed with filled jars. A quick glance didn't reveal eyeballs or formaldehyde-soaked brains, but I wouldn't have been surprised to see them or something even more shocking.

Glass-topped display cases also lined the sides of the shop, sitting upon wood floors too scuffed to save. A narrow line of shelves stood at the back of the space and in front of another display case. The back case was adorned with a behemoth cash register that was sure to have big, button keys when we moved up there and could see it better.

At first, I didn't focus on the specific items, but when I looked again at the display cases I realized nothing inside of them had anything to do with medicine. They were filled with Loch Ness Monster items. Key rings, sunglasses, jacks games, paddle ball, and more.

The sound of a door shutting behind the back counter made some of the glass containers on the shelves rattle. The three of us made our way toward the counter and waited for the person attached to the shuffling footsteps to make it around to us.

Turning the corner, the man jumped when he noticed us there.

"Oh! I didnae hear the bell jingle," he said from underneath his long bangs.

He was slightly hunched, his thick, shoulder-length black hair parted so one side seemed to hang lower with the tilt of his shoulders.

With a flourish, the man swept back the bangs and stood up a little straighter. "Edwin MacAlister! What a lovely surprise."

With a better view of him now, I concluded that he must have had a stroke at some point. But though his face drooped on one side and was lined with wrinkles, he smiled them away and his dark eyes lit up while greeting Edwin. He recognized my boss immediately, and if he'd been angry at him at some point, he wasn't now. Albert Winsom, I presumed.

I also made another assumption—Albert Winsom was in no shape to have physically bested Gavin MacLeod. If he snuck up on him, maybe, but he wouldn't have been able to win a physical battle.

However, because we'd gone there with suspicion already on

our minds, I let another thought take seed: Could he be faking it? The second the thought cemented, though, I was embarrassed at myself for thinking it. No, he wasn't faking. But there was still the sneaking-up-on-Gavin theory.

I noticed that he didn't seem to show any sign of stress from perhaps being questioned by the police, and he obviously hadn't been arrested.

"Albert! Lovely tae see you." Edwin reached his hand forward and seemed to know that Albert shook with his left hand and arm.

"Tae what do I owe this honor? Coming here, tae my neighborhood? And who're the lad and lass? I dinnae remember ye having any wee-uns of yer own."

"Not my children, Albert. This is Delaney Nichols. She's working at the bookshop, come from the United States. And this is her brother, Wyatt Nichols. He's visiting for her wedding."

"A wedding? A lovely union, even if some of us have trouble keeping one together." He smiled and then immediately frowned, then smiled again. "I wish ye all the luck though, lass."

"Thank you," I said.

He extended his left hand to me and then to Wyatt. We both shook, and I wondered if anyone else noticed the cuts on Albert's hand. Edwin probably had. The diminishing well of suspicion filled back up a little.

"I brought Delaney here today because she's helping me with my collections. She has recently become interested in Nessie, the dear beast, and I thought I would show her your place," Edwin said.

On the way over, we'd discussed many things, but Edwin hadn't mentioned any sort of plan about what to talk to Albert about. If he'd known about Albert's physical condition, he didn't mention that either. I knew to play along. By the looks of him—his focused squint and that continuing curious move of rubbing his chin—so did Wyatt, even if he was somewhat too obvious.

"Really?" Albert's eyes opened wide. "Changed yer mind about my 'trinkets' have ye?"

Edwin laughed. "I simply don't know, and Delaney is much better at this sort of thing than I've ever been."

"Aye?" Albert looked at me, a seriousness now clouding his eyes. "Have ye seen her? Have ye been up there tae the dark waters, tae her lair?"

"I have been up to Loch Ness, but I haven't seen her." I paused. "Though I did hear something curious."

"Aye? When ye turned away from the water?" Albert asked.

"Yes."

He nodded knowingly and then leaned forward. "Ye've been kissed by her, then. It's her way of saying hello."

"Kissed?" I said with a smile. "I like that."

"Och, my own term, but I think it fits well. If ye go up again she might decide tae show herself. She needs time tae adjust tae the idea, but a kiss is a good beginning, I always say."

I thought of Norval's father and the similar words he'd used to explain why he couldn't introduce Norval to her until the next night.

"That would be wonderful," I said.

"Aye, and then ye'd curse that moment from then on. It's impossible tae forget her once ye really do see her."

"You've seen her, then?"

"Aye." He nodded sadly. "A time or two. I've no real proof, though. I'll keep trying tae find her again, snap a picture. It's my life, whatever I have left of it now."

My heart went out to him. He didn't strike me as a killer, but it'd been my experience that killers were pretty good actors too. And there were the cuts on his hand.

"I'll hope we both get to see her," I said.

"I," Wyatt put his hand on his chest and interjected, "slept through the whole thing. Jet lag."

Albert didn't need further explanation. He chuckled once. "Ye'll have tae try again, lad. It is well worth the trip. So, what is it about my collections ye'd like tae see? Many things are out here in the display cases, but I keep the really important things locked up at home. I could bring them back another day or we could make an appointment at my house."

"Can I choose both? I'll look around here, but we can talk about what's at your house too?" I said.

"Talk about what I have at my house?" Albert looked at Edwin. "Ye didnae tell her?"

"No, I didn't. I wasn't sure if you still had it. I didn't want tae get her hopes up."

Albert looked toward the front doors of the shop, but no one was coming in. No one stood outside the windows and peered in. He lowered his voice. "A tooth, lass. I have one of Nessie's teeth."

I was rendered speechless for a moment. When I finally found my words again, I said, "What's it like? I mean, is it sharp, or more like a molar?"

"Sharp! Of course."

"Of course." I looked at Edwin again. "You've seen the tooth?"

"I have."

"What . . . what did you think?"

"I thought it was an unusual find, rare certainly."

"Is it a secret because you don't want the authorities to know?" Wyatt asked.

I cringed inwardly at the question. There were laws in the United States about relics found on public land. In my world of museum work, it was only natural that I knew the laws. Wyatt might have heard about them from me, but I didn't remember us ever having such a conversation. I didn't want him to sound as if he would call the authorities on Albert.

"There are laws in the United States. Things need to be reported," I added.

"There is no law about Nessie teeth," Albert said in a clipped tone. He turned to Edwin. "They're not going tae report me tae anyone, are they?"

"No! Of course not," I said. I sent my brother a stern glance.

"Of course not," he said. "Never."

"Good." Albert shook his head to himself. "Good."

"Is it okay if we just look around?" I asked.

"Aye," Albert said.

"Actually," I continued as I moved to a side display, "my interest in Nessie is because of a man named Norval Fraser. You know him, I'm sure?"

Albert's eyes flashed anger again. "Aye, I know the man, and I dinnae believe his stories one bit. He's a fake. And a killer, most likely."

"You mean, he's not telling the truth about seeing Nessie?" I asked, genuinely interested in that part.

"That's exactly what I mean. He's never seen her and he doesnae respect her either. Norval's father ran off with some harlot; he wasnae taken by the monster. His nephew was a piece of rot too. I'm not surprised Norval did away with him. Ye've seen Norval's papers? A mess! It's disrespectful. He's a nuisance tae the cause. Now, maybe he'll stay put away for good."

"Oh. Well, I don't know," I said. I didn't bring up any newspaper articles I'd recently read; neither the current one nor the copies in Rosie's scrapbook.

Albert's eyebrows came together as he looked at me so fiercely that both Edwin and Wyatt moved closer to me. "Are ye really here for my Nessie collection? Ye ken I worked with Gavin, don't ye? Ye saw my name in the paper. Ye think I might have had something tae do with Gavin MacLeod's murder? Och, I should have ken better than tae think Edwin MacAlister would lower himself tae come see me, look over my things. Well, just so you know, the police did talk tae me, for a time longer than I wanted tae give them, but I have an airtight alibi, I do! They'll not be around tae see me again. I won't be telling you my alibi. I don't owe you three a thing, so don't even ask."

"Albert, that's not why we're here," Edwin said sincerely. "The murder happened recently. Norval is top of mind, that's all. We're sorry for the loss of life. Perhaps Delaney wanted to express her condolences tae you if she thought you knew the lad."

"Well. I knew him, knew him well, and I don't need any condolences!"

I took a step toward Albert. "I am sorry, Mr. Winsom. I've heard Gavin might have stolen a lot of money from a lot of people. I'm sorry if you were one of his victims."

Albert sighed and shook his head again. For a moment, he wanted to be angry at me, but the look on my face must have convinced him that I was on his side.

"I'll be all right. There are others much worse off," Albert said.

"I'm sorry, Albert," Edwin said. "I didn't even think about you losing money. I should have put all that together."

He was a better actor than me.

"I'll be fine," Albert said with a tone of finality.

"Do you still travel up to Loch Ness every weekend?" Edwin asked.

"Not every," Albert said, but he didn't continue.

My eyes went to the cuts on his hand again, but I didn't ask him about them.

"May we still look around?" I asked.

"Aye. Feel free," Albert said, not sure whether he should sound put out or not.

I thought he would leave, go through the door to the back. But he didn't. Instead, he and Edwin fell into an amiable conversation about books. I eavesdropped as I looked up and down the shelves. Albert might have read as many books as Edwin and they were evenly matched in the strength of their opinions about those books. As they talked, Edwin steered them back to a friendly acquaintanceship. He was good at that.

I fell into my own thoughts about the items I saw. There were so many things, and they did seem only to be trinkets, souvenirs, but maybe that was purposeful. Maybe there were other good things at Albert's house with the tooth. Now that was something I'd like to see, but who wouldn't? I'd try to work an appointment into the conversation before we left if it felt like the right thing to do.

We are only as blind as we want to be.

I jumped and gasped at the bookish voice. I covered the noise with a cough, and then I focused on the words Maya Angelou had said clearly in my mind.

Okay, Ms. Angelou, *I understand*. I'm missing something.

I peered with more intent into the display case in front of me. It took a few seconds because there were so many things, but my eyes soon landed on the items I was sure the writer wanted me to see.

A deck of cards. The same deck of cards I'd seen the first day I met Norval. Or a deck just like that one. Yes, there was the same Nessie picture I saw on the back of the cards that Norval had dropped outside the church. I'd last seen the deck as Gavin slipped it into his pocket. I felt my heart start to beat faster, but I calmed myself quickly. Seeing these cards in the possession of another Nessie fanatic probably didn't mean anything at all. Maybe it was, or at one time had been, a common deck of cards, sold in all the places that sell plaid scarves, shot glasses, and other Nessie souvenirs.

I squinted my eyes and looked at the artwork. I wished I'd researched it before now. Had they been designed in last mid-century as I suspected?

The shop was small enough that I wouldn't be able to furtively take a picture with my phone and I didn't want to tip my hand and ask Albert if it was okay to do so. But something told me—something other than Ms. Angelou—that I needed a picture of those cards.

I moved to another display case. I wasn't going to show any more interest in the cards, at least not while Albert was in the room.

"Wow, can you believe all this stuff?" Wyatt said quietly as he came up beside me.

Of all the things I'd told him and Edwin in the car, I'd left out the particulars about the artwork on the deck of cards. I'd just said it was a Loch Ness Monster deck.

"It's overwhelming."

"Can we ask to see the tooth, this week before I go home?"

"We'll definitely try."

The conversation between Albert and Edwin seemed to be coming to a close as Wyatt and I sauntered back toward them.

"Albert," I said when they looked at us. "I know you're a chemist, but I'm not seeing any medicinal items for sale out here. Do you sell over-the-counter medications?"

"Some. Most of my work is as a compound chemist. I mix drugs based on special orders. What do you need?"

"Is there any chance you have some aspirin I could buy? I've got a headache coming on." From where I stood, I couldn't see any bottles of pills or powders in the front part of the shop.

Edwin's eyebrows came together. I hadn't been sick one day since coming to Scotland and I didn't think I'd ever mentioned any aches or pains.

"Of course. Just back in my office. Wait a moment," Albert said before he turned and walked around the shelves to the back.

It was evident that any anger we'd sparked had now mellowed. Edwin had smoothed Albert's tone back to friendly.

I didn't give Edwin a chance to ask about the alleged headache. Once I heard the door in the back close, I hurried to the cards and snapped a picture. I was easily back in my position in front of the counter by the time Albert rejoined us. Edwin and Wyatt had watched me silently.

Albert not only brought me the aspirin but a cup of water too. The cup was adorned with a Nessie picture. I smiled at the picture and thanked him.

"Albert, could we make an appointment to see the tooth?" I asked. I felt Wyatt nodding behind me.

"Aye, lass." He looked back and forth between Edwin and

me. "I'll bring it tae you, at the bookshop. It's been years since I've been there. Will that work?"

"Perfect. Thank you for doing that and for letting us look around today."

I didn't need the aspirin, but I took it anyway. If Gavin had been poisoned, I might have reconsidered.

Albert stood by the giant cash register and watched us leave, not accepting any money for the aspirin. We didn't talk until we were out of sight of the shop.

"The tooth?" I asked first. "What did you make of it?"

"It's a sharp tooth, but I suspect there are a number of non-mythological creatures it could have come from. I don't know teeth well," Edwin said.

"Hopefully, we'll get to see it," Wyatt said.

"Did you see the cuts on Albert's hands?" I asked.

They both had, but they'd also both noticed that the cuts weren't deep, just superficial scratches. I agreed.

"The cards," I said. "They looked like the ones I returned to Norval. Gavin had them with him when he chased me down outside."

"You remember Gavin holding them?" Edwin asked.

"Yes. I remember thinking in the back of my mind that he seemed surprised to have them. He'd probably grabbed them accidentally. And, if I remember correctly, the last time I saw them was as he put them in his pocket. Of course, I know that Albert Winsom displaying the same deck might mean nothing at all, but . . . well, it could be a clue, right?"

I also remembered that Nisa had asked me specifically about the cards. She'd said she just wondered if I'd managed to see Norval, but the question she'd used to get there was about the cards. I didn't mention Nisa's inquiry to Edwin and Wyatt.

"Sounds shaky, sis," Wyatt said. "Both those guys are whipped about that monster. The deck might be something common, in the old days or even now. Besides, he said he has an airtight alibi, and I just can't see . . ."

"I know, he doesn't seem like he could do what needs to be done physically to stab someone." I looked at Edwin. "Do you know when he had the stroke?"

"No idea. He hadn't had it those years ago when he and I first met. I was sorry to see his condition, but he seems to be making the most out of it."

"The cards probably don't mean anything at all," I said. "And, I have to admit, I kind of liked the guy."

Edwin made a noise of agreement.

I looked at the picture I'd taken. "It might be a tenuous connection, but I'm calling Inspector Winters to tell him about the cards. This time with something more important than a closed dress shop, even if not by much."

"Closed dress shop?" Wyatt and Edwin said together.

"I'll tell you in a minute."

I rang Inspector Winters' phone but had to leave another message. I understood that he was a busy man, but I had to squelch some rising irritation. He might have seen my number and thought it was something frivolous again.

Though maybe that's what it was: frivolous. I needed to research those cards, their value, their availability, as soon as I could. But for now, Edwin had another appointment for us to attend.

TWENTY-THREE

"Birk is doing some amateur theater. This is where he said tae meet him," Edwin said.

I peered out at the King's Theatre as he parked the car. "Edwin, this isn't amateur. This is big time."

"It's a group Birk has been a part of for many years. I think this is their first opportunity to perform at King's."

Wyatt whistled. "I bet we find Mr. Shakespeare himself inside there."

Edwin laughed. "In fact, the play is *Richard III*."

Wyatt grumbled something from the back. He wasn't a fan. I had a brief flashback to my high school days when I was given the role of Lady Macbeth. Wyatt had had to read lines to help me rehearse. At the time, he found many opportunities to mock the bard. He'd claimed to be damaged ever since, and broke out in hives whenever the word "sonnet" came up in conversation. Fortunately, that didn't happen very often.

The King's Theatre sat at the end of the street where Elias and Aggie, I, and their guesthouses resided. I walked, traveled in Elias's cab, or rode a bus past the esteemed building almost every day.

An Edwardian theatre built back in 1905, opening in 1906 with a performance of *Cinderella*, it had stood the test of time, and it was one structure in Edinburgh that hadn't burned down and required a rebuild. There weren't many that could make such a claim. However, it had been remodeled in the 1950s. I'd heard that the powers that be were considering another remodel to "bring it back to its former glory" but I liked it just the way it was.

The gallery was made of three tiers, the tall stage ornate with wooden carvings framing the bright yellow curtain. I'd seen a production of *The Wizard of Oz* a few months earlier. My date had been Joshua, my friend who worked at the museum. Joshua was a young, brilliant postdoc, who knew something about almost everything. Like Hamlet, he'd become like a younger brother to me, as well as a museum buddy. Finding other people who liked to move slowly while reading everything through museums was rare. He and I moved at the same museum speed. While watching Dorothy's adventures, he'd nudged me with his elbow every time the word "Kansas" was spoken. Aggie would have enjoyed the play too, but she'd been busy. Maybe I'd take her to see Birk perform.

Tom would have gone too, but I could tell theater wasn't his favorite form of entertainment. Besides, he worked most nights. He liked Joshua too, and didn't mind in the least that I'd gone with my twenty-one-year-old friend.

The front doors were unlocked and no one stopped us walking through the grand lobby and into the expansive auditorium.

Birk was center stage, playing the lead role of Richard III

himself. Though perhaps a bit old for the part, he looked like he used makeup very well, even during plainclothes rehearsals. We only moved about halfway down the aisle before we sat, seemingly unnoticed by everyone else in the theater, including the other actors and three people sitting together in the middle who I assumed were the director and the producers.

Now is the winter of our discontent . . .

The actors were currently at a different point than the bookish voice in my head, but I couldn't have stopped it if I wanted to.

"Delaney." Edwin nudged me lightly with his elbow.

"Yes," I answered after a brief delay. "Sorry."

"He's not bad, is he?"

"No, he's great!" I said, but I hadn't really paid attention. I did now, and he truly was very good.

Wyatt sat on my other side, his arms crossed in front of his chest and a frown pulling at the corners of his mouth.

"Cut!" One of the three sitting in the middle stood up. Once everyone was silently looking at him, he turned to us. "These aren't open rehearsals."

"Sorry," I said. "The door was unlocked." I smiled up at a frowning Birk. "It was very good."

"Nevertheless," the director, I presumed, said.

"Right," Edwin said as we stood.

"Hold on," Birk said. "They're friends. May I have a moment with them?"

The director wanted to say no, but instead he said, "Five minutes, and then we have tae get back tae it."

"Of course," Birk said in a tone that made it clear he would continue to do whatever he wanted to do and everyone else would have to deal with it.

"Edwin, Delaney, young man," he said as he approached. I could see the line of the thick pancake makeup on his face.

"This is my brother, Wyatt," I said.

"Ah, delighted to meet you." Birk smiled and shook Wyatt's hand like he truly meant it.

"You were very good," I said.

A smile pulled at his mouth, but he wouldn't give in to it. "Oh, I have much work tae do, but we will be ready for opening in two weeks, I have no doubt." He looked around. "Come along. No one will be out in the lobby. We can talk there."

We found four folding chairs leaning up against one of the decorative columns and gathered in a corner where we would be safe from eavesdropping.

"What's going on?" Birk asked with a heavy eye-lined blink. He did look like the Richard III I had in my head.

Edwin blinked back. "You asked me tae stop by."

Birk thought a moment. "Oh! I'm sorry. The play has my mind . . . anyway, aye, thank you for stopping by. I had tae let you know. We discussed how I'd recently been talking about Gavin MacLeod with someone, but couldn't remember the details. I wasn't sure if I should call the police, Edwin. I remembered who I was talking to, and I wanted tae talk tae you first . . ."

"Who, Birk?"

"Brodie Watson."

"The writer?" Wyatt asked at the same time I thought it.

"Aye, one and the same." Birk paused and gathered his thoughts, as the most dramatic of expressions passed over his well made-up face. "That article I read that mentioned some of Gavin MacLeod's clients didn't mention Brodie Watson, but I know for a fact that not only was Brodie a client, but he was upset with Gavin, very upset, saying things like he wanted to 'kill him' and such. He was angry, and I'm fairly sure he used those words. I just remembered all of this last night. It was a couple weeks ago. Brodie and I were . . . Brodie was drinking me under the table again. I tried to keep up with him, but it was a bad idea."

"I understand," Edwin contributed.

If Rosie were there, she would probably huff an agreement.

"I'm sorry it took me a few days tae remember; I've been so involved with the play, and I really drank so much that night," Birk continued.

"Aye, you should tell the police," Edwin said.

Birk bit his bottom lip. He looked at Wyatt, at me, and then at Edwin again. "Are you sure, Edwin?"

"Why not?"

Birk said, "I'll be blunt. I hope that's acceptable."

"Certainly," Edwin said.

"Hamlet, Edwin. Remember what Brodie did for Hamlet," Birk said.

Edwin's expression transformed. "I don't know how, but I had all but forgotten. It's been years."

"But it's still important, nonetheless."

"The most important, maybe," Edwin said.

"Aye, that's what I was thinking. What Brodie did for Hamlet could trump the fact that he might have killed that horrible Gavin MacLeod." Birk cleared his throat.

"What did Brodie Watson do for Hamlet?" I asked.

"It was years ago, when he was a lad hiding in bookshops," Edwin said. "Brodie was visiting The Cracked Spine when Hamlet rushed in, after having stolen a wallet from a tourist. The police were right after him, but Brodie, seeing Rosie's protective feelings for the boy, stepped up and talked the police into letting Hamlet off the hook. Not only did the wallet make it back to its owner, but it had double the amount of money inside of it than when Hamlet took it."

"Oh. Well, that's . . . I hadn't heard that story," I said.

"That was the beginning of us bringing Hamlet into the family. Brodie's good will and his celebrity standing with the officers saved the day. Had he not been there, I'm sure Hamlet would have been taken away and we might have never really known what a wonderful lad he is."

"You would have done the same for Hamlet if you'd been in the shop," I said.

"I have no idea, lass," Edwin said. "I'd tried tae be friendly tae him, but he was close tae being a lost cause. I might have given up on him. Brodie didn't, and that was the chance Hamlet needed tae become the man he has become."

"I see," I said. But did that mean Brodie couldn't also be a killer? If I'd learned anything at all it was that Edwin's moral definitions were murky, not quite as clear as my Kansas farm upbringing.

Edwin lifted his hand as if to prevent any of us from asking the question I'd just thought. "Let me talk tae Brodie first. I feel like I owe him that much. And, we'll not tell Hamlet about any of this for now. I don't want to worry him."

Yes, lots of Gavin's clients were probably angry with him, but how many had sought out his great-uncle and given him a gift? And why would he have done that? Brodie Watson worked with Gavin; he had access to him if he wanted to talk to him. Unless Gavin quit seeing him, quit talking to clients. What had Brodie wanted to accomplish by talking to Norval? Just give him a book?

"How much do you think Brodie gave MacLeod to invest?" Edwin asked Birk.

Birk said the number aloud, and I felt my brother swoon in the chair next to me.

"Phew," I said. "That's a lot."

"And that's only the beginning," Birk said. "He took that much at least from many others."

"Will anyone get any back? Has anyone?"

Birk shrugged. "Who knows? I'm sure more investigations will be conducted, but they will take a long, long time, and I'm . . . dare I say, not disappointed, that the world will not have to deal with that man ever again."

"That's a wee bit harsh," Edwin said.

Birk huffed. I didn't add an opinion one way or another, though I personally thought the murder was tragic. However, if Gavin had taken that much money from me, I might feel differently. Even Edwin, who had more money than anyone else I knew, might be more unforgiving if someone had taken that much from him.

"Stolen money is a strong motive for murder. If Gavin's clients were beginning tae see that their money, for all intents and purposes, was being stolen, any number of them might have been motivated to kill," Birk said.

"With a Nessie-adorned knife?" I added.

"Aye, well, many knew Gavin and Norval were related, and Norval's gained quite the reputation. It's all very convenient, if you ask me," Birk said.

"It does sound like that," I said.

"There could be a ton of suspects," Wyatt said.

We all nodded.

"So, you don't think I should tell the police about my night out with Brodie? I was certainly blabberin'," Birk said as he looked at his watch.

I'd heard someone use "blabberin'" to describe their drunken evening before, but I couldn't place who.

"You probably should, but I really would like the opportunity tae talk tae him first," Edwin said.

"I understand," Birk said. "Besides, if the police haven't figured out that Brodie was one of Gavin's clients, they need tae do a better job at their job, I suppose."

"Why would they leave him off the list on purpose?" I asked.

"He's a celebrity, well loved," Edwin said.

"Ah, right," I said, knowing those sorts of things happened all the time, but still not liking it.

Birk stood first, but the rest of us followed behind.

"Birk!" I said, remembering something. "Did you talk to your friends up by Loch Ness? I know Wikenton was a place at one time, but it's not much anymore. Any chance your friends would know more about it?"

"In fact I did. They knew nothing about it, I'm afraid. Sorry not tae have something more."

"It's okay. Thanks."

"Thanks for coming tae talk tae me here. I didn't want tae tell you over a phone call. I've become slightly paranoid in my old age. I wonder if anything is private anymore."

"Of course, Birk. Good luck with the play," Edwin said.

Birk cringed. "No, Edwin. You do not wish a thespian luck, you tell him tae break a leg."

"Of course. Break a leg, Birk. Break two!" Edwin smiled.

"Thank you, friend."

They shook hands and then Birk shook Wyatt's hand and mine.

"You really were very good in there," I said.

"Thank you, lass. You'll have tae come tae a performance."

"I will. Definitely."

We watched Birk disappear back into the auditorium.

"Edwin," I said, "I know we have other plans, but I'd really like to talk to the police first. No, I'd like to talk to Inspector Winters. Could we go there next? Not to tell them about Brodie; something else," I said.

"Absolutely," Edwin said before he set out with long steps to lead us out of the theater.

"This is what you do with your time?" Wyatt said to me as we followed behind.

"Sometimes, though it wasn't in the job description."

"Gotta give it to you, sis, for a book nerd, you've certainly found a way to live an exciting life."

"I'm not sure I need this much excitement," I said with a laugh.

I couldn't help but wonder: Maybe I did.

TWENTY-FOUR

On the way to see Inspector Winters, I told Edwin and Wyatt the information I'd already given to the inspector about Brodie visiting Norval. My comment to the inspector had been more about Nisa than the writer, but I had mentioned him by name. None of us thought that boded well for Brodie, but we hoped it was simply coincidental timing.

Birk had been under heavy influence of alcohol when Brodie had said threatening words about what he wanted to do to Gavin. Brodie probably had been too, although from what I'd heard, perhaps Brodie was immune to the effects of alcohol. I went along with Edwin talking to Brodie before we threw him further under any bus, only because I trusted Edwin enough to think he'd tell the police whatever they might need to know when the timing was right. I hoped I was correct, but a small part of me doubted.

I held tight to the fact that it seemed Edwin was fond of Norval. If so, he'd do what needed to be done if it meant catching a killer. I hoped.

I knew this—lots of people said they were going to "kill"

someone. Most of the time it was just an expression, not a real threat.

As we waited in the police station lobby, more than once I felt the urge to leave, embarrassed by my call about the dress, worried I'd come upon something unimportant. But I didn't leave.

I did, however, feel the urge to nudge my brother and ask him to put a less guilty look on his face, but he managed it himself by the time Inspector Winters appeared.

"Delaney, I got your messages about the dress shop and the cards," Inspector Winters said as he came around the wall dividing the officers' offices from the front open area. He sent Edwin a nod and Wyatt questioning glances. "I will ask someone to try to find the shop owner. What is this about the cards?" He scratched the side of his head but didn't say aloud how ridiculous my dress shop request had been. I was relieved, but still embarrassed.

I stepped forward. "Thank you. I'm sorry to interrupt your day, but, well, I felt like you needed to know something about Gavin MacLeod's case."

"I'm listening."

I nodded. "This is my brother, Wyatt. We've been . . . well, can we all come back and talk to you a minute?"

"Sure," he said after a long pause.

Once formal introductions and handshakes were made and we were cramped into the small interview room I'd become familiar with, I pulled up the picture I'd taken of the cards.

"On the day I met Norval," I began, and then told him about the card connection.

"I see. We have talked to Mr. Winsom, but I didn't know about the cards. Though I'm not sure that two Nessie collectors having the same deck of cards is of much, if any, significance."

"Probably not, but I'm not sure yet. I need to research their value. That might tell us more, like how available they were and are. If they're rare, well, that's something, and if you didn't find a deck at Norval's or Gavin's . . . it might help nail down a possible trail or something," I said. "I haven't looked through Norval's place yet. Do you know if you guys found any cards?"

Inspector Winters fell into thought as he continued to look at the picture on my phone. He looked back up a moment later, and I thought he sent a quick sideways glance toward the door just to make sure it was closed. It was. "No, we didn't pick up a deck of cards from Norval's. I don't know if the officers looked for or saw a deck at Gavin's, but I will ask. It's a long shot, but worth looking into." He paused and leaned his arms on the table. "In fact, we found no evidence at all at Norval's. We found a lot of things about Nessie, but nothing that had anything tae do with Gavin MacLeod's murder."

"Other suspects?" Sometimes I tried to sneak a question or two in with the police, but I hadn't intended this one. I blinked at my own surprise gall.

Inspector Winters frowned at me, but he wasn't upset. I'd seen him upset before. This was something different. I was glad when he continued. "Well, I'm not sure we have any other solid suspects. There are some questions about the fingerprints. It's possible there's more than one set on the knife handle. We aren't one hundred percent sure that Norval's are . . . well, enough to count as conclusive, is the best I can explain it."

"Enough to get rid of reasonable doubt?" Wyatt piped up. We all looked at him and his overly earnest eyes. He cleared his throat. "Sorry."

"It's all right," Inspector Winters said. "Aye, something like that."

"Any ideas about the other prints?" Edwin asked.

"None, but other folks are being looked at a little closer. Some of Gavin's clients were pretty upset with his business practices."

"Albert Winsom?" I asked.

"Aye, he's one, but there's a deeper connection there with the Nessie things. Other people too, but I'm not at liberty to say who. You'll have to understand."

"Inspector Winters," I said, "I'm going to tell you something and then I'm going to feel really horrible about it. I've been turning it over in my mind . . ."

"Delaney, what?" Wyatt asked. His question, along with Edwin's raised eyebrows made it clear that they didn't know a thing about what I was going to say.

Along with wrestling with whether I should bring it up to Inspector Winters, I'd wondered if I should tell Edwin and Wyatt, but I hadn't.

"G'on," Inspector Winters said.

"I'm . . . I don't *really* think it's possible that she was involved, but do you know the reverend at Norval's church? Nisa? I mentioned her earlier."

"I do. She confirmed that Norval said that the author Brodie Watson paid him a visit, but there didn't seem to be anything else there. Are we missing something?"

I felt both Edwin and Wyatt hold their breaths, but I didn't go where it looked like I might be headed.

I finally said, "She talked to Norval right before I met him, later telling me that she thought Norval and Gavin were having a row. They were going to meet later to discuss it, but the meeting never happened. Did she mention that part?"

"No."

I nodded. "Tom and I saw her coming out of his flat right after the murder, and right before the crime scene tape appeared. The timing seems weird."

Nisa had ultimately ended up with Mr. Watson's book. I really hoped she wasn't a killer—for more reasons than the fact that I'd have to find yet another officiant if she was—but as we'd talked to Birk, it had become clear to me that the police needed to know more of what I knew about the friendly and open-minded reverend. However, it didn't change the fact that I was cringing inwardly. I'd just brought up Reverend Nisa regarding the investigation of a murder. Talk about gall.

Any other police officer, I probably wouldn't have said anything, but I trusted Inspector Winters. Elias thought I trusted him too much. If he was here, he would have kicked me under the table.

"I see," Inspector Winters said as he took notes in his small notebook. "Thank you, Delaney, we'll check it out today."

I hoped I hadn't made a huge mistake, but it was done now.

"How's Norval?" Edwin asked, easing the tension in the room.

"He's fine." Inspector Winters sat back in his chair. "Do you know him?"

"Not well, no, but it seems . . . I'm glad he's been moved to a hospital instead of a jail cell."

Inspector Winters squinted at my boss. I couldn't tell if they liked each other or not. Maybe they respected each other, maybe not. Neither of them would give me a straight answer whenever I asked.

"Let me be clear. We are keeping a tight rein on Norval because we believe he *might* be a killer. We are investigating all other avenues because, as a police force, we like tae be thorough. We have dropped the murder charges for the time being, but we wouldn't detain Norval if we didn't feel it was the right thing tae do. Additionally, we also think it's the right thing tae have him see a doctor," Inspector Winters said. "We aren't done with Norval Fraser. Please don't think we'd look the other way just because he's a sweet, old man."

Edwin nodded. "I understand. Does he have legal representation?"

"Yes, the court appointed him an attorney."

Edwin's mouth made a straight line as he thought a moment. "May I offer tae hire a different attorney for him?"

Inspector Winters sighed. "Sure. That would be fine, but he might like the guy he already has."

"Is he in any shape tae determine who would serve him the best? He is in the hospital."

"I can't answer that question, Edwin."

"Of course. I will proceed with attempting tae acquire someone else. I will ask them tae tread carefully as not to offend anyone."

"That would be fine."

"Thank you."

Inspector Winters turned back to me. "How quickly can you determine the value of the cards?"

"I'm not sure. I'll start with my friend at the museum, Joshua, but I'm not sure he'll be able to help. He might know where to direct me, though. Maybe I could just do a quick search on the Internet if you have a computer I could use for a minute. It would be better than my phone."

"Aye, come along. I'm going tae have you work with another officer, one of our information specialists. She'll know what we might need tae save." He turned to Edwin and Wyatt. "Can I get you some coffee while you wait?"

"Only if you pass a machine. Thank you," Edwin said.

"I'm good. Thanks," Wyatt said.

Inspector Winters led me out of the interview room and down the hallway. But this time, instead of leaving out the front doors, I followed him down the other side of the building, a side I'd never seen before.

We moved through a short, almost cramped, hallway, stopping outside a plain door. Inspector Winters knocked.

"Enter," a voice from inside said.

"She's got an attitude, but she's the best at what she does. Don't let her offend you. She'll try."

I nodded. I just needed a computer with an Internet connection. I didn't think there would be time for offense.

"Kari," Inspector Winters said as we went through. "This is Delaney Nichols. She needs tae do some research, but I'd like for you tae monitor just in case we need a record of what she's looking at."

Kari was the youngest police officer I'd ever seen. She couldn't have been more than about twenty, with thick black eyeliner and jet-black short hair that stuck up in every direction. She nodded at Inspector Winters and then sent me a critical frown.

"Got it," she said. "Sit here." She pulled a chair over next to her. "Type. I can do what I need to do just by watching."

"Okay." I took a seat. "I'm just looking for some artwork that was on the back of a deck of cards."

"Don't need to tell me. Just do. I'll watch." I couldn't quite place her accent. It didn't sound Scottish.

"Right."

I started by typing a general question about Loch Ness playing cards but had to refine my search to get real results. It wasn't until I figured out who the artist was that I could narrow things down enough.

Bottom line, the artist who'd created the picture had been on staff at a newspaper, *The Scotsman*, back in the 1940s. He'd created a one-panel strip that featured Nessie. The strip wasn't long lived, but the artwork was popular and ended up on souvenirs and promotional items like the deck of cards. There had been many decks created, which made the cards only somewhat valuable. The deck at Albert's shop as well as Norval's— if they were, indeed, the same deck—might go at auction for only as much as about £200, but that was just a semi-educated guess. Not bad for a deck of cards that was originally used for promotional giveaways, but not too hard to find nowadays, particularly for serious collectors.

"Cards, huh?" Kari asked after a few minutes.

"Yes. This deck specifically." I put the cursor over the appropriate picture.

Kari huffed. "That ridiculous monster story. Haven't we squeezed it for all we can get?"

"I don't know. I guess that ultimately depends on if she's ever proven to exist or not."

Kari rolled her eyes. "Whatever."

"Are you from here? Scotland?"

"Nope. I'm originally from Iowa. Not far from where you're from."

"Oh!"

"Yeah, your reputation precedes you. Everyone here knows about the nosy redhead from Kansas. You've given me a lot to live down. American behavior and all."

I swallowed the offense I said I wouldn't take. "I think that's all I really need. Can I print a couple pages and take them back to Inspector Winters?"

"Sure."

"Thanks," I said as I took the pages and stood to leave.

"You're welcome," she said as she looked at her screen.

The last thing I had ever intended was to attain a reputation at an Edinburgh police precinct. And, yet, here I was, known by everyone from the revolving door of officers at the reception desk to the rude woman in the computer room. A smile tugged at the corner of my mouth, though, as I thought about Wyatt's admiration of my "job."

I looked at the papers as I made my way back down the hallway, smiling and nodding at the current reception officer and then moving back into the interview room, where Edwin and Wyatt waited.

"How'd it go?" Inspector Winters asked as he rejoined us.

"I found what I was looking for, at least enough for now. It's more than feasible that both Norval and Albert have a deck of the cards. I guess the question would be if Norval's can be tracked down. Are they at his home, or did they go with Gavin back to his? And did the killer take the deck? I can't imagine Albert would kill Gavin, grab the cards, and think to display them," I said, "but who knows?"

"Aye, you might be surprised by a killer's behavior. I know I frequently am. We'll try to find Norval's cards." He looked at me. "I take back my permission and request to check Norval's flat. I'll let you know if I clear it again, but for now it's off limits."

I nodded, disappointed I hadn't already searched.

"Can I see Norval?" I asked. "Or talk to him on the phone or something?"

At first he looked like he was going to say no, but his expression softened and I thought he might say yes. When he followed it all with a frown I knew what the answer would be.

"Not right now, Delaney. Maybe later."

I was disappointed, but not sure I had a right to be.

Inspector Winters walked us out of the station, promising me that he had someone trying to track down my wedding dress. Once inside the car, Wyatt tapped my shoulder.

"Sis, if your dress is gone, it's meant to be. You didn't think that one through very well, did you?"

Even Edwin lifted his eyebrows at my brother's tone.

"What in the world are you talking about?" I said.

He *tsk*-ed and rolled his eyes at me, and suddenly, ever so clearly, it came to me.

Oh, I was a horrible, horrible person.

TWENTY-FIVE

I was as horrible as I could be. Okay, maybe not as a person, but at least I was a horrible daughter. I looked around at everyone, wondering how I was going to find the right moment to fix my mistake.

I'd had another sleepless night trying to figure out what I should do. Hopefully, an opportunity to right my wrong would present itself.

"Oh, what a lovely day. I'm very excited to give this a try," Mom said as we looked up the path that would lead us to Arthur's Seat.

They'd wanted to go for a hike. They were now plenty refreshed from the trip across the ocean. The weather could change at any moment, but for the time being there was no rain and my parents wanted to take in the view as soon as possible. To top it all off, it was cool enough to make a good hike enjoyable.

My parents, Wyatt, Artair, Tom, and I were the hikers today. Edwin had declined joining us; I was sure he wanted to try to get in touch with Brodie Watson after yesterday's meetings, but he wouldn't give me more details. Hamlet and Rosie had also decided not to come. Rosie wasn't interested in the hike, and though it was clear that Hamlet was, he had other commitments. When we'd gotten back to the bookshop the day before, Rosie and Hamlet had been the only ones there. My parents, Tom, and Artair had gone off to the Writers' Museum and then a dinner that kept them out too late for me to try to find a time to apologize.

When we'd gone into the bookshop, I'd looked at Hamlet in a new light. He'd been given a second chance when he'd most needed one. He'd been fortunate, and the rest of us even more so since we had him in our lives.

"Everything all right?" he'd asked after he caught me staring at him with a woeful expression.

I'd smiled and assured him everything was fine. I wasn't sure he believed me, but further displays of my mushy sentiment were diverted as I remembered how completely terrible I had been.

I'd wanted to grab my mom and apologize the second I saw her, but I hadn't. Maybe there was a better way to handle my mistake. Maybe I'd find a way along this hike that would help me ease my conscience.

"This looks easy," Dad said, but there might have been a tiny bit of doubt in his voice.

"The weather is perfect today, at least," I said.

"Aye," Tom added.

The sound of an approaching motorcycle pulled our collective attention toward the road. A second later, Reverend Nisa, dressed in leather pants, a leather jacket, and a bright silver helmet, brought her bike to a stop next to Elias's cab.

I swallowed hard and tried not to paste on a fake smile.

It was good to see that she hadn't been arrested, but I was still surprised she was there. Maybe she'd come by to tell me that as a rule she didn't officiate weddings whose participants had sicced the police on her. I'd have to go back to searching for someone.

Tom, knowing what I'd done, lowered his voice as he talked to me. "Artair told her we were going on the hike. He called her with a question about some sort of church committee task. She called him back right as we were leaving the museum yesterday, and he told her we were going here today. She said she might join us, but I honestly didn't think she would. I didn't even think to mention it tae you."

"It's okay. I'm glad she's here," I said with more enthusiasm than was probably called for.

"Aye? Very good then," Tom said as before he greeted our leather-clad officiant.

Introductions were made all around. I was pleased that my conservative parents didn't behave as if they were bothered by the female, motorcycle-riding reverend. I needed to give them more credit. As I'd shared some Scotland stories with Mom over the year, glad she'd laughed when I wondered if she would protest in silence over some less-than-proper behavior, she'd said, "We do have a television, dear. We both like to read. Our worlds are much bigger than our farm in Kansas. You forget that sometimes."

She was right.

But, again, I was a terrible daughter.

"Shall I lead the way?" Nisa asked, not even sending me a small sideways glance.

As she, Tom, and Artair fell into their own conversation, and Wyatt set off at his own pace a little ahead of the rest of us, I wrangled my parents, hooking my arms into one of each of theirs.

"I messed up," I said as I kept a slow enough walk that no one else in our group could hear us.

"How, dear?" Mom asked as Dad sent me some tight eyebrows.

"I totally forgot about the wedding dress," I said, my heart plummeting with the words.

My grandmother's simple wedding dress was the same dress my mother had worn to marry my father, in that diner after the barn burned down. It was also the dress she and I had talked about over the years as being the one I would wear when I got married.

"All I can say is that I totally forgot. I don't know how or why. Maybe Tom's proposal was just a huge surprise, maybe things have been busy, maybe being in Scotland is like I've gone to another place where wedding dress heirlooms don't exist anymore. Maybe I just plain got so caught up in myself and the wedding that I forgot."

Dad patted the arm that I'd put through his.

"Oh," Mom said. "Did Wyatt remind you?"

"He didn't mean to. He'd told me that you had been clear that you didn't want anyone to mention the dress."

"But he did," she said.

"Kind of, yes," I said.

"It's fine, dear," Mom said, only about 80 percent convincingly.

"No, it isn't. I mean, I should have at least talked to you about it."

"You sent me pictures as you tried on wedding dresses. I was included."

I cringed. Yes, but I hadn't even thought about the other dress once, not even a "What am I forgetting?" thought. Really, how had it slipped my mind so completely? This had been the thing she'd kept asking me about—what could she bring or send? I can't believe I didn't pick up on it even then.

"Yes, and I never once mentioned the other dress." I stopped walking, causing them to stop too. "Here's the thing; it would have been the dress I would have chosen to wear. I'm not making that up. I'm just trying to say that I truly and honestly forgot. And, I'm so sorry I was so self-involved."

Dad patted my arm again, looked at Mom, and then disengaged himself from our trio. He took off in a hurry up toward the other group.

"Delaney, it's all right." Mom put her hands on my arms. "My feelings aren't hurt."

"But it was rude of me and I apologize."

"Actually, I think it's kind of funny." She let go, but we took off walking up the hill again, slowly.

"You do?" I kept up with her.

"I love what your life has become and I'm so happy we're here to see the wedding. I remember my own fiasco and I know how it goes." She paused. "Okay, I'll be honest, at first I was a little bothered, but not at all anymore. I'm well over the bother and just thrilled. Your brother was just . . . being your brother, I guess. It's all good. And, I'm helping Aggie with the cake now, so . . . I'm just happy to be here."

"Me too, Mom. Me too."

"All right, I want to get to know your reverend," Mom said. "Let's get up there."

We hurried to catch up. I felt a little less terrible, but I knew I would always kick myself for forgetting. Maybe Tom and I needed to hurry up and have kids like he wanted, hope for a girl who would grow up and remember to use the dress for her own wedding. Or maybe that was a slightly crazy plan.

Nisa had already had the chance to get to know Tom and me, and it was refreshing to get to know her, particularly since she had neither been arrested nor seemed upset at me because I'd talked to the police about her.

The nonexistent accent I'd noticed was for a reason. She'd only been in Scotland, a reverend at Artair's church, for five years. Before that she'd grown up in Oregon—yes, that Oregon—making a brief stop at a Texas church before moving to Scotland, the place she'd always wanted to live.

It was precisely as I was thinking about Scottish accents versus Texas accents that a big Texas accent walked toward us. I had to blink twice, wondering if I'd somehow conjured Angus Murdoch. But, though I had a good imagination, it wasn't that good.

The man was larger than life, with his boots that should have been adorned with spurs and that ten-gallon hat that towered so high.

"Well, howdy!" he said as Tom and I both nodded toward him and he recognized us. "How about that? Here we are together again! And, hello to you too," he said as he moved past both Tom and me and extended his hand to Nisa. "Remember me? I stopped by your church the other day."

"Oh!" Nisa said as she seemed to be trying to process the moment. It looked like she didn't remember him, but lots of people probably stopped by that church. "Good to see you again."

Angus put his hands on his hips and tipped his hat back. "I know so few people in this country and it seems we're all destined to be together." He laughed. "What are y'all doing? Taking in the sights? I'll tell you," he looked at me and nodded up the hill, "if that's where Camelot was located, that King Arthur fella had some good taste. Whoa, doggies, that's a beautiful view."

Once again more introductions were made and I explained the possible connection to the legendary king.

"I can't wait to see," Wyatt said before he took off again, on his own.

Angus turned to my parents. "Y'all have a farm in Kansas! Well, thank you for feeding the world, my friends. We'd surely all starve to death if not for folks like you. We're mighty grateful."

He was genuine in his over-the-top-ness. I might feel uncomfortable if many people spoke the way he did and seemed to take up all the space in a room, but with Angus it seemed natural.

It was time to be on our way, but as everyone else started up the hill, Angus gently put his hand on my arm and stopped me. "So, did your boss remember anything else about the book?"

It was an oddly intimate gesture and I caught myself before reflexively pulling my arm away. He didn't mean anything intrusive by the move. Tom sensed my discomfort and hung back with us, keeping close by but appearing unbothered. He'd be bothered if I needed him to be. They all would.

"I don't think so," I said. Angus had let go of my arm. "You should call him. He'd be happy to talk to you."

"I will." Angus rubbed his chin. "Do you suppose I could ask him to dinner? I'd enjoy getting to know the man. He's interesting."

"He's very interesting. I think he'd enjoy that, if he has the time."

"Will do." Angus smiled big at me and then winked at my pub owner before he turned back to me again. "Maybe you can join us."

I was caught in between not wanting to be rude and not caring. I settled for, "Maybe." Though he made me uncomfortable, I might have been misinterpreting his actions. "Have a lovely day, Angus."

"Y'all too," he said, unfazed. He tipped his hat again, and set off down the hill.

"Ready?" Tom said with a smile.

"I think so."

The next few seconds were strange: I'd turned to watch Angus walk down the hill just as he was turning away from looking in my direction. He didn't notice me looking but I felt caught and I flipped back around quickly. As I did so, I caught Nisa looking back at me from higher up. Though, she hadn't initially been looking at me, I realized when her eyes did a minor readjustment. She smiled when she saw me see her. She'd been looking at Angus too. She and I had both been caught, but I wasn't sure what we'd been caught doing.

"I'd like to talk to Nisa," I said to Tom.

"I think that can be arranged."

We set our sights on the reverend and made our way up the hill.

———

Nisa smiled at me. "The police came by yesterday evening. I thought it might have been you who told them about Norval and Gavin's argument and seeing me walking back from Norval's flat. Well, you or Tom." She quit smiling. "And, so you know, I shouldn't have mentioned the argument between Norval and Gavin to you two. I was flustered, and I shouldn't have let myself become flustered. But there's confidentiality and all. My timing of leaving the flat was fine, by the way. It was a police officer who let me in, and I told him why I was there—to check the appliances. He stayed by my side as I checked things. They aren't suspicious of me now, at least as far as I can tell."

"I'm truly sorry," I said. "It seemed like the right thing to do, but I've been a little sick about it since I said something."

"It's okay. I want the police to find Gavin's killer. I'll help in any way I can. I really should have told them on my own about whatever might be going on between Gavin and Norval, but I didn't want to cross any bounds, you know. People are supposed to feel secure that I won't share their secrets. It's not confession or anything, but I want to remain trustworthy."

"Oh dear, I am so sorry."

"No, no, it's okay. There wasn't much to tell the police unfortunately. I knew a little of the difficulty between Gavin and Norval, but I was only going to learn the details at our next meeting. I told the police what I could."

"Any chance you'd want to tell me?" I said, surprised again at myself, but I tried to look unsurprised.

Nisa smiled, almost sympathetically. "No, Delaney, I'm afraid I can't tell you."

"I know, but I thought I'd ask." I looked up ahead as we'd almost reached the top. "Still okay to officiate at the wedding?"

"Even more so than before, frankly."

I smiled at Nisa this time. She was either telling the truth or not. If not, she was hiding something big. And I really did like her.

"Oh, Delaney, I would never leave this place if I were you," Mom said as she turned in a full circle ahead of us.

"No plans to."

"This. Is. Amazing," Wyatt said.

"I couldn't agree more," Dad said.

While everyone else admired the full view of the city, "from castle tae sea," as Rosie often described it, I leaned toward Nisa again.

"Not quite like Oregon or Texas, huh?" I said, though I'd never been to either place. Like my mom, though, I watched television and read books.

"No, not quite."

"You didn't remember Angus stopping by the church, did you?"

It either took her a second to remember who I was talking about, or she wanted to behave as if she had to try to remember him.

"I didn't. Was I rude?"

"No. I bet lots of people visit the church."

"Yes. It's right there near Dean Village, and the building *is* beautiful. I think some people are disappointed with the inside. They expect something Old World, but our insides are much more contemporary."

I nodded. I'd have to take a closer look at the interior of the church myself.

I loved that my parents and my brother were falling in love with Scotland, one old building, one spectacular view at a time. They couldn't leave their farm in Kansas and Wyatt had his own adult life back in the States, but maybe they would all at least visit me more often. I hoped so.

We made our way back down from Arthur's Seat; this time my dad and I walked together. It was good to ask him about the farm and be reassured that my mom was in top notch health. So was he, he said, but I'd have to make sure to get the full story on him from Wyatt.

My adult relationship with my family was made up of love and now friendship. It seems like even my decision to up-and-move to Scotland hadn't disrupted us much.

My dad was the only other person in my family who knew about my bookish voices. He'd been the one to hurry to the school when I was a little girl and the teacher thought something was wrong with me. It turned out my problem was that I loved books, and perhaps took all stories a bit too seriously. I listened and digested the words. They became a part of me, and they spoke to me through my intuition. It wasn't a terrible problem to have, but my conservative father knew that I probably shouldn't advertise the exact reason for my distractions.

As we reached the bottom of the hill, Dad patted my arm again.

"He's a good man, Delaney," Dad said.

"I'm glad you think so. I think so too."

"I'll kick his butt if he ever breaks your heart."

"I wouldn't expect anything less."

"And that will be after your brother takes care of him."

"Good to know."

"We'll make sure Tom knows too."

I hugged him tightly. "Thank you, Daddy."

TWENTY-SIX

When I'd first arrived in Scotland, I'd hit the ground running. I'd seen some of the sights, taken a few pictures on my phone, explored the city a bit, but I'd never really been a tourist.

However, as we gathered in The Cracked Spine after the hike, I was the epitome of a tourist: two cameras hung around my neck; one was my dad's and one was mine. Thanks to the hike preparations, I had the perfect walking tennis shoes on, sunglasses, and a cap on my head. Neither the sunglasses nor the cap were necessary for shade any longer because the clouds had arrived and covered the sun, but I looked the part.

"This is the plan." Dad spread a paper map out on the bookshop's front desk so I could see it and the lines he'd drawn and the notes he'd made. Mom and Wyatt were at the back table with Rosie and Hector, enjoying some sandwiches from the bakery next door.

I tried to act interested in what my dad was showing me, but my mind was wandering to thoughts of the murder, Norval, Gavin, Nessie—so many things.

Hamlet came through the door at the top of the stairs, carrying the behemoth scrapbook. I tried to give my attention to Dad's map as I sent lifted eyebrows to my coworker. He nodded toward the back table as if he wanted me to join him there.

He had tucked a folder under his arm. He pointed at it with his chin. He also wanted me to see something.

"Delaney?" Dad said.

"Sorry, Dad. I was wondering what Hamlet was doing with the big scrapbook. It's got some good stuff in it. Want to see?"

"Uh. Sure."

We joined the others at the back. Rosie directed Hamlet where to put the scrapbook and asked him, "What's in the folder?"

"Something from class. I wanted Delaney tae see it."

"Share it with us all?" Rosie said.

"Aye."

Food and drinks were removed from the table as the scrapbook and folder were situated. Hamlet opened the folder as Hector, on Rosie's lap, put his front paws on the table to better observe. I thought my mom's heart would melt right out of her chest.

"I know. He's something, isn't he?" I said to her.

She nodded and reached to scratch behind his ears. I didn't have the time at that moment to think about it deeply, but I suspected that Hector was another link in the chain of things that might be binding my family to Scotland. Everyone has to retire someday, right?

Hamlet continued. "We're studying legends and folklore in a class I'm taking. It's interesting, and more difficult than you might think. I wish I had a better imagination, but, anyway, we hadn't studied Nessie when the murder occurred, but the professor brought her up yesterday. I paid extra attention. The professor has collected things over the years and it only makes sense that here, in Scotland, there are many things tae collect. I could have brought you a box of information, but much of it was repetition. I did bring you something, one item in particular I thought was interesting, and something you might like tae know. In fact, I think it's something the police might like tae know. Maybe. Here," he turned over a page from the folder, "take a look."

It was a copy of something from a university yearbook page. In the early 2000s, it looked like the University of Edinburgh had hosted a symposium all about Nessie. The page was one half a picture, one half information on the subjects of the picture; younger versions of Norval Fraser and Albert Winsom were pictured, with a woman in between them, holding them back as the two men came at each other. This was not taken at the same time the earlier feud had occurred. The men were older here. I read the copy beneath the picture.

"Self-proclaimed Nessie authorities were the highlights of the symposium, particularly when they battled. Mr. Winsom claimed that Mr. Fraser was a 'phony to the cause' and had, in fact, never seen the monster. When the battle of words escalated toward a physical fight, Mr. Fraser's sister Millie jumped onto the stage to stop it. Side note: The yearbook staff heard that it was rumored that Millie was also involved in a personal relationship with Mr. Winsom. Oooh, fun symposium."

"Obviously, not hard journalism," Hamlet added.

"Rosie, where in the scrapbook was the article about their feud?" I asked.

"I'll get there," she said. She'd already started to search.

It was that last sentence of the yearbook copy, so casually

placed there, that made me think I—or maybe all of us—had missed something very important? Were Millie and Albert involved, now or at one time? Did the police know? Did it matter in the least?

"Here, right here," Rosie said as she pointed. "Not the same time at all. The scrapbook article is twenty years earlier than Hamlet's article."

"Do these two men fight whenever they're together?" Wyatt said.

"I don't know. Maybe," I said.

"That last line got your attention, huh?" Hamlet said.

"Yes. Millie. And I think she's still alive."

"She is," Hamlet said with a smile. "I found her address, if you're interested."

"Good work, Hamlet," I said.

"Thanks. I researched and didn't find anything about Mr. Winsom and Millie being together. No marriage, and no other sign of them knowing each other. I did discover that Millie has, in fact, never married. Mr. Winsom's one and only wife passed about ten years ago."

"Weel, if we've seen anything over the last year or so, old love can cause a whole boytach of trouble," Rosie said.

My parents, brother, and I all knew to look at Hamlet for translation.

"Lots. Maybe 'bundle,'" he said.

"Maybe," I said, still wondering if the police knew about this connection and if it was solid anyway.

How sad and bad and mad it was—but then, how it was sweet!

I jumped at the bookish voice. It was a well-known quote about the past from the poet Robert Browning. Was he telling me the past was important to the present? I couldn't focus and didn't hear any other words. If nothing else, at least my intuition was telling me to pay attention; the voices were talking again.

"Delaney," Dad said gently, nudging me back to the moment. Everyone, including Hector, was looking at me.

"May I get a copy of this?" I asked Hamlet.

"These are all copies for you. The whole folder, though I doubt there's anything else interesting in there."

"Thank you."

"You're welcome."

The bell above the front door jingled. Most of us, including me, were so caught up in the discoveries that we ignored the sound. But Rosie didn't. She stood and walked around the wall to greet the visitor.

Her enthusiastic greeting pulled me out of my thoughts and the chair, and I joined her.

"Delaney, is that Brodie Watson?" my mom asked in the worst stage whisper I'd ever heard. I didn't know she'd come with me.

"I believe it is," I said.

Edwin was with the writer, who was holding onto Rosie's hands and smiling affectionately at her.

"It's been too long, sweet Rosie," he said.

"Aye," she cooed.

Edwin sent me a look that said he'd roll his eyes if he could get away with it. I'd never thought of Brodie Watson as dashing, but he was that, and more.

My mom gushed a bit when they were introduced, all the while using the author's book titles and story lines in her sentences. He gushed back at her and praised her knowledge of his themes and characters. I had no idea my mom had read so many of his books. I needed to pay better attention to my parents' hobbies.

Edwin pulled me aside.

"Do you want tae talk tae Brodie with me?"

"You haven't asked him anything?" I said.

"No. I thought it best tae have someone else with me. We'll talk tae him here, in my office, probably safe from any murderous intentions, but someone other than just me needs tae be there. I'm fairly confident in my assessment that the police wouldn't trust me, but they would you."

I smiled and remembered the cameras around my neck. I really shouldn't abandon my family again. I looked at my mom and dad as they watched Brodie Watson pull Hamlet into a genuine hug. My parents would love the real story behind that hug.

I'd tell them later, after I went with Edwin and Brodie. So much for needing the comfortable shoes, I thought as I took off the cap and sunglasses and the cameras from around my neck. I signaled my brother over.

"I'm going with Edwin. I'll catch up with you later," I said.

"Sure," Wyatt said as he took the cameras. "Work comes first. I'd join you, but I think I'd like to see more sights today. That okay?"

"Sure," I said with a smile.

In fact, it didn't matter much that I wasn't going with them. Elias showed up with his cab and they would be more comfortable inside it without me anyway. I was happy they had plenty to do.

Edwin, Brodie, and I made our way to the dark side, not to the warehouse, but to Edwin's sparse office instead. I doubted

Edwin would ever want to advertise the warehouse to any author, even one who was a good friend.

I caught Brodie's curious glance down the stairway, but
Edwin only said, "This way."

There wasn't time for me to gush over the famous author,
which was a shame, but maybe my mom had gushed enough.

TWENTY-SEVEN

"The police did talk to me," Brodie said with a shrug. "I was home alone at the time the murder occurred. I have no way to prove that. They have told me they want to question me further. I will make myself available to them."

"So they know you were one of Gavin's clients?" Edwin asked.

The back of Brodie's jaw twitched, but I couldn't tell if he was anxious about the murder or bothered by Edwin asking him about it. The two men struck me as genuine friends; they had a history I couldn't possibly understand but I could sense their closeness in the way they listened to each other and their apparent comfort in speaking freely, even with me in the room. Before Edwin started asking about Gavin MacLeod, they'd talked about Brodie's next book, the author sharing the plot but not the twist he hoped he'd skillfully added in the last few pages. Both Edwin and I said we were excited to read it.

When Gavin's name came up, Brodie tensed, but he didn't make a move to leave or behave as if he wanted to stop the conversation.

"Yes, they know I was a client, though I wasn't mentioned in the newspaper article. I was pleased about that," Brodie said.

"Did you know about the article beforehand?"

"No."

Edwin leaned forward, placing his arms on his desk. "Brodie, Birk said you mentioned to him that you were very upset with Gavin MacLeod, that you wanted tae 'kill him.' Now, I'm not holding you to that because we've all said that sort of thing in the heat of the moment, but I wanted you tae know what Birk said."

Brodie smiled sadly. He looked down and then back up at Edwin. "I did say that, Edwin, but I didn't mean it, not literally. I can't deny that I said the words, though. The police haven't asked me specifically if I vocalized such an idea, but I won't lie to them if they do." His smile transformed to a sarcastic tilt. "I am a master manipulator of words, but Birk knows when I'm just blowing off steam."

"I think he thinks you were just talking, influenced by the whisky," Edwin said. "Frankly, I think he's more concerned about you than Gavin MacLeod. I suspect Birk wants you to cover your tracks if there are any tracks that need covering."

"Ah, well, it's a rare moment that the whisky influences me in any way, but I have no tracks that need to be covered. As I said, though, I have no way to prove that. The police won't find any evidence that I killed Gavin MacLeod because I didn't."

I liked Brodie Watson, even if he did describe himself as a "master manipulator of words."

"However," Brodie continued with a sigh, "I *was* by Gavin's flat early the evening he was killed. Yes, I did tell the police I was there, if you're wondering. A bookshop over there had several of my books that required my signature. I stopped at the door that leads into Gavin's building, debating whether I should ring him or not. I decided not to, because I was too angry. I didn't think I would handle it well, so I went on my way."

"How did you know where he lived?" I asked.

"I know where everyone in my life lives, lass. But particularly ones I've entrusted with my vast wealth."

"Had you visited him there before?" I continued.

"Aye. When I first suspected what was going on some six months or so ago. I stopped by to give him a chance to make it right, or tell me the truth, or pay me back my money. He lied then. As far as I can tell, he never told the truth, but . . . well, unless his plan was something he was going to follow through with, and maybe it would have worked. I simply don't know."

"Plan?" Edwin said as he and I looked at each other.

Brodie's eyebrows came together. "Has it not been in the articles? No, probably not. The police know, though."

"Know what?" Edwin said.

"Gavin MacLeod wouldn't admit to stealing money, but he did tell me that he would never have to steal, that he would never, ever have a problem coming up with whatever funds he might need, even if someone rich like me needed their money back. He was convincing."

"Aye?" Edwin said, much more patiently than I thought he wanted to.

"Aye. He said his great-uncle had items that would prove to be worth millions of dollars. That he would someday be the owner of those items. He even mentioned Norval's name. Of course, I knew who Norval was, but that was the first I heard they were related."

"His uncle's papers about Nessie?" I said. "But, Brodie, even if his uncle had papers or proof or whatever worth millions of dollars, the amount of money that had been invested in his company was probably even more. I mean," I cleared my throat, "I would imagine there are more than a few investors like you, who have millions and millions of dollars. Even a fortune in Loch Ness proof wouldn't be enough to cover it. Would it?"

"I doubt it, but who really knows?"

"Brodie, did you visit Norval last week, maybe give him one of your books?" I asked.

Brodie looked momentarily surprised. "No, lass."

I looked at Edwin, but Brodie continued.

"I visited Norval Fraser six months ago, right after that conversation with Gavin. I gave him a book then, but I haven't seen him since."

"You're sure?" I asked.

He sent me an impatient glare, but I tried not to look intimidated. "I'm sure."

"I think he thought it was a recent visit. He seemed to say as much to his reverend."

"Aye? No, it was a while ago. Perhaps he's confused about the timing?"

It didn't seem unlikely that Norval took a book to Nisa he'd had for six months. Nisa might have only *thought* Norval had recently seen Brodie. It takes time to get through a to-be-read pile. Still, I was curious about the seeming confusion, even if I might be the only one confused.

"Was it a bothersome meeting, between you and Norval? Was he upset?" I asked.

"Not at all." Brodie held back a smile. "He was thrilled to meet me."

"Did you talk about Gavin?"

"No, I was going to, but I didn't. Mr. Fraser didn't seem in his full right mind and he was very sweet. I do remember him looking at me like he couldn't quite understand why I'd stopped by. He told me the story about Nessie and his father. It was a brief visit and only friendly."

"You didn't tell Norval what Gavin's plans were?" Edwin asked.

"No, I got a quick sense of the man and his papers. The place was a mess. If there was anything of value in there, it wasn't obvious. I left disappointed in Gavin's 'plan' and sad for Mr. Fraser. I was sure he had no idea his nephew was saying the things he was saying." Brodie paused. "I've thought about this, though. If Norval learned what Gavin was up to, could he have killed his nephew? I simply don't know. But if Norval learned of Gavin's plans, it wasn't from me and it wasn't a week ago. Any number of Gavin's clients might have told on him."

Perhaps Norval did kill his nephew. The man was adamant that money not exchange hands for his items, but only that someone continue his work. Maybe Gavin threatened to steal Norval's things from him and sell them, and that was just too much for the older man to bear. I still couldn't see Norval as murderous, but those papers were his life's work. His obsession.

"There's a little more," Brodie said. "It seemed harmless then, but now I wonder."

"We're listening," Edwin said.

Brodie squinted toward the office's open doorway.

"No one can hear us," I said.

"Aye, I'd still like for you to close the door, lass. Would you mind?"

He could have stood and closed it, but I was closer to it by about a foot. I did the honors.

"What?" I sat back down.

"I . . . after Norval told me the story of his father and Nessie, he said that he was afraid that Nessie would somehow kill more of his family, specifically his nephew, Gavin. It was a curse upon his family, he said. By the way, I *didn't* tell the police that part."

"Why not?" Edwin said.

Brodie's eyebrows came together again. "I just . . . it was like me telling Birk I wanted to 'kill' Gavin MacLeod, but with Norval, it seemed odd and made of fantasy. I didn't think he should be held to those words."

I nodded, but wasn't sure I agreed.

"I see," Edwin said.

"I don't believe in her, the monster," Brodie said. "She can't be real. There would be more evidence than, say, some obscure papers in an old man's flat. Over time, I decided that Gavin was lying about everything. He was a skilled liar."

"Did you offer to buy Norval's papers from him?" I asked.

"No, lass, I didn't. I don't think he ever understood that I was there for anything more than to meet him and give him a book. I don't know, though. I didn't hurt Gavin, though he made me angry enough to be violent. That's why I didn't ring him the night he was killed. I didn't trust myself. And, I'm sure I wasn't the only one angry with him. I'll never get my money back now, and I'll never forgive the man."

If Gavin had, in fact, stolen all that money, he'd probably ruined more than his fair share of lives.

"I'm sorry, Brodie. I really hope you get your money back," I said.

"I do too, lass. I do too."

Rosie grabbed Brodie as we escorted him to the door, and

asked him to sign a few of the shop's copies of his books. He signed the books and then spent a few moments in quiet, private conversation with Hamlet. He didn't wear a cape, but my mind conjured an imaginary cape rolling nobly as he left through the door with the tiny bell jingling above.

TWENTY-EIGHT

The place didn't look any more ransacked than it had the first time I'd been there. I couldn't determine that the police had done anything at all inside Norval's flat. Other than the fact that someone (maybe Norval) had placed the projector and some of the developed films on the coffee table, making me think whoever put them there wanted someone (probably me) to pay attention to those items. Would something on the films help clear Norval of murder? That was my best guess, but with the projectors placed where they were, it seemed a more ham-fisted clue than something he'd have to put in a cryptic note.

"Should we watch the films?" Edwin asked.

"Not here. I don't want to take the time. Let's take everything back to the bookshop. I know it's okay that we're here, but I'd like to get through all of this quickly."

Shortly after we said goodbye to Brodie, Inspector Winters called me to say it was again okay for me to go to Norval's flat. He didn't seem as anxious that I go, but he said the police were again done. I didn't want to miss another opportunity, so I asked Edwin to come with me immediately.

As we were on the way, Angus Murdoch had called Edwin, asking if he was available for dinner, and if I could join them too. Edwin neglected to mention that I was sitting in the same car with him, and instead said he'd track me down and check. I'd given up trying to catch up with my family for the day. I wasn't going to put off searching Norval's flat another moment, and I wouldn't miss dinner with Angus and Edwin either. My family was going to have to experience more of Scotland without me.

"Okay. What are we looking for?" Edwin asked as he plopped his hands on his hips, his feet placed precariously between a couple of stacks of papers.

"I really have no idea," I said. "Something that would assure the world that Norval isn't a killer."

"Well. Okay. Let's get to work."

There were so many pieces of paper that it was impossible to digest much of anything. It was interesting and somewhat alarming that many of the papers were covered in handwriting, Norval's I presumed. I'd seen movies or read books where someone was compelled to write and repeat themselves on paper or over walls. That was the same sort of compulsion I saw on many of the papers. One folder was full of pieces of paper with "Loch Ness/Nessie" scribbled on them over and over again. I realized that Norval's mental health might be more challenged than I thought. Perhaps he couldn't take care of himself, his basic needs. Or, maybe he'd created these files planning to hide things inside of them. It would take someone with more time, patience, and knowledge than I had to make such a determination. As it was, I tried to flip through everything I came upon, but I knew I wasn't being thorough.

We found more interesting first-hand, handwritten accounts of Nessie, and those slowed our search a bit. Still, though, we were there with a purpose in mind, and I didn't want to get caught up in anything that didn't ring of real proof of Norval's innocence.

"I don't think we're focused enough," Edwin said not long into the search.

"I know. I feel like we're looking for a specific piece of hay in a haystack, but there's no way to know which piece of hay we need." I pulled open a short drawer tucked underneath the lip of an end table. "Film. Photographs, not video. Negatives."

Just like the kind my parents had in envelopes back home, the drawer was full of strips of negatives. I reached in and, using my fingertips along the edges, grabbed a few. One at a time, I held them up to the light.

"Uh, Edwin," I said a moment later. "Come look at this one."

Edwin high-stepped over stacks and then crouched next to me as we looked at the negative.

"May I?" he asked as he reached for it.

He took it and angled it in a couple of different directions toward the diffused light coming from the back of the apartment; today, all the windows and the sliding glass door were covered in shades.

He looked at me with an expression I'd never seen before. "Do you think?"

"It's hard to tell on a negative."

"Delaney, could it be possible?"

"Anything's possible," I said.

In the tiny rendering, we could see a young man on one knee on the shore of a body of water. But it was what was in the water behind the man that truly got our attention. A dragon, or a dinosaur, or a mix between the two was there, its head and long neck out of the water. Maybe there were flippers on its front, keeping it afloat. It was the clearest proof I'd seen. It was also a tiny negative that might illustrate something altogether different when developed and enlarged.

"Do you think that's Norval with . . . well, with her?" Edwin asked.

"Hard to tell," I said. "I wonder if we can get it developed and analyzed for authenticity."

"Let's take some of the negatives, that one for sure. You can let Inspector Winters know if you want, but I won't tell."

I gathered a stack of negatives, put them in a plain envelope, and then inside my bag. We found a box for the projector and the films, but we didn't find anything that pointed to Gavin's killer or Norval's innocence. No note, knife, or deck of cards. If the police had found any of those items, they'd probably taken them in.

In fact, I wondered briefly why they hadn't taken the negatives or the films. Though anyone might be curious about Nessie, the police had had the singular purpose of finding evidence—of a killer. However, if even an officer of the law had come across conclusive proof of Nessie, he or she might have been compelled to pocket the proof themselves. It was impossible to know if something was missing.

I hoped Norval wasn't a killer. I hoped Gavin's killer would be found. And, I hoped to find out if Nessie existed. No, that wasn't it exactly. I hoped Nessie was real, and I wanted irrefutable evidence. I didn't want credit for the discovery, but I wanted to see it, digest it. Know it.

We packed up the projector and the developed films, a few files with handwritten firsthand accounts, and took pictures on my phone of a couple notes we found by Norval's phone with Gavin's name. One simply said, "Call Gavin." The other one said, "Gavin lunch cancelled. Move to another day."

If one of those held a clue, neither Edwin nor I picked up on it.

We made a few trips out to Edwin's car. After we had everything, I felt I should take one last look.

"Give me a minute," I said to Edwin.

Edwin watched me over the top of his car as I jogged back down to Norval's door. I put my hand on the knob and made myself be still. Was my intuition trying to tell me something?

I got nothing.

But as I unlocked the door and pushed it open, I noticed a flash of color sticking out from under the edge of the Nessie welcome mat, the one that had made me smile that first day.

I bent down and lifted the mat. It was a business card. And it came from someone I knew. Angus Murdoch. I bit my bottom lip as I stared at the card. Tom and I had seen him by the church and he'd been curious about the crime scene tape. Had he come over to check out the tape, or to talk to Norval at some point? Or, had the card fluttered here in the breeze and finding it now wedged under Norval's mat was just happenstance?

I put the card in the inside pocket of my jacket. In only a

short time, I could ask the man himself why it was there, under the welcome mat of the man who'd been arrested for killing his great-nephew.

I hurried back to show it to Edwin. Now I couldn't wait for dinner.

TWENTY-NINE

It was just Edwin, Angus, and me. My family was having too much fun at an outdoor reenactment of a famous Scottish vs. English battle to leave the subsequent pig roast that was to take place. I couldn't blame them, and I wondered if maybe Tom and I shouldn't just be tourists for a little while during our honeymoon. I'd seen a reenactment or two, but never one with a pig roast. Tom was busy at the pub and Artair, Elias, and Aggie were with my family. However, I'd asked everyone to meet us later at The Cracked Spine for a movie event.

Edwin had told Angus that we'd meet him at Vanessa's restaurant, and our new friend from Texas was right on time. He sauntered in with a cowboy walk that matched his cowboy smile. He lifted off his hat when his eyes landed on mine and his smile got bigger. He wove his way through the crowd to what was probably the best table in the house, set in a cozy, windowed nook that was somewhat private.

His style made an impression, and it was interesting to watch others watching him as he made his way to us.

"Hello y'all," he said, greeting us.

Edwin stood and greeted him. As they sat, Angus reached over the table to shake my hand. "I'm pleased as punch that you could join us too, Delaney."

"Thanks for the invitation," I said.

"It's just us," Edwin said. "I asked everyone else at the bookshop but they were all busy."

"Well, I think three's aplenty." He looked at me. "And some time to get to know this lovely lady without her . . . everyone else, is a welcome opportunity."

A waiter, who seemed to know Edwin, approached and began by letting us know that Vanessa would be out to greet us later, but she was currently busy with something in the kitchen. Edwin ordered wine for the table and then made dinner recommendations. I chose the lasagna, Edwin the macaroni and cheese, and Angus the rib-eye steak and some smoky whisky.

"So, what have you seen in our fair country, Angus?" Edwin asked as the waiter left with the menus.

"Just about everything in Edinburgh, and I even found my way up to Loch Ness for a short trip. I'd like to get to Glasgow and Inverness, but I'm leaving tomorrow, so I've run out of time."

Opportunity handed to me, I said, "Did you like Loch Ness?"

"I did. It was . . . bigger than I thought, but I didn't see Nessie." He laughed and winked at me. "Have you seen her?"

"I haven't."

"Edwin?" Angus asked.

"I haven't seen her either," he said.

"Are you particularly interested in her?" I asked.

"Not really, but I would love to see her," he answered as he reached for a piece of sourdough from the breadbasket on the table.

"Me too," I said.

I wanted to ask about the business card under Norval's mat but I wasn't ready quite yet. Angus turned to Edwin.

"Edwin, have you remembered anything? Have you checked any of your old records or . . . well, found anything? Have you found *any* evidence of the book ever being in your shop, proof of my grandfather's theft?"

As the waiter placed our drinks in front of us, I noticed something different in Angus's tone. It was now full of emotion. I tried to put myself in his shoes. He'd come to Scotland to return the book, get some answers. But he had no distance from what his grandfather had done. I would feel guilty too, but not *that* guilty. I would probably have called the bookshop in question and then mailed them the book—after insuring it to the gills. I wouldn't have felt as terrible as he felt, and my life was all about old books. What were we missing?

Had he not trusted his grandfather? Did he feel as if he had somehow been lied to, posthumously? It wasn't just affection; there was more going on here. What was it?

"I can't remember a thing," Edwin said. "I've tried, but I've got nothing, lad. I'm sorry about that."

Angus's mouth pinched tightly, but only briefly. He nodded. But then his shoulders relaxed. Was he relieved? "I understand."

"In fact, I'd truly like tae give the book back tae you," Edwin said.

"No!" Angus cleared his throat. "I mean, no thank you. It's yours, somehow. If you ever figure out the story behind it, I'd appreciate hearing it, but I won't be taking that book back."

"You're relieved," I said aloud.

"I am, particularly since it's so valuable. It's out of my hands now. No, ma'am, I don't need to be responsible for such a thing."

I nodded. Okay, I thought. Maybe that's all it was; freedom from responsibility. Maybe.

"If I sell it, together we can come up with a viable cause or charity for donation," Edwin said.

"You wouldn't keep it?" Angus asked.

"I don't know. Would it bother you if I didn't?"

"No," Angus said unconvincingly. He cleared his throat. "No, of course not. It's your book." He lifted his whisky and said, "One for all and all for one!"

Edwin and I looked at each other. Did Angus think his quote was something from King Arthur? Well-known words from *The Three Musketeers,* it was a strange comment. In the span of a few seconds and with our eyes only, Edwin and I shared our surprise at the mistake. Mistakes, misquotes happened all the time. No one was immune to them. Maybe Angus hadn't intended to toast with a quote anyway. Maybe it was just something he said.

"Aye," Edwin said as he and I lifted our wineglasses.

We toasted and for a long moment, the buzz of the restaurant crowd and the bread took center stage. It was really good bread.

Angus looked at me. "Congratulations on the marriage. Your fiancé is a lucky guy."

"Thank you," I said.

"You're welcome." Angus paused and wiped his mouth with his napkin. "Did you two meet here or did you move here for him?"

It wasn't a rude question, but there was an edge to his voice, maybe something like a challenge. I bristled.

"We met here," I said, clipped.

Edwin studied Angus as one of his eyebrows lifted.

"And how long have you been here in Scotland? Did you tell me that yet?" Angus asked.

"Just over a year," I answered.

Angus chuckled a little. "Taken in by a kilt, I imagine."

"He's . . ." I was going to say how wonderful Tom was, but I realized it would have sounded both immature and defensive. "Yes, he's lovely in a kilt."

Angus leaned back in his chair and wrapped his hand around his tumbler. He lifted the glass and swirled the liquid inside as he smirked in my direction. "It's too bad you didn't come to Texas first."

Now Edwin bristled while I fought a rise of heat in my cheeks. In another tone, maybe something playful, perhaps there would be nothing wrong with what he said, but it certainly sounded strange. I hoped Edwin wouldn't jump in and say something, but I knew he wanted to. I tried to give myself time to think of an appropriate response, one that I wouldn't replay later and wish I'd worded differently. I realized in the small beat of time that perhaps I (Edwin too) was taking Angus's words too seriously. He probably thought he was being complimentary, not arrogant and offensive.

"Good evening," Vanessa said as she stopped next to Edwin. "I'm sorry I couldn't say hello earlier."

"Not tae worry," Edwin said as he gallantly kissed the top of her hand. "This is Angus Murdoch, a visitor from Texas in America."

"Pleasure," Vanessa said.

Angus stood and shook her hand and smiled. "A pleasure to meet another beautiful woman."

Edwin and I exchanged a glance. Maybe this *was* just Angus's way.

"Can I get any of you anything?" Vanessa said.

"We've ordered dinner," Edwin said. "Can you join us?"

"I'm afraid I can't." She smiled at him.

I suddenly realized how similar Edwin's and my love lives had become. We were both dating night workers, a pub owner and a restaurant owner. My boss and I were doomed to many evenings alone. I smiled at the similarities.

"This is a great place," Angus said, still standing.

"Thank you. Please sit. I'm just flying by," Vanessa said.

Angus sat and grabbed the whisky again. The way he leaned back in his chair and looked at Vanessa made me certain that his way was just his way, uncomfortable. It verged on creepy, but maybe I was just being too sensitive. I looked up at Vanessa, who seemed to only have eyes for Edwin. If she knew how Angus was looking at her, she didn't care. I sat up straighter. Okay then, I didn't care either.

"The bread is amazing," I said.

Vanessa laughed. "You're not the first to tell me that. Some people come in just for the bread, but I hope you enjoy the rest of the meal too."

"I have no doubt that we will," I said.

"Well, thanks for coming by tonight. I must run, but I hope to see you all later."

Dinner was served moments after Vanessa took off back to the kitchen. We didn't mention the films waiting at The Cracked Spine, but they must have been on our minds because the conversation turned to movies. Angus jumped at the topic with gusto. He loved movies and enjoyed sharing his expertise. I liked movies, but they weren't part of Edwin's typical routine. However, Angus's enthusiasm and knowledge of plotlines and cinematography kept both my boss and me intrigued through dinner and dessert, and I managed to put Angus's over-the-top personality traits aside.

"Can I get the bill?" he asked when dinner, dessert, and more drinks were finished.

"It's taken care of, but thank you," Edwin said.

"That's mighty kind of you, Edwin. Thank you."

"Can we give you a lift back tae your hotel?" Edwin asked.

"No, thank you. I enjoy walking around the city."

I was glad to step outside into the fresh air. Vanessa's restaurant was comfortable and the food delicious, but dinner with Angus and his big personality had been work.

However, I had one more thing I wanted to ask him.

"Well, it's been a pleasure," Edwin said. He took in a deep breath of the chilly evening.

"The pleasure has been all mine," Angus said, his eyes on mine only.

I shook it off. "Oh! Angus, I just remembered something. I saw your card."

"My card?"

"Yes, your business card was tucked under a welcome mat."

"Really? How strange. Where?"

"Remember the crime scene tape over that door, close to the church? My friend lives there?"

"Sure. I remember," he said, his tone cool.

"Your card was under his mat. Did you run over and take a look?" I smiled.

"No, ma'am," he said as he fell into thought. "I must have

dropped a card by the church and it blew where you found it. I did visit the church. You and your fella said it would be okay if the door was unlocked."

"Right." I nodded. "Makes sense."

He shrugged. "Must have been it. Listen, y'all, it's been a pleasure." He swung his attitude back to friendly, pumped our hands, and smiled big.

"Let me know if you remember anything at all, alrighty?" Angus said to Edwin.

"Definitely," Edwin said. "Safe travels, Angus."

"Thank you. Best of luck to you and your fella," Angus said to me.

"Thank you."

"And off he rode into the sunset," I muttered quietly to Edwin as we watched Angus walk away. "The star of the upcoming film, *A Cowboy in Edinburgh*."

"I guess," Edwin said, not laughing at my joke.

"You don't trust him?"

"Not even a wee bit," Edwin said. "I suspect we'll learn more about him as time goes on, but, no, I don't trust him. He's too . . . much."

"He wouldn't take the book back. I think that's a good thing."

"Mmhmm."

"What?"

"Nothing, lass, let's get back tae the bookshop," Edwin said with a quick glance back inside the restaurant. Vanessa wasn't anywhere to be seen, but he'd see her later, I was sure.

"She's amazing," I said.

"Aye, she is," Edwin said with a happy smile.

I wondered if there was another wedding in our near future.

THIRTY

As Edwin steered us back toward the bookshop, my phone buzzed.

"Hey, Tom, what's up? Uh-huh. Really? That sounds wonderful! Great. We'll be there in just a few minutes." I ended the call and looked at Edwin. "They're getting in the spirit. We should have given them more details. It sounds like they think it's a full-length movie, and it looks like we've got a full house. Rosie even had Hamlet run out for popcorn and something called Cola Cubes. Candy?"

Edwin laughed. "Aye. A chewy, fruity candy that no adult should ever consume, but it sounds like they're having a good time. I'm glad to know your family. We all are."

"They're glad to know you too. I hadn't planned on this, but I'm plotting to try to get them to move here."

"Let me know what I can do tae help," Edwin said.

"Will do."

Though it was verging on chilly, the night was beautiful, with a rare cloudless sky. As Edwin drove down darker streets, I could peer up and see some stars.

I'd taken the envelope with the negatives out of my bag and put it in the inside pocket of my jacket, with Angus's business card. It was a light jacket, one I could keep on at all times, particularly in Scotland, and the pocket was an inside breast pocket like in men's suit coats. This way, the negatives and the card were with me, on me, in fact, and the photos weren't being bent. I'd told Tom about the pocket's contents but asked him not to broadcast that I had them only because I wanted to see the films before determining if I should develop someone else's photographs. He asked why I kept the card there too. I didn't have an answer other than it felt like the right thing to do.

"Rosie?" Edwin asked as we went through the front door. She was standing on a step stool and tacking a sheet over the front window.

"Ah, ye're here," she said around the tacks she held with her lips. She took a couple and stuck them into the sheet and the window frame. "We're going tae be watching films of Nessie herself. I dinnae want the world tae see us."

I looked at Edwin. "They're just in the spirit."

"Be careful up there," he said to Rosie.

"Ayeways."

"Always," Hamlet translated as he hurried by, carrying some plastic cups and a pitcher of lemonade. "She wouldn't let me do it."

"I'm not surprised," Edwin said.

My parents and Artair were placing chairs in the small space around the back table. Tom was moving books. The projector and another sheet that would serve as the screen had been set up in the back. I silently wondered where the sheets had come from, but I hadn't even known about Rosie's scrapbook until recently.

Elias and Aggie were busy too and didn't notice Edwin and me. Hector did, though. Through the crowd, he spotted me and trotted over. I picked him up and we managed a brief snuggle or two.

Everyone I cared about most was in the same room, again. I could get used to this.

"Lass, I havnae found the wicked woman who has your dress. I'm not giving up my search, though. I'll find her," Aggie said as she set a book on the front desk.

"Thank you." I stepped toward her but had to veer so I wouldn't run into Wyatt walking by. "Don't worry about it too much. I appreciate everything you're doing."

"Och, not a problem."

"What do you think of all this Nessie stuff?"

"Nessie is as real as you or I, there's no doubt."

"You've seen her?"

"Maybe. I'm not sure, but I know some who have without a doubt and I believe them. Elias told me he showed you the place by the castle." She leaned closer to me. "I think he's seen her, but he just doesnae want tae tell."

"Really?"

"Aye!" Her eyes lit. "This is an exciting evening. Who knows what we'll discover."

We were set up only a few moments later; all of us with small bowls filled with popcorn and candy. Hamlet loaded the first film onto the machine. Tom sat next to me and we managed a brief kiss and hello.

Hamlet said, "There are only two developed films. The

other three containers held unused reels. And, I don't think we have an audio mechanism on the projector," he said as he inspected it. "There's a line of audio that's been recorded along the film, but I don't think we'll hear anything. We'll have tae read lips."

"Some of us actually remember silent films," Edwin said in the mostly darkened shop, the only light from the bright bulb on the projector. "We'll be fine."

"Reminds me of an elementary school film," my dad said quietly when the machine whirred to life.

I'd watched videos via TVs with VCRs when I was in school, but I remembered seeing some projectors stored in a back room at the elementary school I'd gone to. It had been the same school both my parents had attended.

Immediately, the film took us back to a time when little boys wore woolen shorts and little girls wore dresses to play in. We surmised that the young boy we saw was Norval and the two little girls, older than Norval, were his sisters, Millie and Jean. I saw no resemblance to the adult version of Norval, but it seemed a logical guess. The person behind the camera might have been their mother, since their father did pop into the picture.

From first indications, this was a happy family, but it could have all been an act for the camera.

They were standing on a shore of Loch Ness. It was easy to determine the location because at one point the camera angled to the right just enough that the remains of the castle came into the frame. The three children and the adult man played tag, smiling and laughing too big. I studied the older Fraser. He was a handsome man with slicked-back black hair, a tall, thin frame, and a face that verged on funny-looking, with big eyes and a crooked nose, but stopped short enough to be appealing. I saw neither Gavin nor Norval in the man on the screen.

We learned nothing about Nessie from the first film, but it was interesting to note that we now knew what Leopold Fraser looked like. Rosie stood to flip on the overhead light so Hamlet could see to thread the next one.

"That was pretty close to the same spot you took us to by the castle," I said to Elias.

"Really?" my mom said.

"Yeah, again sorry."

Mom nodded absently; she hadn't meant to make me feel guilty this time.

"Verra close," Elias said. "Do ye suppose there's anything tae make of that?"

"I wouldn't know what," I said.

"But that spot's a distance from where the wee lad Norval lived. That's not Wikenton."

"How far away?" Tom asked.

"A good three miles," Elias said.

"And his father was right outside their house in Wikenton when Norval was told about Nessie, or so he said." In my mind I worked through the locations. Maybe it wasn't so strange that Elias had driven us to that spot. You could see the castle well from there, and it was only partially private. Maybe lots of people over the years enjoyed that "hidden" place.

As if reading my mind, Tom leaned to my ear. "I've been there. I think many have."

"I wondered."

"Next film is ready," Hamlet said.

Rosie flipped the switch and our attention turned back to the sheet screen.

It was the same location; the Loch Ness shore with the castle ruins in the background. This time, though, there were only two people in the picture. Norval was one. He was a teenager, close to twenty, probably, and this time I could see a resemblance to the old man I'd come to know. It was something in the set of his eyes, the shape of his head, and the angle of his shoulders. I was certain it was him. I couldn't tell if the woman with him was Millie or his other sister, Jean. The two in the frame looked nothing alike.

They moved together, sliding their arms around each other. The woman stood up onto her tiptoes and kissed Norval on the cheek. He put his hand to the spot and smiled sheepishly. The woman smiled and shrugged at the camera.

"Not a sister," I said aloud. She looked familiar. It didn't take me long to realize we were seeing Ava McMasters Keaton. In the film she was about the same age as in the picture on her cottage wall. I didn't announce her identity, and I didn't pull out my phone to check the picture.

Besides, as we were all looking at the adorable couple, who seemed to either be in love or headed in that direction, we gasped in awe, and were then suddenly struck silent.

Behind the couple, though grainy with time and old film, we clearly saw something the world would probably want to see too: a tail. It swished up out of the water and then slapped back down. It might have been twenty feet long but it was hard to tell. It had a pointed tip, and two spines jutting out from it. The couple seemed to hear the splash as the tail slapped the water just before it disappeared under again. They turned and watched the water for a second. But it was how they turned back around that was the most interesting part.

First, they looked at each other and said something as they

both nodded. Neither of them seemed surprised in the least. They faced the camera and Norval spoke. We couldn't hear a thing, but his lips were easy to read: "Did you get that, Millie?" and then both he and the woman he was next to said, "Good," before they both walked toward the camera and then out of the frame. That was the end of the film.

"Hamlet, back that up and play it again," Edwin said. The rest of us made mumbles of agreement.

He played it back three times; it was the same each time.

Finally, when Rosie flipped on the light, Aggie was the first to speak. "We all saw the tail, aye?"

We all did.

"Do ye think it was . . . it was her?" she asked.

There was no way to be sure. Time, imagination, and old film were all involved. There was also the behavior of the couple. Did it look like they were trying to set something up? It was hard to tell.

"Lass, it's . . . this cannae be," Artair said, a small amount of distress in his voice.

That was the first thing I'd heard him say about Nessie. Tom stood and moved over to his father.

"Delaney, you came to Scotland and found Nessie?" Mom said. Dad nodded.

"I wouldnae be the least bit surprised if she's the one tae break open the story," Rosie added.

"Me either," Tom said.

But I was looking at Artair. "Are you okay?"

Now everyone was looking at Artair.

Artair's frown turned into a wince.

"Oh. Well, I think this could be something verra big," he said as he looked around at us. "Look, I'm not into conspiracies, but if this is real—and, I'm not sure it is, lass. Perhaps it's a prank of some sort—but if it is real, it simply cannot just be thrown out tae the world. We all know that, don't we? There are proper channels and authorities. I don't know who or where they would be, but I think we need tae take care, and work on authentication first."

We all blinked at him as reality fell back into place. Of course, he was right.

I thought about the negatives in my pocket. I would find a way to get them developed, some secret way. Edwin or Hamlet would know someone.

I suddenly understood something I couldn't have comprehended beforehand. Some things just needed to remain secrets. I wasn't sure yet if this was one, but Artair was correct, we would definitely need to take proper steps before unleashing this information on the world.

Luckily, I thought this was the perfect group for keeping something to themselves. The saying about a secret remaining a secret if only one person knew it might not apply here. Rosie was the most gossipy of all of us, but even she'd kept a few secrets over the years.

"You're right, Artair." I looked around. "We will keep this to ourselves? For now at least?"

They all must have come to the same conclusion because the agreement was quick, unanimous, and firm.

We'd only needed about half an hour to view and discuss the films. When we were done and everyone fell into a thoughtful haze of sorts, Tom and I said we'd handle the cleanup. No one argued, probably thinking the bride and groom-to-be wanted a little alone time together.

Once everyone else left and we'd cleaned up and removed and folded the sheets, Tom and I sat side by side on top of the front desk. We left the lights off, so no one could readily notice us sitting there looking out at Grassmarket and the nighttime activity. There was always something going on in the square, even if it was just people walking through.

"Four more days," Tom said. "I'm glad we're almost there."

"Me too," I said.

Tom laughed. "Are you sure?"

I looked at him. "Oh, I'm so sorry. I'm just distracted, and I'm very excited for us to be married. I might be wearing jeans to the ceremony, by the way."

"It doesn't matter what you wear," he said so quickly and easily that I was sure he meant it.

"Just so you know, I'll be pretty disappointed if you're not in your kilt."

He laughed. "I know." He kissed the top of my head. "If the murder isn't solved by Saturday, do you want tae postpone the honeymoon?"

I looked up at him, one side of his face lit by the glow of a streetlight. "You'd do that?"

"Of course. We've got the rest of our lives together. If you would have a more relaxing, enjoyable time, let's postpone it a wee bit."

"No, I don't want to postpone our honeymoon, but I think it's pretty amazing and wonderful that you asked."

"All right. Now, what about those negatives you found at Norval's? Do you want me to see if Artair can find someone to develop them?"

"That's a great idea, but . . . I think he was correct. Let's make sure we're doing everything properly here. So, not yet."

"Sounds good." Tom paused and then leaned his shoulder into mine. "What is it?"

"I have no idea what Norval wanted me to look for, Tom. While that film and the negative are shocking and interesting, there's nothing that I've found that would clear Norval of murder."

"But he's not under arrest anymore, right?"

"For now. He's being detained, but I can't help but think I've failed him. I have no idea what he wanted me to find."

"Delaney, he's not in his right mind, and he's getting help, it sounds like."

"I just don't know. Is there any chance you'd drive me somewhere?"

"Anywhere. What's going on?"

"I need to . . . see a man about a monster."

"Lead the way."

THIRTY-ONE

"Lass?" the receiving officer said. He made a big deal of looking at his wrist as if there were a watch there; there wasn't. "A wee bit late, isn't it?"

It was almost ten.

"A little, yes. Is Inspector Winters in?" I didn't expect him to be there. I expected to be turned away at the door, at which point Tom and I would leave and go home. But I had to try.

"Aye. One moment," the officer said.

"Oh. Good," I said and looked at Tom. He shrugged and smiled. He was surprised too.

"Delaney? Tom?" Inspector Winters came around the wall and removed a pair of reading glasses I'd never seen him wear before. He was also in plain clothes—jeans and a sweatshirt. I'd seen him once before in plain clothes, on Christmas Day in a cemetery.

"Hi," I said. I looked around. The only other officer was the receiving officer, but that still felt like too many. "Can we talk in the interview room?"

"Certainly."

I caught the eye roll from the receiving officer, but I was pretty sure Inspector Winters sent him back something stern.

"What's up?" Inspector Winters asked once we were closed inside the windowless interview room.

"A couple of things," I began. "First of all, I looked through Norval's flat and didn't find anything that might prove his innocence, or who might have killed Gavin."

"I'm sorry tae hear that, but thank you," Inspector Winters said as if he wasn't surprised. "I appreciate you looking."

"Okay." I looked at Tom and then back at the inspector. "You said you were getting help for Norval."

"Aye. Medical help."

"Does that mean he's still in a hospital?"

"Aye." Inspector Winters caught himself and put up his hand in a halt. "Delaney, you can't visit him."

I nodded, but leaned my arms onto the table and said, "Well, why not? I mean, he's no longer under arrest and I'm just a friend."

Inspector Winters' eyebrows came together. "You want to question him about something."

"I might ask a question, but I'd like to talk to him, just see how he's doing. Maybe there's something in his apartment that *will* clear his name, or point to the real killer, that we couldn't find. Maybe he'd tell me more specifics. You could come with me."

I really hoped I could talk to Norval without the police there, but I'd make do if I had to.

"He's doing all right. He's getting medication."

"Good. Have you asked him if there's something inside his apartment that would clear him? How about if Gavin threatened to steal his papers from him and sell them to pay off some debts?"

"Aye." Inspector Winters paused. "And he didn't give us an idea of something that would clear him, no matter how many times we asked. He also said that Gavin never once threatened tae take his papers and sell them. He doesn't tell us much."

"Don't you think he would talk to me more easily than he would talk to you? He asked *me* to help him, Inspector Winters. He was afraid, he didn't think the police would do right by him. I know you've helped him, but he doesn't trust authority figures. That's normal for conspiracy theorists."

"Aye."

"I don't think he killed his great-nephew. If he could tell me something more specific that might help his case, I owe it to him to try to talk to him."

"Look, Delaney, Norval isn't well, but he's not totally un-well either. He went through some things when he was a child that affected him terribly, but he's capable of taking care of himself, maybe even of having a job. He's still a person of in-terest in the murder of his nephew, though. I just can't let you talk tae him."

"You know I met Norval the day before the murder, don't you?"

"I do."

"And he wanted me to take over his work. I'm not going to do that, let me make that clear. However, what if I looked through his things more like the archivist that I am. I know how to search, catalogue, and file things. Your officer, Kari, was impressive, but I'm older and have more experience. I know how to do this sort of research. But there's a lot there, and time is always of the essence. Maybe Norval could tell me exactly where to look, or exactly what more to look for. Maybe another conversation with him could help save time?"

I felt I owed this battle to Norval. I didn't know if it was because of all the information I'd learned—about him and Gavin—or if it was simply the film with the tail. I'd become fully invested in helping him, but I wasn't sure at what moment it had happened.

Inspector Winters thought another long moment. "I must be out of my mind, but you're making good points, God help me. All right, you can have a few minutes with Norval."

"Really? I mean, that's great, thank you!"

"Tonight?"

"Yes. If he's asleep I won't wake him, but I'd like to try to talk to him tonight."

"All right. I like him. I can't help it. He's a likeable person, and he's not telling us everything. I think it's worth you having a wee conversation with him tae see if you can find out."

"Where should we go?"

"He's in a hospital, guarded by an officer, but I'll call him and tell him tae let you in."

I cringed.

"He's not being hurt, lass."

I nodded and tried to look more confident than I felt. I wanted to do right by him. I couldn't help it, I owed it to Norval and Gavin to try to figure out who the killer was.

Didn't we all?

THIRTY-TWO

The smell of antiseptic didn't override the other scents, the bad ones. I wished it had.

"Hospitals," Tom said quietly.

"Sorry," I said.

Tom had spent too much time in hospitals lately. His aunt suffered from dementia which, combined with her elderly years, had brought on other conditions requiring frequent emergency medical and long-term attention.

He blinked as if he was surprised he'd said it aloud. "Sorry."

The worn linoleum floors and lathe-and-plaster walls were clean but old, harkening back to a time when mental health issues weren't treated with compassion. The noises inside only added to the overall ambience, which forced a chill through my limbs. The yells and screams weren't frequent but the few that we heard were enough to be distressful.

At the front desk, we'd been directed to the seventh floor, the "mental health" ward. Patients weren't roaming the halls or being visibly mistreated in any way, but there were sounds coming from behind the closed doors that made me think people were struggling—physically, emotionally, or mentally. It was bothersome, and it was late—darkness visible through the random windows.

"Room 706," I said as we continued down the hallway.

"Aye. Right here. Do you want me to come in?"

"Yes. Where's the guard?"

Tom and I looked at the vacated chair next to the door.

"Taking a break?" Tom said.

I looked through the window in the door but could only see sheet-covered feet, and then pushed through. Tom followed behind.

"Lass?" Norval said when he noticed us. He was wide awake, staring at the wall, as far as I could tell. There was no television in the sparse room.

"Hi, Norval," I said as we approached.

He scooted into a more upright position as his eyebrows came together. "Did ye find it?"

"Oh, Norval, I don't know exactly what you wanted me to find," I said as I took a last hurried step to his side.

Disappointment pulled at his mouth as his eyes darted back and forth between me and Tom.

"This is my fiancé, Tom," I said, introducing them. "You can trust him. How are you feeling?"

He studied Tom a moment and then said, "Oh, I feel fine. They're giving me some medicine that makes me much less nervous about everything, but I'm not so sure I should be takin' it."

"Being less nervous is good, isn't it?"

"I dinnae ken. I feel muddy in the head. I think I'd rather be nervous." He smiled sadly, and his dentures shifted slightly.

Tom and I nodded.

"It's so good to see you," I said.

"Good tae see ye too, lass."

"Norval, I have questions, okay?"

He blinked as if it was okay for me to continue. I hoped to tread lightly, but still get the answers I needed.

"Norval, had you already seen Gavin's body when you came to the bookshop to get me?" I asked.

He looked at me with surprise and then admiration. "Ye figured that out?"

I nodded. It had been the least difficult mystery to solve, but probably the most important answer I'd needed.

"Aye, lass, aye, but if I'd called the police, they would have arrested me on the spot! I would have been locked away."

"Oh, Norval." I put my hand on his. "I'm so sorry for what you've been through, but why? Because . . . of the knife?"

More admiration filled his eyes. "Aye, lass, that's exactly why. When I saw Gavin, I rushed away, rushed back home and looked for my knife. I couldnae find it. If it was my knife that killed the lad, it wasnae with my hand, but I ken it would look that way. I thought if I had you with me, it would seem . . . better, and then I thought you would figure out what you needed tae find."

"The knife. You wanted me to find your knife?"

"Aye, that's it! See, if ye found it—if someone other than me found it—I would look less guilty, I suppose?"

He seemed so convinced of his logic. I didn't want to argue that part. "No, I didn't find a knife. The police didn't find another one in your flat either. Did you ask them to look for one?"

Norval's face fell. "No, lass. They would never have believed me without seeing it, and I couldnae find it when I went back home. I looked!"

"But you do have a knife . . . you did?"

"Aye."

I put my hand on his arm. He would never trust the police. No amount of medication would change that.

"But Norval," I said. "That doesn't mean it was your knife that killed Gavin, or even if it was your knife, that doesn't mean you were the killer. That knife . . . like the cards, there were many made."

"Aye, but . . ."

"No, listen to me." We locked eyes. "The police aren't sure about the fingerprints on the knife that killed Gavin. Yours are there, but there's some question, and that's why you're not in a jail cell. There are also some other prints on it too. The police are trying to figure out whose. Help me remember, who was in your flat that might have taken the knife from you? Think, Norval. Who was in your flat in the last . . . I don't know, month or so?"

He blinked at me. "Other than you and Gavin, I don't know." He fell into thought again. "Oh! An author stopped by, gave me a book and everything. Brodie Watson."

"Norval, this is very important. Did Mr. Watson stop by within the last month or so?"

Norval closed his eyes. They shot open a moment later. "No! It was longer ago than that. In fact, I'm not sure exactly when, but months, maybe."

"Okay," I said, glad that maybe Brodie Watson hadn't lied about the timing. "Now, try hard to remember this—when is the last time you remember seeing your knife?"

"Lass, I ken that exactly. It's all I've thought about. It was there on the floor beside my couch a week before Gavin was killed. I saw it! I kicked it under, thinking it was dangerous and I should find a better place for it. I couldnae think of a better place at the time, so I just hid it under there. I searched and searched for it, but it wasnae there. I hoped you'd find it!"

"Okay, now, I need you to think even harder. After you saw the knife, after you kicked it under the couch, who else came into your home? Delivery people? Your landlord? Anyone else? Would Gavin have picked it up and taken it with him?"

Norval had been shaking his head as he looked at and listened to me. "I can't think of one other person who came into my house, lass. Not one other. Gavin would not have taken it. He thought my things were silly."

"Remember the cards I brought back to you the day we met?"

"Aye."

"Gavin had those on him when he chased me down to talk. He picked them up. He could have picked up the knife."

Norval's eyebrows came together as he shook his head again. "No, I don't think Gavin would have taken the knife."

"Did he leave the cards with you later?"

"I . . . I don't know. I dinnae remember." Frustration pulled his voice tight.

"All right. It's okay. I want you to keep thinking about any other visitors. I forget those details a lot, customers who came into the bookshop only briefly, phone numbers on my phone I'd forgotten I'd called or who they belong to. It's only human to forget brief interactions. Just relax and keep thinking, even after we're gone, okay?"

"All right."

I took a deep breath, hoping to calm Norval down too. I

wasn't sure it worked, but I had more questions. "Norval, any chance Albert Winsom stopped by to see you?"

"Gracious no! I wouldnae let him in anyway."

"Right. I understand. Can you remember the last time you saw Mr. Winsom?"

"I dinnae remember."

I was curious about Winsom's relationship with Millie, but it seemed such old news that I didn't want to further bother Norval by bringing it up. Maybe later. I looked at Tom and then back at Norval.

"I think you have to come clean with the police. You have to tell them that you saw Gavin dead before you came to the bookshop. You need to tell them you were afraid and why, and that you couldn't find your knife. They aren't out to get you, Norval, they want to help you. I promise." I hoped I was correct.

"Oh, lass, I don't want tae do that."

"I know, but it's the right thing to do, and it might help find Gavin's killer. That's what we need to remember, okay?"

Frankly, I felt like a bully, pushing him to do things he wasn't comfortable doing. I didn't want to cause harm, but it had to be done.

"Norval," I continued. "When we first met and you were talking to me about how important it was to find Nessie, you mentioned how important the truth was. It's still important. The police need to know the truth about the knife, Norval. It's important."

A long moment later, Norval said, "Okay."

"Good, good." I smiled. "Would you tell me why you and Gavin were planning to meet with Nisa? You were having an argument, right?"

"Aye," he said, though he'd quit looking at me.

"What was the argument about?"

"It's not important."

"I think it is."

He looked at me and sighed. "I'd heard he was lying to his clients, lass, telling them he had a way tae pay them back."

"By selling your things?"

"Aye."

"It made you mad that he was going to take money for your research?"

"No, lass, when I'm gone, I'll be gone. I was going tae give Gavin everything if I couldnae find someone to continue my work. I didn't want money for my work, but I wouldnae cared what he did with it. I loved the lad. I was upset that he was telling his clients that he could get *that much* money. He couldnae have, lass. My work isn't worth that much. I just wanted Gavin tae quit lying tae his clients. I wanted him tae come clean. I was going tae have Nisa convince him. He wouldnae go with me when he realized what I was up tae."

"I'm so sorry."

Norval knew his things weren't worth enough to cover Gavin's debts. But they were worth something.

"I, uh, took the films and the projector."

"I wondered if ye'd be curious. Did ye watch them?"

"We only found two films that were developed. One was of you, your sisters, and your dad, right?"

"Aye," he said with a genuine smile, wiping away the concern and fear that had been there only a moment ago. "I was a wee lad, but I still remember that day, or I've seen the film enough tae remember it."

"The other one, though, with an older you and a young woman, and . . ."

"The tail?" he said matter-of-factly.

"Well, yes."

"That was her, Nessie," he said. "We saw her often those days. Or we saw bits and pieces of her. A tail, a nose, a snout, eyes. She showed herself much more back then. Then she started tae hide more. Finally, I thought she'd died, but I still saw bits of her once or twice a year. She's auld. Verra auld."

Out of the corner of my eye, I saw Tom's eyebrows lift.

"There's only one Nessie?" I asked.

"I'm not sure," Norval said. "That's part of my work. I've been trying tae understand if there's one or two, or many. I just dinnae ken."

"Was the girl with you Ava?"

"Aye, Ava McMasters. She was . . . a friend."

"A girlfriend?"

"Aye. Maybe." He looked up at the wall and his mouth made a firm line.

I didn't tell him I'd been to Wikenton, or that I'd been inside Ava's cottage.

"You two didn't work out?" I said.

"No, lass." Norval smiled sadly at me. "I wouldnae work out with anyone. I have a job tae do and I cannae put anyone before that job."

I nodded and tried not to be too sad for him.

"Norval, any chance someone with a big, Southern American accent, with a big cowboy hat and boots stopped by your house?" I reached into the pocket where I'd put Angus's card, but all I felt were the negatives.

"No, lass, no one like that," Norval said.

I dug around in the pocket a moment more but couldn't locate the card. I checked a couple of other pockets but gave up searching quickly. Norval would have remembered Angus, surely.

I tapped the outside of my jacket. "I also grabbed some photo negatives. Do you mind if I get them developed?"

"Not at all." Norval smiled at me. "You're going tae take over my work, aren't you?"

Despite everything, I couldn't help but laugh once. "I doubt it, Norval, but I'm mighty curious."

Norval nodded. "You'll see. Get the negatives developed and you'll be hooked, I promise."

"We'll see."

As Norval leaned his head back onto his pillow, it seemed we'd asked enough questions.

"We'll let you rest," I finally said.

Norval Fraser's mind was not dulled to the point of use-lessness. Was his obsession part of a mental illness, or would anyone who'd claimed to see what he'd seen, had a film of a tail, be obsessed? I still needed to research the authenticity of the film, but in viewing it I was convinced that we'd seen something that *might* be proof of Nessie's existence. I wasn't ready to de-vote my life to finding her, but, then again, my father hadn't al-legedly been stolen by her. Who knew how I'd feel after I saw the pictures?

Tom and I said goodbye and turned to leave.

"I'll talk tae the police, lass, right away. Send in the officer from outside if ye will."

"We will. We're your friends, Norval, and we hope you get out of here and get to go home soon," I said.

"Aye."

Tom and I made our way out. The officer was back from his break, surprised we'd made it by him. We sent him into

Norval's room with the promise that the man inside had some things to talk about.

I hoped we were right. We weren't invited to stick around and listen.

However, unbeknownst to me was what I left behind. Something had escaped the pocket inside my jacket and fallen to the floor, under the corner of Norval's bed, and that something would prove to break the case wide open.

Just not quite quickly enough.

THIRTY-THREE

Thank goodness my family and Artair had forged a fast bond. Any thoughts I had about imposing on my soon-to-be father-in-law deflated a little as he enthusiastically joined us for breakfast at the bookshop, bringing along a list of sights for them to see that day.

"He's having more fun than they are," Tom said to me as we sat at the end of the table. Our parents and Wyatt were looking over brochures Artair had handed out.

"I've been neglectful," I said. Not to mention the dress debacle, but I was still too embarrassed to go into detail on that one with Tom.

"I don't think you need tae worry. And, we'll visit them in Kansas," Tom said. "As often as you'd like."

A surge of emotion worked its way to the spot behind my eyes. I blinked and swallowed hard. We'd had this conversation before and it had never made me emotional. Of course, the fact that my parents were there, and that they were there for my wedding, was bound to wreak a little havoc on my emotions.

"You're the best," I said.

"Well, I'm marrying the best, so I'd better be."

I liked it when we verged on nauseating.

Elias promised to be the driver again, but Aggie had guest-house duties, Tom had to work, and Edwin was curious enough about Millie to want to come along with me. Besides, he said he had something to talk to me about and the trip to Millie's flat would give us some privacy.

After we bid everyone else goodbye, Edwin grabbed a brollie from a shelf by the front door, commenting on our growing collection. I played innocent, and we took off on the short walk to Millie's flat. I'd called her earlier, and though she hadn't sounded thrilled by us stopping by she'd sighed and said we would be welcome.

I shared with Edwin the details of Tom's and my visit with Norval. He didn't like the idea of forced medication, but we both thought that Inspector Winters would watch Norval carefully. He hoped Norval had told the police the truth of his actions the morning of the murder. I did too. I would let Inspector Winters know what he'd said, but I was giving Norval a chance to come clean himself first.

"Are you going tae search for the knife again?" Edwin asked.

"I think so, even though I think we would have seen it if it was there. Want to come with me after we talk to Millie?"

"I do."

"You're distracted, though. What did you want to talk about?" I asked as we turned a corner and both of us eyed the threatening clouds above. No rain yet, but it was on the way.

"Aye. I can't stop thinking about Mr. Murdoch. I believe he's left Scotland, but . . . I keep thinking about his story, and the more I think about it, the more I believe it didn't happen."

"You think he lied?"

"I don't want tae believe that he lied. I want tae believe he was mistaken, or the story was just something his grandfather wrote on a note tae entertain him in some way, though I don't think that makes much sense."

"Do you think you should give the book back to him?"

"Not really, though I do think I should give it back tae him if it isn't mine. I've tried tae figure out what he might be up tae, if he is up tae something. What would be the point of making up a story? He hasn't seemed the least bit curious about the warehouse, so I don't think he's someone who's heard about it and is intrigued. After going through things in my mind more than a few times now, I wonder if he might have stolen the book from another bookshop, maybe one here in Edinburgh."

"Really? Why such a story, then? I can't pinpoint a motive to do such a thing."

"I've been trying to figure that out. Maybe he stole it and bringing it into the shop was a way tae hide his theft, but I don't see how. He refused tae take it back. What else would be behind it?"

I'd met few people as smart as or smarter than Edwin, but it seemed that Angus had him confused. It didn't make sense that Angus would steal the book and bring it to Edwin, but if that was what happened, there must have been a solid reason for him to have done so.

"Do you think you actually knew his grandfather, and maybe something happened between the two of you?"

"Maybe. But I don't remember knowing him."

"Let's ask other shops in town if they're missing the book. We're part of that Facebook group, remember? Do you want me to post a question? I'd been working under the assumption that the book was Angus's and then with everything else I haven't done one thing to check the provenance. Maybe there's a clue there somewhere."

"I thought about that, but no, I don't want you to ask the group. Delaney, while there are many booksellers I am friends with and whom I trust, there are some that I don't. I don't want tae start asking questions when I don't already have more of the answers."

"Okay. What should we do?"

"How would you feel about you or me asking Inspector Winters if any of the shops have reported the book stolen?"

"Good idea."

"Well, I think so, but I wanted your input. He doesn't trust me and I don't want tae make you look guilty of anything."

I sighed. "I'm afraid neither you nor I are considered absolutely innocent, Edwin, but we haven't done anything wrong, and I believe Inspector Winters is thorough enough to trust us."

"All right, then. We'll give him a ring when we're done here."

The narrow brick facade of the three-story building was decorated with small gargoyle statues. They weren't attached to the building but arranged on stoops on each side of the dark wood door.

I confirmed that Millie Fraser was on the list next to the buzzers and pushed the button.

A long, silent moment later I buzzed again.

"Who is it?" an old woman's voice said from the small speaker.

"Delaney Nichols. I called this morning. I'm here with my boss, Edwin."

"Who?"

I repeated myself, and when she grumbled incomprehensible complaints, I thought we were being turned away. But she buzzed us in.

There was no lift. I'd been in several buildings in Edinburgh with no elevators, but as we climbed the stairs up to the third floor, I wondered how the woman attached to the old voice maneuvered the stairs every day. The building was clean, with beige linoleum over the floors and a black wrought-iron banister that guided us up a polished wood stairs. It was a beautiful place, full of character.

The door to room number 402 was ajar so we pushed through as we announced ourselves.

"Well, come on in, then," Millie said, sitting on an old, towel-covered, leather recliner. A walker was propped on one side of the recliner; a tall lamp with a table extending around the pole in its middle sat on the other side. The table was covered in used and unused tissues, medicine bottles, and a fanned and frayed paperback.

Millie seemed much older than Norval, and Norval seemed old. Millie's short, gray hair was sparse over her head. Her thick glasses magnified runny eyes on a face made of wrinkles and a sour frown.

She coughed, grabbed a tissue, and put it to her mouth as she coughed some more. She nodded toward the couch; obediently, Edwin and I took a seat. The brown furniture reminded me of the scratchy fabric that had covered my grandmother's couch. I could feel the itch already coming through my jeans.

The flat looked like it had been furnished and decorated sometime in the 1960s or '70s and hadn't been updated since.

However, everything was clean and in good shape. The entire space was charming and would probably make a popular link to pictures of a bygone time. The only mess I saw was made up of the used tissues on the lamp's table and overflowing from a small garbage bin beside the chair.

Once the coughing fit stopped, Millie looked at us with impatience. "Ye've come tae talk about my daft brother?"

"Well, yes," I said. "Edwin met him years ago, and I did recently. Edwin owns a bookshop, The Cracked Spine. I work for him. Norval wanted Edwin, years ago, and then me recently, to continue his work."

"Of course he did, the wee pain in my arse," she said. "I wish ye would have taken the papers and burned them all. I wish someone would."

"They've been quite a burden, then?" Edwin said.

Millie laughed with a noise that was a cross between a hack and a cackle. "They've been a curse. No, he's been a curse. My brother's the curse."

"How has he hurt anyone?" I asked, not trying to hide my sudden dislike for her.

She didn't seem to mind my tone. "Imagine living your life having tae take care of yer brother, make sure he's fed, takes a bath every now and then, and has food on his table. It's a full-time job, and now without Gavin tae help, I'm sure both Norval and I will wither away tae dust." She paused and shook her head to herself. "I told the police the same thing, mind, and they dinnae care in the least."

I tried to imagine it, taking care of a sibling all her life. But it wasn't as if Norval needed constant care, was it? He just needed people to check on him.

"I'm sure it's been difficult," Edwin said. "And, we're terribly sorry for your loss."

"Loss-es, ye mean? I lost my great-nephew and my brother all in one fell swoop."

"Aye," Edwin said.

"Do you think your brother killed Gavin?" I asked.

"No! Of course he didnae, but I cannae prove a thing. Told that tae the police too. They just looked at me like I was the daft one. I'm not daft, I'm old!" She shook her head again and dabbed at the corner of her nose with a tissue. "Norval adored our nephew." Tears welled in her eyes.

Chances were pretty good that Millie wasn't a hateful old woman, but one who was grieving and, as she'd said, old. I needed more sympathy, less judgment.

"Millie," I said more gently now, "what if Gavin threatened to take Norval's papers and sell them?"

She sat up straighter and blinked a few times. "Never would have happened."

"Probably not, but what if it did?" I persisted, but I wouldn't mention the row I'd heard about.

She shook her head again. "Norval would have burned his papers before taking money for them, before letting Gavin sell them while he was alive. Even *for* Gavin, he wouldnae have allowed money tae change hands. He would have burned his papers to ashes." She leaned forward in her chair. "However, once Norval was gone away tae the dead, he wouldnae cared what Gavin did with the papers. If he couldnae find someone tae continue his work, he wouldnae cared what happened after he passed."

I nodded. He'd told me as much the night before. "What

happened to Norval, Millie? You don't believe your father was acquainted with Nessie? That he was taken by her?"

She sighed out of her mouth. It came out tinged with a wheeze and I felt even more badly for her. "I don't know if he knew the creature or not. I ken though that he ran away from us the day after filling Norval's head with stories, off with a woman other than our dear, sweet mother, may she rest in peace. That sort of thing was bound to influence all of us, and it did, but it hurt sweet Norval the most. Imagine being a wee lad and yer da did what our da did tae him. And we didnae have all the resources tae take care of making sure our brother was all right. Now we have doctors and people tae talk tae about such things, but not then. And it's far too late tae fix Norval. It's been too late for a long, long time."

"I'm so sorry," I said. I looked at Edwin and then back at Millie. "Do you believe in Nessie?"

She brought her eyebrows together and sent me a stern stare. "It's not a matter of believin' or not believin'. She's real, tae be sure, lass. All ye have tae do is," I thought she was going to say "have faith" or something similar, but she surprised me, "look long enough. She's there, just waiting. I have no time for ye if ye need me tae convince ye. I'll not even try." She punctuated her words with a strong blow of her nose.

"Do you know the woman who your father left with?" I asked.

"Aye, of course. I remember her still. She was young and beautiful and my da was taken by her, so much so that he left the family he loved. And he did love us—until he met Flora Folsom, and then she blinded him tae the rest of us."

"Do you know where they went?" Edwin asked.

"No, I never wanted tae know. My sister and mother never

wanted tae know either. We told everyone not tae tell Norval. We told everyone not tae tell us a word. Maybe it was a mistake, but it seemed like the right thing tae do at the time."

I sat up straighter. "Does that mean that some people knew?"

"Certainly. Our mother took us away from Wikenton shortly after Da left. We moved here tae Edinburgh. And it wasnae easy, mind, my mom an uneducated, country woman, but she made do. Here, we wernae everyone's blether. She thought it would be better for all of us that way." Millie shrugged. "Who's tae say if she was right or not? And she could never have predicted what Norval's problems would turn into, she never could have known that he'd become the subject of the blether. Och, 'tis all a long time ago."

It was and it wasn't, but I didn't want her to dwell on the recent tragedies. "Is anyone left in Wikenton who would know where your father went?"

"I didnae ken if anyone even lives there anymore. Who's still alive?"

"Ava is," I said. "Norval's girlfriend, or something like that."

"Och, not girlfriend. She was kind tae us when we went back over the years and over time she came tae care for my brother as he continued to visit Loch Ness on his own, but even she knew he was too much work. Too much."

I looked at Edwin, who nodded at me. I didn't know why I needed to gather my courage for the next question, but I did. "We saw the film with the tail," I said. "I think you were the one holding the camera."

Millie's mouth fell open and her runny eyes blinked heavily behind her glasses. "Aye," she said quietly.

"You remember that?" I asked.

"I do."

"Was it real?"

"What does that mean?" she snapped. "Did we put something in the water and make it look like a tail? No, lass, we didnae make it up."

"But, was it real, Ms. Fraser?" Edwin asked.

"That's up tae you tae decide," she said.

I still wasn't sure, but I was believing more and more every day, and I really wanted to go back to Loch Ness.

"I see," Edwin said.

Millie continued. "I moved on. My sweet, strong mother tried tae move along, my sister moved along, but Norval just couldnae." She shook her head again. "I ken he's in hospital. I think it would be best if they keep him there, but not because he killed anyone, mind, but because he needs the help. I hope they help him."

"I do too," I said. I hoped they helped him, but I also hoped he'd be free again someday if he didn't kill Gavin.

I looked at Edwin. He didn't have any other questions. I turned to Millie again.

"I'm so sorry about Gavin."

"Aye, the wee lad," she said as tears filled her eyes again. "He made some mistakes tae be sure, and it seems he's had tae pay for them. I wish I knew the people he worked with. If I did, I imagine I could spot his killer. As it is, I'm useless, an old woman stuck in her flat, unable tae do much of anything."

"What can we do for you?" I said. "Can we go grocery shopping? We have plenty of time today."

"No, lass, thank ye, though." She smiled for the first time since we'd arrived. "I'll be okay for a few days. I have help here in the building."

Edwin reached for his wallet and pulled out a card.

"Please call me or Delaney if you need anything at all," he said.

"I'm sure I'll have tae move into a home," she said. "I've got tae come tae terms with the idea and soon, now since Gavin and Norval are gone."

I wanted to remind her that Norval really wasn't gone, but that seemed impertinent.

"You know, Millie, I have some friends who have a lovely place. Would it be presumptuous of me tae send them over tae talk tae you?" Edwin said.

"I . . . weel, I dinnae ken."

We fixed her a fruit and cookie plate and some tea before we left. She gave Edwin permission to send over his friends, and she seemed to appreciate the snack. But she was tired and glad to get rid of us so she could close her eyes for a bit.

"You know someone at a lovely old folks' home?" I asked as we walked down the stairs in between the gargoyles.

"Aye." He winked at me. "Or I will very soon."

"All right. Let me call Inspector Winters on the way to Norval's flat. Let's grab the bus from that stop." I pointed. I knew the bus system well by now.

"Very good, I'll make some calls as we go too," Edwin said.

He became so busy making sure Millie was taken care of that he seemed to enjoy the bus ride, a form of transportation I'd never seen him take. Maybe it was just Millie he'd enjoyed.

THIRTY-FOUR

Edwin and I felt defeated by the time we made it back to the bookshop. Inspector Winters didn't tell us what Norval had said to the police the night before. He did, however, tell me that he would look into a possible stolen King Arthur book but he hadn't heard of any, and we didn't find a Nessie knife in Norval's flat—we looked everywhere, more than once.

However, it was only shortly after we were inside the warehouse that Edwin did receive a call back from someone with a lovely home for the elderly. He excused himself to his office, crossing his fingers at me as he left. He was determined to help Millie. She'd be in good hands.

I tried to call Ava again. She answered the phone but then hung up on me before I could ask her where Leopold Fraser and Flora Folsom ran off to. She did not like talking on the phone. I wished I'd written down the other Wikenton resident's name and phone number so I could call and ask him to ask her, but I hadn't.

The good news was that I finally got to show my family the

warehouse. They returned after lunch an hour or so later and it seemed the right time to share my work space.

"This is . . . your office?" Mom said as even in the shadowed light I saw her eyes get big.

"This is it." I walked to the wall and flipped up the switch.

"This is amazing," Dad said. "Is it a bunch of junk, or is it all worth something?"

"Some of both." I put my hands on my hips as I thought back to the first time I'd seen it, and tried to look at it through their fresh eyes.

A smallish, cramped space in the back of the building, its walls reached up the full two stories and were topped off by short but wide windows that let in some natural light, and kept me apprised of both the weather outside and the time of day, when I lost track of it.

Shelves full of items lined the walls. When I'd seen it the first time, it had been messy, the myriad items stacked willy-nilly with no regard for their value or safekeeping. I'd done some organization, but I still had a way to go. I eyed the old box mousetraps that had caused me some trouble last Christmas and the miniature treasure chest–like container that still held some priceless medical instruments back from the time when William Burke and William Hare were killing people so they could sell the bodies for money.

It was impossible to digest it quickly, that's what I remembered. In fact, I'd swooned at the sight of the priceless desk—it really had seen the like of kings and queens. And now it was mine. Of course, I covered it with paper every time I worked on it, but I wasn't as afraid of it as I had been when I'd first come to Scotland.

There were times when it did all seem unreal. I put my finger on the edge of the desk. It was real.

"Sis?" Wyatt said.

"I know. Pretty cool, huh?"

"Unbelievable that my nerdy sister . . . anyway, it's really great."

"Thank you."

"This is so you!" Mom said. "If I could have picked a room for you to work in, it would look just like this room."

I smiled. "I love that."

"Do you get antsy, claustrophobic?" Dad asked.

"Well, it's not a wide-open wheat field, but it's not too small, and it has windows." I pointed up.

"It's quite the room," Dad said, though I could sense that he felt the packed shelves could close in on him.

I laughed. "You'd get used to it." Though, I wasn't sure he ever would. And any indoor work space would be too small for him if it was any smaller than a Kansas plain. I needed to keep that in mind in my pursuit of convincing them to join me in my new country.

Mom stepped closer to a shelf I'd recently stacked with some small bejeweled jewelry boxes. I was pretty sure the jewels weren't precious stones, but not completely convinced. I hadn't figured out the answer, and when I had time to work on the project, I wouldn't be surprised to find something valuable. I'd found a Fabergé egg last month, on the back of a shelf, tipped over and reminding me of Humpty Dumpty, but, fortunately, without the cracks.

I remembered the egg and Edwin's surprise at its discovery. He hadn't remembered ever owning it. At first. He had remembered it eventually. It seemed he remembered most things, eventually, but perhaps not everything.

Angus's book had been away from the shop for at least twenty years. Maybe that was asking too much of anyone's memory. But it was such a memorable book.

It's so much darker when a light goes out than it would have been if it had never shone.

The bookish voice was from John Steinbeck's *The Winter of Our Discontent*. It was about loss, but not the loss of something like a book. It was about a bigger loss, something heart breaking.

My mind, dreams included, had had been filled with Nessie and Norval since the moment I'd seen the cards on the ground by the church door. Angus and his priceless book had taken up some of my thoughts, but I wondered if that bookish voice was trying to tell me about Angus and the loss of his grandfather. He'd waited so long to open the trunk that held the book and note that the discovery had probably been like losing him again. It was sometimes better to leave things in the dark. Sometimes we found ourselves illuminating things we didn't even know were lacking the light.

"Delaney," Mom said. "You with us?"

"Oh. Sorry. Yes," I said.

"My girl still has her moments, huh?" Mom said.

I looked at Dad as Mom turned to face the shelf again. He and I shared a smile as he furtively put his finger up to the side of his nose. I liked our continuing secret.

"I guess so," I said. "What were you saying?"

She turned toward me again. "I wondered if your job would be over when all of this is organized, though I doubt that will happen any time soon."

"I haven't asked that question." I looked around. "Maybe I'll make sure I never finish."

"Oh, you don't have a thing to worry about. You've found a place and people who will welcome you forever. Besides, you have the pub too, if you ever need a job," Dad said.

"That's true. We'll see, but I'm not worried." I wasn't. At all. However, business ownership would certainly be different than anything I'd ever done before.

"Tom served us some of his favorite whisky the other night. I didn't know I liked whisky," Mom said.

"I didn't know you liked whisky either."

"Well, I'm not interested in drinking a lot of it, but if I'm going to drink any at all, I want something that tastes like that."

"Delaney, have you seen these?" Wyatt held up some old handcuffs. "I bet there's a story here."

"I have seen them, but I haven't researched them yet."

"So cool." He placed them carefully back onto the shelf.

I heard muffled noises coming from the other side that included an uptick in the tone of Rosie's voice. We hadn't consciously intended for that to be a signal that she might need some help, but when I heard it now, I hurried over to check on her.

I herded everyone out of the warehouse, locked the door, and led the way up the stairs. The door at the top opened just as I was reaching for the knob.

"Oh! Hello," she said.

"Everything okay?" I asked.

"Aye, aye," she said. "There's a woman here tae see ye."

"Who?"

"I didnae get her name, but she said she had tae put her ears in. She's old, that's all I know."

"Okay." I turned back to my parents and handed them my keys. "Feel free to go back and look around all you want but lock the door when you're inside and when you leave, three turns of the key."

All three of them sent me questioning looks. Why had I made them leave in such a hurry only to send them back? It had been unconscious, a habit made from being so aware of the warehouse and making sure it was always locked up, always secured, for the past year. They chose to go back and explore some more.

As my family turned to head back down the dark side stairs, I followed Rosie down the other side.

Our visitor sat in Rosie's chair behind the front desk. She held a happy Hector as she scratched behind his ears. He noticed me but sent me a rare "Do Not Disturb" pair of eyes. He did not want to be removed from his new person's attention.

She was old, older than Rosie, but there comes a point where sometimes eighty and ninety have an equal shot at being correct. Her short, gray hair peeked out from under the red scarf over her head. I thought she should be wearing a warmer cap to match her thick, fleece winter coat and her dark woolen, fingerless gloves. Bright green eyes behind thick glasses looked up at me when she was able to pull them away from Hector.

"Och, lass, I love the wee dogs," she said.

"Hector's especially wonderful," I said, recognizing her voice, I thought.

"Aye," she said a beat later.

I noticed hearing aids, but I also thought she had read my lips.

"I'm Delaney," I said when she was looking up at me again. "Are you here to see me?"

"I am," she said. "You were in my cottage up by the loch. Ye rang me a couple hours ago. I was coming into town anyway. I thought I would see what's so important that ye've rang me twice now, as well as visited me at my home."

"Ava. I wondered."

"Aye. I cannae hear well on the telephones, and my neighbor told me ye seemed particularly inquisitive. I read yer note and ye seem like a sweet young woman. I had tae see so for meself." She squinted at me playfully. "Ye look awright, but I have a question before ye ask me what ye wanted tae ask me."

"I'm listening."

"Ye didnae take even one wee slice of the bread. Why?"

"I thought it would be rude."

"Och, then ye have a lot tae learn. If someone bakes a bread, that someone wants it eaten and enjoyed. Next time, ye should take a piece." She smiled.

"She's right," Rosie added. She hadn't even tried to pretend to look busy doing something else. "It's an insult ye didnae cut a piece."

"I'll do better next time," I said, wondering if the rules were the same in Kansas. I'd have to ask my mom.

"Good. Now, what is it ye want tae ask me that ye'd ring me twice and then drive all the way up tae see me?"

"I have questions about Norval Fraser," I said.

Ava's smile saddened but remained in place. She looked down at the contented dog on her lap. "Norval Fraser was the love of my life, even though I didnae have much opportunity tae know many a young man. But him not coming home again tae stay was the best thing that ever happened to me. I married, had a child of my own, my boy. My husband's long gone now, but it all turned out for the better. I heard the news about Norval being arrested for killing his great-nephew, but I have no way of knowing if he was capable of such a thing. Is that what ye wanted tae know?"

"Well, not really," I said. "Though I'm sorry to hear that he left behind a sad story."

She'd watched my mouth again and her eyebrows lifted ever so slightly. "Weel, it wasnae him as much as it was his father's abandonment. I ken who was tae blame."

I looked toward the front door and then back at Ava. "How did you get here? Your son?"

"No. Train and cab today," she said as if I should have figured that out already.

"I'll make sure you get home easily, but can we move to the back of the bookshop, where there's a little more privacy?"

I felt bad that I asked her to move, but she stood and walked easily. The train and cab probably hadn't been a challenge. She kept hold of Hector and resumed scratching his ears when she sat again. I excused myself for a moment to get her some tea and to let my family know I would be busy for a while. I told them they could join us, but they didn't want to overwhelm Ava; they decided to stay and explore the warehouse, a place my dad seemed to find more interesting and less claustrophobic each minute that passed.

I called Edwin, who'd left for lunch too, and asked him to join us if he could. He could and was already headed back, arriving only a few minutes later. Hamlet also came in, and after he introduced himself found things to keep him busy away from the back table. In her always reliable way, Rosie placed some shortbread on the table that she'd made just that morning. Her Scottish shortbread deserved accolades and blue ribbons.

I also called Elias and asked if he would take Ava back up to Wikenton when we were done talking. It was a huge favor, but he didn't mind, and I knew he would have been offended if I hadn't thought of asking him.

I hadn't meant to make such a big deal about our visitor from Loch Ness, but every step I took to make sure our conversation was somewhat private and that she was comfortable gave me time to think about the questions I wanted to ask her. She'd known Norval and his family a long time ago, but since she wasn't a part of his family, maybe she had some emotional distance that would help clear up some of the mysteries.

And, she'd been in the film, not to mention the photo in her house.

Edwin and I sat at the back table with Ava and Hector. Rosie hovered nearby, and Hamlet went over to the dark side to make sure my family was doing okay.

"Ava, can you start from the beginning?" I asked. "Back when you first knew Norval. You knew him, then, before his father left, right? They moved to Edinburgh shortly after that, correct?"

"They left Wikenton a few months after Angus disappeared. Norval and I were wee-uns, only seven, eight by the time the family left. Norval and I were connected from the verra first. We were born on the same stormy Scotland night." She chuckled once. "Or, that's the way our parents told the story. For all we knew, it could have been clear and beautiful, but this is Scotland and stormy gave it more drama. I asked Norval's sisters once if the story was true, but neither of them could claim tae remember the weather. All they could remember was the screaming child that joined their family and that he and I arrived at aboot the same time." She paused and sighed.

"You were always friends then. Close?" I asked.

She nodded slowly. "We were always close, aye, but we both took our coorse turns."

I knew she meant "naughty," and was pleased I didn't need a translator.

She continued. "We were together all the time, with no other bairns around our age. It was a small community. And when my da went off to war and his—Leopold—didnae, the families became even closer. With all the men gone, we had tae look after each other. Leopold looked after many families. He was a good man, until he made that terrible decision tae run away with Flora Folsom."

"Did you know Flora?"

"Everyone knew Flora. 'Flora the Floozy,' I believe we all, at one time or another called her. Even us kids. She was young and beautiful and when her husband went off tae fight, she became bored quickly. Och, probably not her fault. She *was* so very young. Too young tae be married and then left on her own." Ava blinked before her eyes unfocused in thought. "There are days that I remember that time like it was yesterday. The sirens, the bombs. The sounds were terrifying, and they never leave ye." She looked at Edwin and me. "It made sense tae me when the men came back different. How could they not?" She shook her head. "Anyway, my da didnae make it back. In fact, he was killed only two weeks after leaving tae fight. Leopold took care of us all. And when he left, we all had tae figure oot how tae pick up the pieces, particularly Norval's mother. My mother was there for her, and though my mother would never take the credit, she probably saved them from a fate worse than the streets. She made sure they had money be-fore they came here, tae Edinburgh. She was a good woman." She shook her head again.

I looked at Edwin with a question in my eyes. He nodded that he thought she would be okay.

After a few moments, I asked, "If they moved to Edinburgh shortly after Leopold left, how did you and Norval remain friends?"

"Once he could figure out how to get rides from his sisters or others, he was there every weekend, searching for the monster. Many times one of his sisters brought him, but not all the time. I went with them on their explorations. It was a natural friendship at first, but then it turned romantic." She *tsk*ed and smiled wryly. "One of his sisters should probably have come with him every time tae save us from . . . We . . . well, we were young and nothing happened that caused any problems. Anyway, believe it or not Norval wasn't as . . . obsessed before the age of about eighteen. He was curious and wanted to find Nessie, of course, but the real obsession didn't begin until he was almost eighteen. Before that, we all just spent a lot of time having a good time."

"What happened at eighteen?" Edwin said.

"He quit believing, I suppose."

"In the Loch Ness Monster?" I asked.

"Oh, no, lass, he would have never quit believing in her. No, he quit believing that the monster would give him back his da. That was a difficult pill for him tae swallow. I thought it was something else too, but Norval would never admit it—I think he, deep down, came tae believe that his father might have truly abandoned him. I think his obsession became more about prov-ing the monster did take his father, than finding his father. If the monster took Leopold, then he didn't leave by his own accord. So many men left, but the only one in our village who chose tae leave was Leopold. It ruined Norval, and ruined us eventually. The realization ruined his relationships with everyone. His family had tae take care of him. He couldnae keep a job. He would have been on the streets if not for them."

"That had to be tough," I said.

"Aye. 'Twas."

"I don't understand," Edwin said. "Did he just become mature enough tae change the way he thought or was it something else? An event?"

"I believe that Nessie, herself, told him."

I cleared my throat. "Nessie spoke to him?"

"Not with words so much but she can communicate. Her eyes are a funny blue. Ye can spot them under water."

"Did you . . . do you talk to her much?" I asked.

"I havenae in decades. I told her tae leave me be. Once Norval wasnae a part of my life, I couldnae bear tae even see her swim by."

There was no hesitation with her words, no tone of apology as if she might be weaving some sort of fabrication. No wink.

"And all you had tae do was tell her tae go away?" Edwin said.

"Aye. She was friendly tae us. We were friendly tae her. Once she's been seen, she kens she cannae hide anymore and she likes company. Or she used tae—too many people nowadays. Toys, pictures, lies, cameras everywhere."

I thought about Norval's collection. Was it research or a tribute?

I still didn't believe in the Loch Ness Monster, but I knew

World War II, that time in history, was traumatic in many ways, and there was no doubt in my mind that all the trauma that Norval and his family, and in some way Ava, went through, was bound to affect them all, one way or another.

I'd seen pictures now. I'd heard stories. I'd read first-hand accounts. What would it take to convince me? I wasn't sure.

"Do you know if Norval ever heard from his father again?" I asked.

"No. My mother and I exchanged some letters with Leopold over the years. Just a couple. They were brief. He was apologetic, but not coming back, that was certain."

"Where did he go?" Edwin asked.

"He and Flora went tae America," she nodded at me, "yer neck of the woods, though I dinnae ken if the place he went tae is close tae you. America is such a big place."

"Do you know what city?" I asked.

"Oklahoma," she said. "Oklahoma City, Oklahoma. It's funny sounding."

Not far from Kansas, it turned out, and even closer with the Internet. My fingers itched to do some deeper research.

"Did he ever come back to Scotland, even just tae visit?" Edwin asked.

"Not that I'm aware of," Ava said.

Edwin sat forward and leaned his arms across the table. "Ava, I have a strange question if you don't mind."

"Aye?"

"Do you, by chance, remember if Leopold Fraser, or anyone in the Fraser family, was particularly interested in the legend and stories of King Arthur?"

My head turned so quickly to look at Edwin that Hector sent out one tiny whine. I'd wondered about Angus's card under

Norval's mat, but King Arthur hadn't quite made it into my Norval thoughts.

Ava looked at Hector before she looked up at Edwin. "No, not that I remember."

I brought my eyebrows together as I looked at my boss.

Edwin shrugged at me before we turned back to Ava.

"Ava, has anyone named Angus—tall guy with a cowboy hat—come to see you in Wikenton?" I asked.

"When?"

"Recently."

"No, lass, ye're the only one tae visit as far as I know."

I'd walked right into Ava's cottage. I'd looked around unimpeded. I didn't like the idea of Angus doing the same, and now Edwin's question had made me wonder if there might truly be a connection there.

"Can you lock your cottage door?" I asked.

Ava laughed. "Lass, I havenae locked that door in decades." But she saw my expression and her mouth formed a line. "Who is Angus and why should I lock my door?"

"It's fine," Edwin said. "No need tae worry."

But he was worried, I could tell. When Elias came by, Edwin asked him to make sure the cottage was clear and that her locks worked. Elias agreed without one question.

Edwin and I watched Elias's cab disappear with Ava inside.

"I'm going to grab my laptop. I'll be right back," I said.

But the shop's phone rang before I could get halfway up the stairs.

"Aye, she's here," Rosie said as she signaled to me. "One moment."

Rosie held the handpiece to her chest, covering the mouthpiece.

"Delaney, it's a representative from the psychiatric hospital. She wants to talk to you." Rosie's eyes were big.

I wasn't exactly sure why, but dread washed through me as I made my way back down the stairs and took the handpiece.

"This is Delaney Nichols, can I help you?"

THIRTY-FIVE

"Ms. Nichols, my name is Dr. Sellers and I'm here with Norval Fraser. He's become quite agitated and said he would like to talk to you. I'd like to medicate him, but first, do you have a minute?"

"Of course," I said as relief washed through me. When Rosie told me who was calling, I was immediately concerned for the worst. At least Norval was still alive.

"Lass?" Norval said as he took the phone.

"It's me, Norval. What's wrong?"

"I'm glad ye're there. Did ye drop something in my room last night, perhaps a business card?"

"That could have been me, yes. Why?"

"Angus Murdoch?"

"Yes, it was in my pocket." I'd put the jacket on again, and now I absently touched the spot on the outside of the pocket. I felt the outline of the negatives.

"That's my da, lass! Angus Murdoch. I need tae know where ye got the card."

A million thoughts sprung to life in my mind, but I zoned in on what I thought was the most pertinent one. "I thought his name was Leopold Fraser."

"Aye. Leopold Angus Murdoch Fraser! How did ye get the card?"

"Oh, Norval," I said.

Every Scottish man I'd met had at least four names. Tom had five. Thomas MacIntyre Lucas Frederick Shannon. I'd been working on reciting them just so I'd get the vows straight. Why hadn't I looked up Leopold Fraser yet? It had never occurred to me that other names would be at play.

"Norval," I continued, "he's not your father. He's a man from the United States who brought a valuable book into the bookshop. The name is probably just a coincidence."

But it wasn't, I knew that much. I was just trying to say the right things to keep him calm.

"A King Arthur book?"

"Yes," I said. Immediately after I said the word, I held my breath.

"A tall, handsome lad all dressed in black?" Norval said

I started breathing again. "Yes, with a cowboy hat and boots?"

"No, no hat and I didnae look at his shoes. He stopped by my house about a week ago and offered me the book for all my papers. I cannae remember the name he gave me, but it was-nae Angus Murdoch. I would have remembered that. I have no use for King Arthur books, even valuable ones. I sent him away."

"Did he have a big Texas accent? Southern United States?"

"He had an accent, but it wasnae strong. He said he was

from . . . Oklahoma. I wish I could remember the name he gave me. Something like John or something else easy like that. It was like ye'd said, I forgot all aboot him because he was such a small part of my day. I didn't have time for him and sent him away quickly."

"Norval, this is very, very important—is there any chance he could have come into your flat and taken the Nessie knife without you seeing him?"

Norval was silent for so long, I thought maybe the call had become disconnected. Just as I was about to say something else, Norval spoke.

"Aye! He asked for a towel, a paper towel was fine. He'd gotten rained on and water was dripping from his face. I walked around to the kitchen and got him a towel and then gave him an extra brollie I had. All he'd had tae do was just hurry in a few steps and reach under the couch. I probably didnae kick the knife far under; he probably saw it from the doorway."

I laughed a release of stress. "A brollie, a towel. Well, that makes sense."

"Aye?"

"Yes, Norval, this is great. This will all help with a bunch of mysteries."

"Will it help us know who killed my Gavin?"

Not will it help to get him, Norval, released, but will it help find the killer of his great-nephew. Norval's mind might not have been exactly right, but his heart was.

"I hope so. I'm going to talk to the police. Hang in there, they might come talk to you again too."

"All right. Find the killer, lass. I'm going tae miss Gavin."

"I'll do my best. I promise."

We disconnected the call. I didn't explain anything to anyone as I hurried over for my laptop. I brought it and my whole family back over to the light side.

———

"I didn't look him up," I said, my attention on my screen. A crowd had formed around me. Everyone was there. If a customer came in, chances were good they'd be ignored, though. "Too many other things going on."

"I didn't think about looking him up either," Edwin said.

I typed into the search engine. "Angus Murdoch, Oklahoma."

A number of Angus Murdochs popped up, but none of them were ours.

"Hang on," I said. I poised my fingers on the keyboard. I listened hard to the still silence. I didn't really need a bookish voice, but I would have welcomed one. I was rewarded.

Inhale confidence, exhale doubt.

I smiled to myself. It was an anonymous quote. That worked. I knew I was on the right track.

"I'm not thinking straight. Of course." I typed in "Leopold Angus Murdoch Fraser" and in the flash of seconds we were rewarded, with pictures and everything.

"Oooh, Delaney, you did it, lass, you really did it," Edwin said as we all looked at the screen. "There he is."

Our Angus Murdoch was also actually Leopold Angus Murdoch Fraser. The third.

"Mr. Fraser's grandparents came from Scotland during World War II and settled in Oklahoma. The first Leopold Angus Murdoch Fraser opened a dry-cleaning company, which was the beginning of Fraser Clean Enterprises, now a chain of one-hundred-sixty dry cleaners throughout the state. The first Leopold passed his entrepreneurial spirit onto his son, deceased, and his grandson, Leopold III, who now runs the company and goes by the name Angus. Mr. Fraser III has never married and when not running the businesses, devotes his extra time to his horses and the Oklahoma land his grandfather purchased eighty years ago."

"I'll be," Wyatt said. "Sis, you did it. You solved the mystery."

"Not really. We don't know for sure that this Angus killed Gavin. I suspect he wanted the papers, but he didn't kill Norval. And the King Arthur book—I still don't understand."

"We need tae call Inspector Winters right away," Edwin said.

"Yes." I pulled out my phone.

———

"He brought you a King Arthur book? Is that why you asked me about one being stolen?" Inspector Winters said.

"Aye," Edwin said.

"Give me a moment." Inspector Winters looked around the bookshop.

Everyone was still right there. All my families—the one from Kansas, the one from the bookshop, and the one I was marrying into. Tom and Artair had joined us too. There didn't appear to be any space for Inspector Winters to make a private phone call.

"Would you like to use my office?" Edwin asked.

"No, I'll step outside a moment." Inspector Winters was already pulling out his phone and moving toward the front door.

Edwin looked at me and I shrugged. There was still much more to the story but Inspector Winters stepped outside before we could get another word in.

However, he walked back inside a moment later and said, "Do you have the King Arthur book, Edwin?"

"Aye." Edwin hurried up the stairs and disappeared to the other side.

I thought he'd taken the book home, but maybe he was carrying it with him wherever he went.

"What?" I said to Inspector Winters.

"In a moment. I need tae see the book. You believe he's related to Norval Fraser?" Inspector Winters asked me.

"Yes. Our Angus is Norval's father's grandson, from his second family."

"Okay."

I drew him a couple of quick family trees, and he seemed to understand that our Angus was actually Leopold the first and Flora's grandson. I thought that also made our Angus Norval's step-great-nephew, but I wasn't sure titles mattered anymore.

"And, perhaps Angus killed Gavin so he would legitimately be next in line to get Norval's papers when Norval died," I said. "That's my guess."

"Maybe," Inspector Winters said more agreeably than he ever had.

Edwin had come back with the book and he handed it to Inspector Winters, who carefully opened to the title page.

"I'm sorry, Edwin, when you called earlier, I didn't . . . well, I didn't investigate your question as thoroughly as I should have," Inspector Winters said. "I'm sorry, but yes, this book has been stolen from another bookshop. I'll need to take it with me."

"Of course," Edwin said.

The two men looked at each other and I sensed something that might indicate that a truce was in the air. An understanding. Some mutual respect. Whatever it was, it felt positive.

"Do you know how valuable this book is?" Inspector Winters said.

"I do," Edwin said. "I would have called you immediately if I hadn't fallen for the lad's story for a few days. It was a good story."

Inspector Winters nodded. "It's certainly interesting."

My cell phone rang in my pocket. I pulled it out. "It's Elias. Hello."

"Lass," he said amid clicks and in-and-out static. "There's a visitor at Ava's. I believe he's the man ye mentioned that Ava needed tae be wary of . . . Angus . . . I'm not so sure." The call died.

I still held the phone as I looked at the inspector. "You need to call someone to get up to Ava's cottage in Wikenton. Will they know where that is?" I stepped around the table. "I can show you. We need to get up to Loch Ness."

"What?" Inspector Winters said.

I pushed the button to call Elias back but it didn't make it through. "The mobile reception must be bad up there. Hang on." I scrolled to Ava's number and tried to redial it. It only rang and rang, with no answer. Panic began to build in my stomach and spread to my fingertips. "I think Angus Fraser is up there with them. I know Elias can handle himself and Angus might not mean them harm, but he also might be a killer." My words were clearer than I thought I had the ability to make them. "We need to get them some help. Let's go."

Inspector Winters looked at me and then asked me a couple

of questions regarding the location. He quickly decided that Wikenton might be difficult even for Loch Ness police to track down.

"All right. Let's go," he finally said. "I'll make calls on the way."

Neither Tom nor Wyatt would let me go without them, so the four of us got into Inspector Winters' police car. I didn't know that my parents had gotten into Edwin's and they followed behind, but I should have guessed. After all, they'd missed Loch Ness the first time they were there; they weren't going to miss it again.

THIRTY-SIX

Inspector Winters made calls, but it was as I suspected, and Wikenton was hard to nail down. I did the best I could and told him about the cove with the two cottages and the ghost buildings up a few miles from that other cove where you could go to get a good view of the castle remains.

I tried Elias and Ava a few more times, but either the calls didn't go through at all or they rang without an answer.

The usual forty-five-minute ride up seemed longer but, in fact, took only about twenty minutes because of sirens and Inspector Winters' skillful maneuvering around the curves on the tight two-lane road.

There wasn't much conversation, since Inspector Winters was on his police radio most of the time, trying to guide Loch Ness officers or asking questions about both of the Leopold Angus Murdoch Frasers we'd now come to know, and what the dispatcher could find out about them.

Turned out, not much more than we'd learned with our earlier online search.

"There, right there!" I said as I thought I recognized the

turn toward Wikenton. I was relieved to come upon the old wood sign. "Yes, this is it. You'll have to drive around the inside of the cove to get over to Ava's. Hurry, though."

Inspector Winters didn't respond but focused on driving down the narrow path that wasn't much of a road. I spotted Edwin's car a few cars back but I didn't mention it to Inspector Winters. Edwin had had to speed too just to keep up.

We passed the cottage with the red door just as the gentleman who lived there came outside. He sent us a long, suspicious look. I sent him a hasty wave, but he didn't return the greeting.

"There's her house. There's the cab, and that must be a car Angus was using."

Inspector Winters stopped the police car just as Edwin's came around behind us.

"Dammit," Inspector Winters said. "I thought he might follow. Listen, stay in the car, all of you. We don't know if there's a threat, but we need tae behave as if there is one. Stay put!"

Tom, Wyatt, and I agreed.

Inspector Winters got out of the car and I could see him signal to Edwin to stay back. Edwin's Citroën backed up enough that it was mostly hidden by the trees.

It had become cloudier on the ride to the Loch, and suddenly, the little bit of sun that had been peeking out became fully hidden by the clouds. It wasn't as dark as night, but shadows suddenly became deep, and the dark water of the loch became even more foreboding.

Inspector Winters, his hand on his holstered gun, made his way to the cottage's front door. He pushed it open easily and disappeared inside. The few seconds we didn't see him seemed to stretch and turn into long minutes, but he was back outside shortly, behaving as if he'd found no one inside. He sent us, and then Edwin's car, "halt" hand signals, indicating we should all remain where we were. I nodded, but I wasn't sure he could see me.

Inspector Winters made his way to the rocky shore and followed a path that took him closer to the water and farther away from our view. Soon, he was hidden completely by the trees. I thought back to Norval's story and how he hid behind the tree when he was a boy, how he came out from behind it and found his father.

"This is the precise spot," I said. I opened the door and got out of the police car. Tom and Wyatt were in the backseat and couldn't open their doors from the inside. I let them out too.

And then Edwin and my parents were out of Edwin's car and hurrying toward us.

"I . . . I need to go over there," I said.

"No!" rang out from everyone.

"He told us to wait," Tom said as he stepped next to me.

"I know," I said. I looked at my fiancé, my boss, my parents, and my brother. "I have to go over there. I'm pretty sure this is where Norval saw Nessie. I have to look. I'll be careful."

"No!" my father said. "We'll wait right here, until the police give us the okay."

I nodded, but then everything changed. We heard a splash, a big splash, and then a voice, maybe female, but indistinguishable enough for us to wonder, came to us, loud and clear. "Delaney!"

We all took off in a run. The small rocks were slippery and the trees were even thicker than I remembered them to be, but, shortly, en masse, we came upon the scene.

Ava, Elias, Inspector Winters, and Angus stood on the shore and looked out to the water. Inspector Winters didn't have his gun drawn and no one seemed in much distress, but they were all looking out toward the same place.

"Lass," Elias said.

"Delaney," Inspector Winters said. "I asked you all to wait back there. We were just talking, and we were on our way back to the cottage in a moment."

"I saw her!" Angus said. "I just saw her! She was beautiful."

I looked at Ava, who nodded solemnly. I looked at Elias, who shrugged somewhat helplessly. Finally, I looked at Inspector Winters, who was just trying to take in everything at once and remain calm.

"Someone yelled my name," I said.

"No one here," Inspector Winters said.

I looked at Tom and Wyatt. They both said they thought they heard it too, but it could have been something else. I wanted to ask what else it could have possibly been, but there were more important things.

"Why are you all over here?" I asked.

"This is where I told them they could see her," Ava offered, seeming to have heard me just fine, even over the increasing wind. "I'd told her tae leave me alone a long time ago, but I knew she'd come back. He," she nodded toward Angus, "wanted badly tae see her."

She looked at me with wide, fearful eyes. I didn't see a weapon on Angus but he must have seemed threatening in some way. Elias would have punched him if he thought it would help the situation. He must not have thought it would help. Maybe Elias just wanted to see Nessie too.

"Okay," I said. "You saw her, right, Angus?" I said.

His eyes darted to me. "I did."

"Good. You've done right by your grandfather, Angus," I

said, but then I hesitated. What I was about to do might upset him. But I knew the truth needed to be spoken. I knew the killer needed to be discovered. And Inspector Winters was right there. Now, before Angus had a chance to think about it, was the time. "You came here for your grandfather, didn't you? He told you stories, didn't he? They weren't about King Arthur. They were about her, Nessie." I smiled at him, but he didn't smile back.

"You know who I am?" he said as he turned, and I finally saw a reason to be concerned. A gun stuck up from the side of his jeans' waistband. His accent was lighter than it had been. There was no hat on his head. He wasn't over-the-top Texas anymore, but something wasn't right. "I thought you might figure it out sooner, but you didn't."

"No, I didn't, but why didn't you just tell us who you were from the beginning?"

"I just wanted what was mine. I wanted the papers," Angus said. "They were mine, you know. My grandfather knew her." He nodded out toward the water. "Oh, the stories I heard, you're right about that, Delaney." He looked at me a long moment. "At first I thought you wanted them. I'd already tried to talk to Norval and then I'd been watching him. I saw you go in and talk to him, and then Gavin came out to talk to you too. I thought you were going to get the papers. You would never give them to me."

"So, you shortened your name, hid your identity, stole a book, and made up a story about King Arthur?" Edwin said.

"Yes." He stepped toward Edwin, and Inspector Winters put his hand back on his holstered gun. I really hoped he wouldn't have to take it out. "I thought it was all pretty clever. And if you or she got the papers, I was going to come back and remind you about the priceless book I crossed the sea to return to you.

Maybe you'd be kind enough to give me the papers. It was a good plan."

Not for people like my boss and me. None of that would have worked with either of us. Edwin wasn't even going to keep the King Arthur book. It would probably have been donated to a library if we didn't find its owner.

"Oh, Angus," I said. "It was a good plan, but why did you have to kill Gavin?"

I heard my mom gasp quietly behind me.

"He wouldn't give me the papers either. He told me he would sell them to me, but he changed his mind. He wouldn't take them from his uncle. He changed his mind! If he was gone, all I had to do was prove who I was and I would get them. They were mine anyway. Leopold Fraser was my grandfather, and he cared the most about me, about us. He left Norval and the rest of them and never looked back. The papers were rightfully mine."

"You grabbed the knife from Norval's apartment and used it on Gavin?" I asked.

"It was easy! Even that crazy old man wouldn't take the King Arthur book. You said it yourself, that book is priceless! Even if there's proof of Nessie, the book would be worth more. I don't understand why he wouldn't trade with me."

Thunder boomed with the spark of a nearby lightning bolt. I ducked reactively and lifted my arm up protectively. As if someone had just turned on a fan, the wind picked up even more.

"A storm's coming," I said. "Come on, Angus, we'll give you a ride back to Edinburgh."

"Oh, I'm not going back to Edinburgh," he said. He looked out to the sea. "I'm going with her." He looked back at me as emotion, and probably grief, twisted his face. "I miss him so

much, you'll never understand how much I miss my grandfather. He was such a good man. I loved him deeply. If he's
still to be found anywhere, it's with her, with that monster he
talked about and longed for, forever. I'm going with her."

I noticed that he wasn't wearing his boots. Momentarily, I
wondered where they'd gone. I looked back at the tree line. The
boots were there, on their sides.

Angus threw the gun to one side, and was out of his jacket,
shirt, and jeans faster than any of us could register what he was
doing. Wyatt ran and gathered the gun, emptying the clip as
Inspector Winters and Elias hurried to Angus and tried to grab
his arms. Once their shoe-clad feet hit the water they had
trouble keeping their balance, so they just grabbed at air as
they missed his arms.

The rest of us hurried to try to help, but seconds later, as we
were all standing there, our own shoe-clad feet in the water, the
wind only knocking us further off balance, Angus went under.

"What do we do?" I said as the rain started to fall.

"Let the police take care of it, lass," Elias said as he wiped
his hand under his nose and looked out at the water. He wanted
to dive in, but was smart enough not to.

I lifted a foot from the slog it was sinking into and tried to
step backward, but staying upright with the water, the mud,
and the wind was tricky. My foot went deeper into the water
instead.

"Delaney," Tom said as he took hold of my arm. "Step back,
lass."

"I'm trying." I tried to lift my foot again, but it seemed I was
stuck.

The sound of an approaching siren set me further off balance as I turned my head and tried to see around the trees.

"More help is coming," Inspector Winters said. "Get out of the water, Delaney."

Easier said than done. The water, even only as high as my knees, was pulling me in with more strength than Tom could pull me out.

At the same moment another flash of lightning and boom of thunder turned our world blindingly bright, I was tipped all the way over. One moment Tom had hold of me, and the next he didn't. I wasn't even sure which way I had gone, other than under. I'd heard that the loch fell off into deep waters close to shore, but this depth seemed ridiculously close.

Surprisingly, I didn't panic. At first. I was too shocked, maybe, but my thoughts came to me with laser-like precision. I had to get above the water to get oxygen. It was all too dark to figure out which way was up, but I knew I would float in that direction if I just let myself. I hoped the small amount of oxygen I had in my lungs would keep me alive long enough to make it.

But I didn't really float. I churned, but not quickly. Not floating was unfortunate, I thought, as panic finally began to balloon in my chest.

I opened my eyes big and looked all around. I didn't see anything but a lot of the same—more darkness in every direction. My chest started to burn in ways I'd never felt before when my eyes finally caught something, one thing—okay, two things— that didn't look like everything else.

Did I see two glowing blue orbs, small, but round? Reactively, I blinked a few times trying to focus, to no avail. The orbs came closer. And I saw her.

Or, at least that's what my imagination said happened, because if I had to describe exactly what my eyes saw in that watery place it would be unreal: two glowing blue round things that might have been eyes sunken deeply into what might be something like a dragon's head. Maybe. But I couldn't be sure. And the vision only lasted a few seconds, since after that something seemed to push on me from behind. My hand grazed the long, solid but yielding thing that ran along my back. It felt scaly, or maybe bumpy.

With a *whoosh* that made me take in more brackish water, I was shoved hard. Just as I thought I couldn't take it anymore, I was released into the open, on the shore. I was a good twenty yards away from everyone else who I thought were yelling my name, but I coughed exuberantly enough to get their attention.

Tom won the race to get to me. It would have been lovely and romantic if he'd taken me in his arms and kissed me passionately, but the elements and the water I needed to get out of my lungs prohibited me from doing anything but coughing, and him from doing anything but kneeling next to me, his hand too tightly around my arm, as I recovered.

Inspector Winters crouched on my other side when I was better. "Are you all right? I need tae help Angus. Are you all right?"

Mid-cough I nodded that I was, but I lifted my head. Where *was* Angus?

Even farther down shore, but only by about twenty feet. He was there, in his underwear and socks only, splayed out on his back. With his face aimed our direction, his vacant stare made me certain that he was dead.

I tried to stand.

"Hang on, Delaney," Tom said. "Inspector Winters will take care of him."

I still tried to stand.

"Oh, Delaney, take it easy," Mom said. I caught her wide, frightened eyes, and I suddenly felt terrible that I'd come to Scotland for the most wonderful job in the world, only to marry the most wonderful man in the world, and had now forced her to watch her daughter almost drown in the world-famous Loch Ness. Never mind about that damn dress.

I was going to be fine, though. I found my voice. "Let's all get to him."

Tom and my mom and dad helped me navigate the way, and I could breathe fine by the time we got to Angus as Inspector Winters worked CPR on him. The rain came down in sheets and thunder boomed and lightning flashed, but we stayed as more police and an ambulance arrived. Even Ava stayed. At moments, when the lightning flashed, we looked like players in an old, choppy black-and-white film. As the imagery came to me, I remembered the negatives in my jacket pocket, the jacket I'd worn solely to keep the negatives with me. I reached inside but wasn't at all surprised that they weren't there. I'd kept them with me to keep them safe, but I could never have predicted I'd be sucked into Loch Ness, and that she'd be there to take them from me.

Or something like that.

And when Inspector Winters managed a watery cough from Angus, followed by real breathing and real life, some missing negatives didn't matter anymore. Besides, we still had the film.

As we left the cove I almost didn't look back. But I did, briefly. I can't say for sure, but I thought I saw a thick tail skim the water, the tail that *might* have pushed me back onto land.

THIRTY-SEVEN

"I know," I said into the phone. "Of course, I'll be there. But I have to do this. You understand? Good. See you soon."

I ended the call.

"Lass?" Elias said as he looked at me in the passenger seat. He'd been baffled since I'd told him to turn right instead of left.

"We'll get there. This is important."

"Awright. Do ye want me tae come tae the door with ye?"

"No. I've got this."

"Awright," he said again.

He parked the cab and then hurried around to the passenger door, opening it and helping me out. I exited the cab, careful to keep the dress clean. My mother's dress. In a million years, I would not have guessed that an old Kansas farm girl wedding dress would turn out to be the most beautiful dress ever made. But it was. Wyatt had hidden it in his luggage. He'd waited until he knew that Inspector Winters and Aggie wouldn't be able to find the closed shop's owner or seamstress before he gave it to me. Fortunately, not only could Aggie and my mother bake a wedding cake fit for blue ribbons, they could both alter and sew things too.

It was simple white, with a lace bodice and a skirt that fell to the ground. It was perfect.

As I walked down the line of apartments, I glanced up at the mostly clear and sunny sky. "Sunny today would be good."

I was pretty sure a small cloud smiled back. I hoped so, at least.

Foil still covered the window. I tapped a three-knock rhythm, and hoped he really was home. Inspector Winters had told me he'd been released.

Just as I was about to turn away and rejoin Elias in his cab, the door opened.

Norval peeked out and then opened the door wide, with a matching, equally wide smile.

"Have ye come tae take the papers, lass?" he asked.

Murder is always a tragedy, but Gavin's, it turned out, had been pointless. Had Angus just told Norval who he was, Norval might have given him everything, if he'd agreed to continue the work. In fact, I'd speculated that Norval would have been so happy to have a part of his father back with him that he might not have even required Angus to do the work. None of us would ever know for sure now.

Angus could have easily proven who he was, but he chose murder. It seemed that Nessie had been meant to haunt Leopold Angus Murdoch Fraser's entire family. Monsters did that sometimes.

There was also a question of Angus's mental health, which begged more questions. Was there something in that family that caused delusions? Perhaps they didn't see the same reality the rest of us saw. Maybe some of it was a better reality, but certainly some of it was worse.

I hadn't learned much more about the man who'd introduced his son and his grandson to Nessie, one in person, one through stories, but through Inspector Winters I'd come to know the elder Leopold Angus Murdoch Fraser as a hopeless romantic. He'd loved his wife until he met Flora. He'd loved his Scotland family until he was compelled to make an American family. But he'd always loved Nessie. I didn't understand people who could abandon their families; I didn't want to try very hard to understand Leopold. I didn't really have to, though, because he was there in front of me, as part of Norval and part of Angus. I'd seen some bad parts, but Norval had shown me some of the good too.

Angus had stopped by Ava's cottage one other time, but she hadn't been home. He didn't know who she was; he'd only gone there because that cove, Wikenton, was a location his grandfather had talked about. When she didn't answer her door, he made his way inside. He saw the picture on her wall too, and when it came time for him to leave Edinburgh, to fly back home to where his crime might never be found out, he couldn't bring himself to board the plane. He had to go back to that place and find out more about that picture, maybe take it with him. She would have handed it over if he'd only asked instead of cornering her and Elias as he ranted about the monster, Norval's papers, and his grandfather, all while a gun was tucked into his jeans.

Gavin MacLeod's clients were upset with him, but none of them was truly murderous enough to kill him, though I wondered if Brodie had gotten closer than he'd admitted. Fortunately, we'd never have to know that answer either.

Maybe Nessie wasn't the monster. Maybe she had brought out the monster in the Fraser family. Perhaps Norval had been correct. Perhaps their family was cursed.

"Well, no, Norval, I'm not here to take the papers. You look well, though."

He shrugged and smiled thinly. His teeth shifted.

We'd returned the projector and the films to Norval's flat. None of us had discussed it, but it seemed unspoken that we wouldn't tell anyone what we'd seen. I wasn't sure why we didn't want to, other than our collective understanding that not everything needed to be illuminated.

The deck of cards had never been recovered. It looked like that mystery would remain unsolved, for now at least.

"I'm so sorry about Gavin," I said.

"Thank you, lass. Ye are lovely."

"Thank you. I'm getting married today."

"Aye? Weel, best wishes tae ye and the lucky lad."

"Thank you. I wondered, though. Do you want to come? I've got a cab right over there. Nisa is our officiant. You'll know her. The police officer, Inspector Winters, will be there."

"He was kind tae me."

"Good. You can meet my family and my coworkers."

He still seemed hesitant.

"The cake is going to be amazing!"

His eyes lit a moment but then dimmed again. "I'm not dressed."

"No. It's come as you are. Very informal, in the bookshop, with the reception in my groom's," ah, my *groom's*, "pub. We'd love to have you join us."

"In The Cracked Spine?"

"Yes."

"How lovely."

"It will be fun and we'd really love to have you there."

"Well, awright, then. Let's go."

———

I always knew a bookshop could encompass whole worlds, but this one had taken on the role literally. My parents and Wyatt, Elias and Aggie, Artair, Edwin, Rosie, Hamlet, Birk, and Inspector Winters were there. Regg had joined Rosie, and Vanessa had joined Edwin. Everyone was going to love her.

Norval was there too. He needed more family, I thought, one that wasn't cursed, and this seemed like the right one to bring him into. Millie was going to be fine in the place Edwin had found for her, but she wasn't at the wedding. I'd asked Ava if she wanted to come, but she hadn't. She was no worse for the wear from the time in the storm, but she had wanted to stay home, and, I suspected, have a discussion or two with Nessie. I didn't ask, though. It felt like none of my business.

I'd even invited Albert Winsom, but he'd also declined. He'd brought in the tooth the day after our incident at Loch Ness. There was no doubt it was a tooth, but it could have belonged to any sort of creature that had once had two-inch-long, sharp teeth in its mouth. It was an interesting artifact to be sure, but there was no way to determine if it was Nessie's.

Tom wore a kilt I'd never seen before. It was a pleasant surprise. When his cobalt eyes locked onto mine as my dad escorted me down the bookshop's side aisle, I had such a sense of destiny that I suddenly felt as if I'd had this place and these people inside me all the time, just waiting to come out and show me I truly belonged.

Reverend Nisa said words. Tom and I said words. I got his

name right. Everyone cried a little, and the city outside the shop whispered things to me. They weren't bookish voices, they were those of passing time and history, and, I thought, probably held the voice I'd heard call my name at the loch, whoever that was.

You are right where you belong, Delaney Nichols. You were meant to be right here, with these people, in this place. We called to you across land and sea, and you heard us. Do you love it as much as we thought you would?

I do, I definitely do.